This is a work of fiction. Names, characters, organisations, places and incidents are either the product of the author's imagination or are used fictitiously, and any resemblance to actual persons, living or dead, business establishments, events or locales is entirely coincidental.

Version 1.0
ISBN: 9781925827057
Cover art by Kellie Dennis @ *Book Cover By Design*

Pilyara Press
Melbourne

ALSO BY JENNIFER SCOULLAR

Brumby's Run (The Wild Australia Stories - Book 1)

Billabong Bend (The Wild Australia Stories - Book 3)

Turtle Reef (The Wild Australia Stories - Book 4)

Journey's End (The Wild Australia Stories - Book 5)

Fortune's Son (The Tasmanian Tales - Book 1)

The Lost Valley (The Tasmanian Tales - Book 2)

COMING SOON - The Memory Tree (The Tasmanian Tales - Book 3)

Wasp Season

For the Wilderness Society, and their work to protect and restore wild places across Australia.

CHAPTER 1

Friday morning. Clare finished the interview and sized up her client. Too thin, junky thin. Red eyes, more than a hint of the shakes and she couldn't stop sniffing.

'I advise you to plead guilty,' said Clare. 'We'll present a plea in mitigation and ask for a bond or a community-based order. It will be better all round.' This week she'd seen too many cases just like this one. The young woman was going to make a bad impression on the court without even opening her mouth.

'Can we nick out for a smoke?'

'Of course.'

The boyfriend was already out the door, and the girl wasn't far behind. Clare started making notes on the file, then looked up. The little boy was still sitting there. Clare walked to the door and called after the two figures retreating down the hall. 'Haven't you forgotten something?'

The boy regarded her with solemn eyes, peeking from beneath cartoon-perfect lashes. An uncommonly pretty child in spite of his snotty nose and soiled, shabby clothes.

'Mummy and Daddy will be back soon.' Clare's voice was bright and encouraging, but the boy's expression didn't change.

'Daddy's dead,' he said in a small voice. His bottom lip began to quiver.

Oh. Tiredness and guilt washed over her, along with a feeling that she couldn't name. A vague dissatisfaction that had troubled her all week, each time she'd looked out of her narrow window to the view of the stunted coolabah tree, and beyond it, the barren car park. A *missing*. Or perhaps a *wishing* for something indefinable. Clare averted her gaze, both from the tree and the boy, and rifled through the files on the desk. What on earth was his name? It was hard to concentrate with him looking at her like that. She glanced down at the interview sheet. The mother was Taylor Brown. But that was it - no mention of the child at all.

'What's your name?' she asked.

He didn't answer. He just maintained that unsettling stare. It didn't matter. How long could it take to smoke a cigarette? Clare turned back to her work, reviewing her record of the interview so far. The plea in mitigation would be simple. Taylor had a depressingly familiar tale: growing up in a series of broken homes, women's refuges and foster care placements. She ticked all the boxes and was an addict to boot, although currently on a methadone replacement program. Clare reread the charge sheet. Theft of a bull terrier puppy. Cute, really. The rest wasn't so cute. Around three o'clock in the morning of May the second, police had stopped and searched her vehicle on Wickham Street in the Valley. They'd found drugs, a large sum of money and various stolen items. The boy had been unrestrained in the front seat. Clare looked up and surprised herself by imagining him with a puppy on his lap. Would the puppy have made him laugh? Put a smile on his serious face? Had Taylor wanted to see that smile?

Time ticked by ... Her next appointment would be here soon. Clare daydreamed out the grimy window. A bird sat in her poor excuse for a tree. She'd never seen a bird there before. A currawong, big and black, with bright yellow eyes and startling white crescents on its wings. It looked straight at her and uttered a wild, ringing cry. The call sounded disturbingly out of place in a city carpark.

With a wrench Clare returned her attention to the boy. What was

Taylor's mobile number? The digits on the legal aid form were a series of uncertain scratches. A quick glance over the rest of the largely incomplete application, revealed her to be barely literate. Under *date of birth* Taylor had laboriously written her age instead — *twenty*. Only twenty years old. Good grief, how old could she have been when she had the kid? Clare began to key the digits into her phone, then stopped. There weren't enough numbers.

'Hey, come back here,' said Clare, as the little boy got down from the too-big chair and went to the door. 'Where do you think you're going?'

The child turned to face her. Pale blue eyes. A tangled lock of golden hair fell over his forehead. Pushing it aside with a thin hand, he said, 'Mummy,' and tugged at the door knob.

The phone rang. Clare automatically reached for it, then let her hand fall and hurried for the door instead. She guided him back to the chair, impulsively putting her hands around his waist and lifting him into the seat. He was light as a feather. She kneeled in front of him on the worn blue carpet. 'What's your name?'

His mouth moved to shape a word, ever so slowly. 'Jack,' he said at last.

The word was no more than a sigh. If her face hadn't been so close to his, her green eyes so close to his wide blue ones, she would have missed it. Clare loved the name Jack. It was her father's name, a father that she'd recently lost, way too early, to cancer.

'Stay,' she said, and reached once more for the phone. It stopped ringing. A knock came at the door. Thank goodness. 'Here's Mummy now,' said Clare.

But it wasn't Taylor. It was Debbie, the legal aid centre's one and only secretary. 'Just letting you know, Clare, your ten-thirty's here.'

'Could you have a look outside please?' said Clare. 'For a young woman, tall and thin, with long brown hair.' She nodded towards the boy. 'His mother — and a man. They went for a cigarette.'

Debbie retreated from the room, looking doubtful. She returned a few minutes later, shaking her head. 'I'm sorry. No sign.'

Clare frowned. She lifted Jack down from the chair, picked up

Taylor's file and took hold of the boy's small hand. 'Ask my next appointment to wait,' she told Debbie. 'I need to see Roderick.'

CLARE FINISHED SPEAKING and watched Roderick stroke his bush of a beard with a forefinger, deep in thought. The child pressed in against her knees, pushing her pin-striped linen skirt up her legs. His skinny warmth radiated through her black tights. Eventually Roderick held out his hand for the file and she handed it over.

'Ring Child Protection and have them send somebody round to pick him up,' he said at last. Clare nodded and tried to prise the child from her legs.

Jack began to scream, a piercing cry that tore through the thin walls of the office.

'My next client ...' she said through the noise. 'I have to go.' The more she tried to detach herself from the boy, the harder he yelled.

'Enough.' Roderick held up his hand. 'He obviously wants to stay with you.'

Clare let her hands fall from Jack's shoulders and the screaming ended as abruptly as it had begun.

Roderick picked up the phone. 'Debbie, send Clare's next one to me, and see if you can divvy up her morning slots between the rest of us.'

Clare looked confused. 'I don't understand.'

'You're looking after the boy until a social worker comes.'

Clare's mouth fell open. 'What do you expect me to do with a four-year-old kid?'

'I don't know, McDonald's maybe?' He fished a wallet from his pocket and plonked some money on the table. 'Get him a Happy Meal.'

Clare dragged herself from the room, with Jack still attached to her leg.

Debbie watched her struggle back towards her office. 'Adam rang,' she said. 'To remind you about the ballet tonight.'

Adam's sister was opening in the lead role of Queensland Ballet's production of Giselle. Clare secretly didn't like the ballet and was bored after ten minutes, but Adam loved it and tonight was apparently a very big deal.

Debbie smiled at the little boy. 'He's a sweetie.'

Clare grimaced as she finally made it to the office and slammed the door behind her.

THE CHILD WAS SITTING in the too-big chair again, watching her with those wide eyes. Every now and then he looked out the dirty window. The currawong had flown, leaving the misshapen little tree looking even sadder than usual. Clare's arm ached from holding the phone to her ear. The department's intake worker was apparently on the other line, trying to tee up a place for Jack. 'Clare,' she said at last. 'I've found something. An experienced foster carer who lives in the same suburb as the boy's mother. It's a stroke of luck that we can keep the child within his community, don't you think?'

Clare bit her tongue. It hardly mattered. Taylor was transient. She'd listed her latest address as a caravan park, where she'd been for two weeks. What sort of a connection were she and Jack supposed to have with that particular community?

'The carer can take him this afternoon,' said the intake worker.

'We'll be waiting.' Clare hung up the phone. 'Good news, Jack. Let's get lunch to celebrate.'

The little boy didn't say anything. As she took his hand he looked out the window again. She followed his gaze to the bare tree. His hand felt warmer than before, and it nestled into hers like a baby bird in a nest.

THE PIMPLY-FACED TEENAGER behind the counter put a colourful cardboard box and a drink cup on the tray. They sat down at a corner booth. Jack pulled ineffectually at the tough plastic bag containing the Happy Meal toy, then handed it to Clare. She used her fingernail to poke a hole and extracted the small item inside: a fat, orange hog-like creature with tall black ears, a yellow nose and a fierce face, like it wanted to bite someone. Clare looked at the instructions. Its name was Tepig, and it was something called a Pokémon. According to the leaflet, its little ball of a tail was supposed to light up. Clare squeezed it a few times. Nothing happened.

Jack wiped sauce from his mouth, then leaned over and took the toy from Clare's hand. He put it on its back. Ah, there was a switch. Jack flicked it and Tepig's tail glowed purple.

'Well, what do you know?' Clare smiled at him. 'You're a pretty smart kid.'

Jack picked up a card that had fallen out along with the toy. It was some sort of trading card with a hologram of a bird on it. His eyes lit up and for the first time, he smiled. He pulled a dog-eared deck of cards from his pocket and proceeded to lay them out, side by side, on the table.

'What's that you've got there?' she asked.

Each card had a picture of an odd animal on it, twelve cards in all. The new card was the only one with a sparkly hologram and Clare guessed it was special. She felt ridiculously pleased about that. Jack handed her the paper cup that minutes ago had been filled with cola. His little box of food was empty as well. The burger and chips hadn't seemed to touch the sides going down. 'Same again?'

Whoever said looking after kids was hard? This was a breeze. Jack let her wipe his nose. 'How about I have a Happy Meal too?' she said. We'll get more cards and toys that way.'

Four Happy Meals later and they were both full. The table was littered with empty food wrappers, Pokémon figures and swap cards. Jack burped, then lay down on the bench seat and patted his tummy. Clare found herself copying him, stretching out on her back along the seat at right angles to his. The tops of their heads were almost touching. Jack reached backwards and touched Clare's face, an unexpectedly tender gesture. Then he started to tickle her. Clare laughed in surprise.

'Jack, no, people are looking—' However her inhibitions were no match for Jack's wriggling fingers. 'Stop,' she gasped, but it only spurred him on. Now he was giggling too – peals of musical laughter shaking his slight frame.

'Clare, is that you?'

Clare felt herself redden. Oh no ... she knew that voice.

Clare sat up to find one of her fellow solicitors regarding her with an expression halfway between curiosity and distaste. What on earth was Veronica doing at McDonald's, of all places? The overpriced tapas bar down the road was more her style. Clare attempted to reclaim some dignity, straightening her skirt and running her fingers through her blonde bob. As she did, she noticed a pink smear on her shirt — tomato sauce.

'We're here for lunch,' Clare said, unnecessarily. 'Would you like to join us?' What a dumb thing to say. Jack's expression was one of rebuke. He was right of course; Veronica would spoil their fun. Veronica would spoil anybody's fun.

The woman was, as always, immaculate; clothed head-to-slender-ankle in Gucci elegance, balanced on high-heeled red Louboutins. Veronica had ambitions to be a trial lawyer. Next year she was reading at the bar with Paul Dunbar, one of Brisbane's top criminal barristers - essentially an apprenticeship. What Clare wouldn't do for such an opportunity. The only reason that she and Veronica were working in the same building was that Dunbar had a social justice agenda. He liked to see himself as a defender of the common man and often appeared for a reduced fee, or even pro bono, if the trial was high profile enough. Dunbar required his readers to spend twelve months as legal aid lawyers, believing that nothing blooded a future barrister better than the world of petty crime. So unlike Clare, Veronica was a reluctant champion of the underdog.

Her mouth twisted at Clare's offer to join them. 'I didn't come here for lunch.' She spat out the last word like lunch was something loathsome, like she'd never eaten lunch in her life and didn't intend to start now. 'I'm here to fetch you back. You're needed at the office.' Veronica's expression was faintly puzzled, as if she couldn't understand why anybody would need Clare for anything.

Clare wanted to say that she'd only come to McDonald's because of Jack, but stopped herself. It might hurt the little boy's feelings, and anyway, what did it matter what Veronica thought?

'Why didn't you just ring me?' asked Clare.

'Ringing you really would have been so much simpler,' agreed Veronica. 'Since I'm absolutely swamped with extra work today. But somebody – ' She took a phone from her bag and placed it on the table in front of Clare. 'Somebody forgot her mobile.'

Clare picked up her phone. She felt about as tall as Jack.

Veronica looked at the discarded wrappers from the four Happy Meals, at the sauce on Jack's sleeve and finally at Clare. 'Enjoy your … lunch,' she said, and swept from the restaurant.

As they walked back to the office, Jack volunteered his hand. It fitted so comfortably into her own. Clare gave it a pleased squeeze. For the first time she tried to imagine where he might be going. An experienced foster carer, that's what the intake worker had said. Jack should be okay with somebody like that, shouldn't he? Until his mother came back?

CHAPTER 2

The person from the Department of Human Services was waiting for them in Clare's office when they got back – a thin, young woman with frizzy black hair and a crooked smile. She introduced herself as Kim Maguire. 'And this must be John,' she said. 'Why don't we all sit down?'

'Jack,' Clare corrected her. 'His name is Jack.'

Kim pulled a thick bundle of papers from her briefcase and examined it, while Jack slipped from his chair onto Clare's knee.

'No, as I said, it's John. Definitely John.' Kim brandished a fat manila folder like a weapon. 'There's already quite a file on him.'

'The kid should know his own name, don't you think?' said Clare. 'And he told me his name is Jack.'

Kim's expression was pained. 'That's simply not possible, Clare. John is autistic, quite high on the spectrum.' She paused. 'He can't speak.'

This was so patently untrue that Clare found herself speechless. Kim stared at her and Jack, nodding and looking slightly sad. The silence dragged on until it became uncomfortable. Jack was looking out the window at Clare's coolabah tree again. He seemed to like trees. She wondered if the little boy had ever been beyond the city limits.

'He *can* speak,' said Clare. 'He told me his name. He told me his father was dead. Didn't you, Jack?' She could feel the child's small body stiffen, but he didn't answer.

'I have no information on file about John's father,' said Kim. 'But there is a wealth of information verifying his autism. Reports from clinical psychologists, doctors, social workers, childcare staff ...' The kid had really done the rounds. As Kim recited each category of professionals, she slapped a corresponding sheaf of paper down on the desk. 'John has been in care before. The last paediatrician to examine him said that with his level of disability, it's unlikely that he'll ever speak.'

'And what about his mother?' asked Clare. 'What does Taylor Brown say about her son?'

Kim shuffled through her pile of papers. 'Taylor reports that John has spoken, but her caseworkers indicate that she is an unreliable witness. Perhaps she understates the extent of her son's disability because she fears she'll be blamed for it.'

'He talked to me,' Clare repeated.

'And told you what?' said Kim. 'That his name is Jack, when it isn't? You must have imagined it, Clare. Files don't lie.'

Clare frowned. Records were only as good as the people who kept them – and from her own observations of the overworked, under-resourced, burnt-out workers of the child protection system, the people often weren't very good at all. A slipshod assessment or a wrong diagnosis could follow a kid around for years.

Roderick peered briefly into the room. 'Finished here, are we?' he asked. 'Ready to get back on the treadmill?'

Clare heaved a sigh, picked up the boy, whoever he was, and placed him on the chair beside her. She tried to be more objective. Jack had to leave no matter what, so they may as well both make the best of it.

'This lady is Kim,' she said stroking Jack's white-gold hair. Kim smiled her crooked smile. It occurred to Clare that, if she was a child, she might think Kim was a witch. 'She's going to take you to another nice lady, who'll look after you until Mummy's home.'

The boy shook his head violently and crawled back onto Clare's knee.

'Come along, John,' said Kim, in a cheerful voice. 'We're going to have a lovely time.' The boy picked up a heavy stapler and aimed it at Kim's head. His throw was surprisingly accurate. Kim shrieked as the stapler thudded into her temple. Her hand found the spot; blood showed on her fingers. Now the boy was screaming. He ran to the corner of the room and started to bang his head rhythmically against the wall. Bang ... bang ... bang. How could he do that? Surely it must hurt? When Clare tried to get close to him, he vomited up his lunch — a projectile stream that hit her skirt and dribbled down her tights.

In a truly impressive move Kim tackled him from behind, pinning his arms and holding him too close for his kicking feet to have much impact. The boy hurled himself backwards and struck her in the belly with the rear of his skull. Kim gasped like she'd been winded, but hung on grimly.

When Roderick rushed in, the boy was still yelling. Not crying, but yelling. Long, angry bellows, like an animal. Clare couldn't bear to watch. She ducked from the room and headed for the bathroom. The boy's cries reverberated through the walls. Clare pressed her palms to her ears. The row grew fainter and fainter until at last, all was quiet again. She checked herself in the mirror. What a mess. Her face was red. Her tangled blonde hair had sticky bits that refused to comb out, and there was pickle on her teeth. Clare dabbed ineffectually at the sick on her skirt with some damp toilet paper.

When she'd cleaned herself up as best she could, she ventured out, tiptoeing down the corridor back to her office. Overturned chairs and scattered files told the story. A suspicious puddle lay on the floor near the door. She picked up the bag of Happy Meal toys, along with Jack's special trading cards. He must have dropped them in the fight. Clare switched on Tepig. His purple light now shone pale and sad.

Debbie came in with a mop. 'Don't worry. Veronica's seeing your next customer.' She looked around and shook her head. 'He seemed like such a sweet boy. I wonder what happened?' Clare began to collect the rainbow of multi-coloured paper clips dotting the carpet. Yes, what had happened? The boy had been in care before. Where? How many times? Was that when the error-filled reports were made? Clare stood up, stepped over Debbie's broom, and went to see Roderick.

RODERICK WAS on the phone when Clare entered his office. He waved her in and she sat down to wait. 'Still no sign, I'm afraid … I know it's not an ideal arrangement for the child, but what do you expect us to do? Produce his mother out of thin air? Potentially she's unfit to retain custody anyway … Of course, you'll be the first to know … Bye.'

'Well?' asked Clare. 'What's the upshot?'

'You know what it's like, trying to put a kid like that with a regular foster carer.'

Clare shifted uneasily. 'What do you mean?'

'I means the placement fell through.'

'So, what happens to the boy?'

'They've found him some sort of short-term emergency housing.'

'He's four years old,' said Clare. 'You're not telling me he's going into a contingency unit?'

'Brighthaven.' Roderick shrugged. 'What can you do?'

'You're not serious?' But she could tell by the look on his face that he was. Contingency units were used as a last resort, usually for older children with multiple behaviour problems. One of her clients had been placed in Brighthaven a few days ago. Aiden: a troubled teenager, in and out of state care all his life — guilty of sex offences against younger boys. Brighthaven was a risky place for any child, let alone a vulnerable four-year-old.

'Jack did tell me his name,' she said. 'And Rod - Aiden's just been placed in Brighthaven.'

Clare watched his face as he made the connection: puzzled at first, then concerned and finally, pale. She handed him his phone. 'You call Kim and tell her to bring the boy back or I will.'

Roderick opened his mouth as if he was about to argue, then smiled. 'That attitude,' he said, 'is what makes you such a terrific advocate. You have until the end of the day to find him a new placement.'

Clare returned to her desk and began to make calls. One call. Two calls. Three ...

FIVE O'CLOCK. Déjà vu, all of them back in Clare's office. Jack sat on her lap again, clutching his bag of Pokémon toys. Kim finished her phone call and wrote something down on a notepad.

'Well?' asked Clare.

Kim looked grim. 'There is nowhere else,' she said. 'He must return to Brighthaven.'

Clare shook her head. 'I'll take him.' The words startled out of her mouth. 'For a little while,' she said. 'Until his mother comes back.'

KIM LOOKED at Clare for a long time without speaking. 'A foster care assessment takes time,' she said at last. 'Months.'

'What about a kinship care assessment? Can you do that?' Clare already knew Kim could. Kinship assessments could be fast-tracked in emergencies, and only rough guidelines existed as to who a kinship carer might be. There was nothing to legally rule her out.

Kim frowned. 'It's a little unorthodox, seeing as you and John aren't related.' Another long pause. 'But the term *kinship* is a flexible concept. For the purposes of this assessment we can perhaps regard you as a person who shares a community connection with the child.'

'Perfect.' Clare could feel herself smiling and tried to arrange her face into a more professional expression. It was no use. She beamed as Jack wrapped his arms round her waist.

Kim gave Clare a probing look. 'Are you sure you want to do this? Jack has very complex needs. He belongs in a disability placement.'

'Do you have one of those?' asked Clare. They both knew she didn't. 'Just get on with it.'

'I've seen people like you before,' said Kim. 'You think that if you just love a child enough, you can cure him - make him normal. Love can't cure autism.'

'Who said anything about love? The kid needs a safe, temporary place to stay. You don't have one, so I'm offering. Nothing more, nothing less.'

'As long as you know what you're getting into. It will only be until we find John somewhere else, so don't get too attached.'

Clare nodded and Kim finally seemed satisfied.

'Okay, let's get started. I need to be finished by six,' Kim said. 'We've got tickets to the football. The Brisbane Bears elimination final.' Her eyes lit up at the prospect, and she began crossing questions off on the form in front of her. 'That's not pertinent to you ... nor that ... okay. How do you propose to meet the needs of such a challenging child?'

Clare didn't have a clue. Kim believed the boy was mute and Clare knew he wasn't, so they didn't even agree on what those needs were. But Clare would play the game if it meant she could take Jack home.

'Suppose John shows aggression,' said Kim. 'What would you do?'

Clare tried to remember what she was learning at puppy school with her new dog, Samson. 'I'd try ignoring it. Provide no response, no talking, no eye contact. Oh, and I'd give positive reinforcement when his behaviour improved.' Clare had almost said that she'd give Jack a dog biscuit.

Kim looked impressed. 'Excellent. I see you've done some child psychology along the way. That will be a great help.'

Clare nodded and smiled.

'What else might you try?'

'Um ... Redirecting. I'd distract him with a toy when he starts to get agitated and refocus him on a calming activity.' Kim beamed, and ticked off a series of boxes. The puppy training technique for children was working like a charm.

'What about discipline?' asked Kim. 'What are your thoughts?'

'No physical discipline, obviously,' She wracked her brains for some more canine tips. Of course, crate training. 'Time out, perhaps?' said Clare. 'Or a naughty chair?'

Kim moved on to easier questions. Stuff about the layout of her flat, and where Jack would sleep. For some reason, when asked about relationships, Clare didn't mention Adam. Was it because they hadn't been dating for that long? No, a year was long enough. It was more that she didn't want Kim talking to him. Adam wouldn't approve of her impulsive decision any more than Roderick had when she'd suggested it. *'You know the golden rule,'* he'd said. *'Don't get involved. A lawyer who breaks that rule is less effective professionally, loses objectivity, can't function. You know all this, Clare. Let it go, will you?'*

'I'll let it go,' she'd responded. 'Just as soon as you tell me you've found somewhere safe for Jack.'

As the assessment continued, Clare wasn't entirely forthcoming about Samson either. German shepherds had a bad reputation with some people, so Samson was magically transformed into a cuddly labrador pup.

'Before we proceed any further, you should see this.' Kim handed Clare a few stapled pages titled *Report by Specialist Children Services on John Brown.*

Her eyes ran down a daunting litany of behavioural problems listed by the clinical psychologist. *Repeated and severe head banging, extreme tantrums, food obsessions.* Clare took a deep breath. *Hitting others, hitting himself, screaming, spitting, biting, bed-wetting, soiling.* What on earth was she getting herself into? *John has failed to develop language. He only communicates through yelling or by inflections of grunting (animal noises). His mother reports that John never cries. Given his diagnosis of mid- to high-range autism, he may never learn to talk.* Perversely, this piece of misinformation cheered Clare up. Jack could definitely talk. If that part of the report was wrong, maybe the rest was too?

An hour later and the assessment was complete. 'You'll need to book him in for a general health check with your doctor.' Kim stood up. 'And get his vaccinations up to date.'

'Of course,' said Clare. That reminded her - Samson was due for his next set of shots too.

'There's funding available for child care,' Kim continued. 'You can arrange that yourself. Just make sure I sign off on it once it's organised.'

Clare hadn't thought so far ahead. What about that crèche just around the corner from home? Jolly Juniors? No, Jolly Jumbucks. And it was right opposite Samson's doggy day-care. She could drop them both off on her way to work. How long would those places care for Jack in one stretch, she wondered? Whole weekends, maybe? As long as they did late nights so she could still go out with Adam. He wouldn't be able to stay at her place for now, not unless he jumped through some hoops, like submitting to a police check, and she couldn't imagine him doing that. But perhaps, despite her misgivings, he might actually warm to the little boy? It was hard to say with Adam.

Kim handed Clare a business card with her phone number and an after-hours contact. 'For emergencies,' she said. 'There's a spare car seat in my boot. I'll just go get it. And I'll give you a ring in a day or two; see how you're getting on.'

As Kim went to shake hands, she reached past Jack, who was still perched on Clare's knee. The boy bit Kim on the arm. Clare could see his little teeth marks, opposing white crescents on Kim's pink skin. Jack growled low in the back of his throat.

'Good luck,' said Kim, rubbing her arm and frowning. 'You'll need it. I'll meet you outside with the car seat.'

Clare nodded her thanks as Kim left the room. Had she lost all perspective? Lost all judgement? Was she just flattered that Jack seemed to like her and nobody else? She stroked his hair and he snuggled into her shoulder. Clare hugged him tight. What did it matter if her motivation was flawed? All that mattered was that Jack stayed safe and happy until Taylor came back. 'Come on,' she said, taking his hand. 'Let's go home.'

the screen. Jack peeped out from under the blanket. 'Do you want some milk?'

He nodded.

Clare pushed the glazed coffee table against the couch. She went into the kitchen and picked up his bag of toys before pouring a glass of milk. Skim. It was all she had in the fridge. That and Chablis. Clare took Jack the drink and the bag of Pokémon. He rewarded her with an uncertain smile, the first since McDonald's. She pulled up a chair next to him. He drank down the milk, curled up and promptly fell asleep. With a great, relieved sigh, Clare pulled Samson's blanket up to his chin. She sneaked back to the kitchen, poured herself a generous amount of wine and sat down to think. The fog of emotion was clearing, allowing a little more clarity of thought. The enormity of what she'd done was finally hitting home and it was giving her a headache.

Her phone rang. Clare scrambled to retrieve it from her handbag before the jazzy tune woke Jack. It was Helga, director of doggy day-care, a veritable Valkyrie when it came to defending the rights of her canine charges - sometimes even from their misguided owners. This was, apparently, one of those times. 'Samson is still waiting to be collected, Clare. May I remind you that this is becoming an all too regular occurrence.'

'I'm sorry,' said Clare. 'Could you perhaps keep him overnight?'

'A dog is a living, breathing, emotional being, Clare. Not some object that you can keep in the cupboard until you feel like playing with him.'

Clare's cheeks burned. 'Sorry. I'm not really set up for a dog.' She regretted the remark as soon as it had passed her lips, although it was true enough. Managing a German shepherd puppy in an upmarket, second-floor apartment was difficult to say the least.

'Then why did you get one?'

'Samson was my father's dog. I only took him on a month ago, when Dad died suddenly.'

There was a long pause before Helga spoke. 'My condolences,' she said. 'You should consider rehoming him.'

'No!' Clare's raised voice caused Jack to stir in his sleep. 'Dad loved that dog. He'd never forgive me.'

'Don't sacrifice Samson on the altar of your guilt,' said Helga. 'Puppies who spend too long in kennels can suffer long-term damage. Aggression, separation anxiety, depression – an inability to properly bond. Particularly with a dog as large and strong as Samson, the risk must not be overlooked.'

'I'll do better, I promise,' said Clare. 'But I honestly can't come and get him tonight. Could you … could you perhaps drop him off?'

Another long pause. 'Will I see Samson at obedience school this week?' asked Helga. 'You missed last Sunday's session.'

That was blackmail. 'Yes,' she said. 'Of course. We'll be there.'

'Very well, Clare. I'll drop him off around seven.'

'Thank you, Helga.' Clare switched off her phone. Adam was out for the night so he wouldn't ring. In any case, the last thing she wanted was to talk to anybody. Clare pulled a stool up to the breakfast bar, sat down and drained her wine glass. She squeezed her eyes shut, trying to ward off the growing ache in her skull. It had been a very long Friday and the weekend wasn't panning out quite like she'd planned.

to the shining tower of the Southern Cross windmill and the dam. More of a lake, really. A shining expanse of sweet fresh water, fed by the Great Artesian Basin. A vast underground ocean, millions of years old. She'd written a story about it at school: a cross between *Journey to the Centre of the Earth* and *Alice in Wonderland*. A girl escapes from her bossy mother down a wombat hole to the shores of the Great Artesian Basin. She makes friends with the plesiosaurs that live there, grows a long neck and flippers, and she never goes home.

Clare hadn't been to Currawong Creek since she was a child. It was the only permanent home she could remember, a precious constant in an ever-changing world. With Dad in the military, she and Ryan had grown up as army brats. Their childhood had been shaped by the constant loss of friendships, by never having a hometown, or any place to belong. It was hard on them and on their mother. Clare must have been about eleven years old on that final visit to Currawong. It was the same summer that Mum had left them. Afterwards Dad had discouraged all contact with her side of the family. Clare had lost both her mother and her grandparents in one cruel blow.

She'd watched her father fight his way out from under the loneliness and grief, fight to obliterate the memories of their former life. And Clare had respected his wishes, all this time. The dreams of Currawong, its creeks and mountains, had slowly faded. Even when Grandma died they'd only sent flowers. That was ten years ago, and now Dad was dead as well. How was Grandad, she dared to wonder? He'd have to be at least seventy by now. Clare could still picture him, a pair of huge clydesdale horses in tow, crossing the stable yard to the cart shed.

Those clydesdales had seemed bigger than elephants when she was a child. But they were gentle giants and she couldn't ever remember being afraid. Not even when Ryan dared her to lead their pony, Smudge, under the belly of Rastus, Currawong's enormous stallion. Eighteen hands, he'd stood. Rastus had spooked and reared, a tonne of horseflesh looming above her, blotting out the sky. His platter-sized hooves had crashed to earth just inches from her head. But she'd known with calm certainty that Rastus wouldn't hurt her, that he would do everything to avoid her.

That was a lifetime ago. Those things had happened to a different person. After finishing school she'd studied law on her father's advice and built a career in the city.

She didn't have many friends, but that didn't bother her. Childhood experience had taught Clare that friendships didn't last anyway. It was an advantage that she didn't have a busy social calendar to distract from her professional ambitions. Her life up until now had suited very well.

Sixteen years had passed since she'd last seen Grandad. At first, each time a hot north wind blew, it had reminded her of Currawong and she'd ached for her grandparents, but she'd learned the knack of letting go. She'd built a fence around her heart, walling out the pain, growing into a self-contained, studious teenager who'd tried hard to please her father. In the end she'd hardly thought of them at all. Until today. It was only natural, she supposed, to think of family with her father's death so fresh. Grandad probably didn't even know that Dad was gone. Who would have told him?

Samson started to bark, then with an almighty tug he wrenched the lead from her hand, dragging her away from her recollections.

Clare jumped to her feet. The sun was still in her eyes and it was hard to see. She shielded her face with a hand and scanned the playground. Where was Jack?

'Jack,' she yelled. 'Jack!'

Clare sprinted down the hill after Samson. The dog ran straight as an arrow, and like an arrow, he seemed unable to deviate from his course. He ploughed straight through a group of children.

'Is that your dog?' asked a red-faced woman nursing a screaming toddler.

'I'm reporting you,' said another, comforting a crying child at the same time. 'Dogs like that should be put down.'

'So sorry,' called Clare, putting on a burst of speed. She was well out of earshot before anybody else had a chance to complain. Clare crested the hill and stopped to catch her breath. In the distance, at the far side of the barbecue area, stood a red and yellow striped marquee. Bunches of bright balloons were strung from poles. Someone was handing out plates to a line of waiting children, while parents milled about. Clare ran closer for a better look. She could see now. A colourful clown held aloft an elaborate, castle-shaped birthday cake. Candles in the shape of fluttering flags graced the towers and turrets, along with tiny chocolate cannons. Its moat, complete with candy swans, glinted in the sun. A truly magnificent creation. A work of art - and Samson was on a collision course with both the clown and the cake.

'Samson!' yelled Clare. She'd never get there in time. It was like being witness to a looming train wreck, and being powerless to stop it. Everything seemed to be happening in slow motion. Too late now. Samson bowled the clown over and the cake toppled majestically to the grass. Toy soldiers leaped from the battlements as it fell. The poor clown landed face down in the ruins, while kids ran screaming in every direction. All except one - Jack.

Jack had crashed the party, and had been standing in line with a plate. Now he trotted over to the smashed cake and, using both fists, started shovelling chocolate and cream off the ground, and into his mouth. One turret. A piece of blue moat. The drawbridge. Then Samson grabbed a mouthful of Jack's jeans. He began dragging the child back towards Clare by the seat of his pants, ripping the threadbare fabric.

'Help!' A woman tried to move towards Jack, but her stilettos sank into the grass. Clare guessed her to be the party host. 'Somebody help that little boy. That brute of a dog's got him.'

The clown dashed forward. Clare winced as he kicked Samson in the jaw, but the dog maintained his grip. The clown grabbed hold of Jack, and played a brief game of tug of war, until Jack sank his teeth into the man's clutching hand. The clown let go, yelling that he'd been bitten.

'Get back,' said the woman. 'That dog's dangerous. It just bit this poor man.'

'Not the dog,' wailed the clown. 'The boy. It was that f**king boy who bit me.'

Some kids gawked at him, open-mouthed. Others stared at each other and giggled. 'That clown's *ruuude*,' said one. 'He just said a bad word.' The parents looked even more horrified than before.

Clare skidded to a halt in the midst of the chaos, planting herself squarely between Jack and Samson and the angry horde. She held up her hands, palms out, and forced her face into a smile. 'I'm Clare,' she said. 'And little Jack here ...' She placed a protective hand on his shoulder. 'He was lost. Thank goodness my dog found him.'

Samson barked and the crowd, as one, took a step back.

'He got a little carried away, that's all. A little too enthusiastic ... a little over-affectionate.' She grabbed hold of Samson's trailing lead and picked up Jack. 'Very sorry about the cake. It was absolutely spectacular, by the way. Let me pay for it.' Clare put Jack down again and pulled her purse from the tote bag slung over her shoulder. 'I insist.'

'Do I know you?' asked the host.

Clare maintained her smile. It was beginning to make her cheeks ache.

'And you mean to tell me that's your boy?' The woman's tone was accusing.

Clare nodded. She could feel her smile fading.

'So, he was never invited?'

'No. Jack's a blow in, I'm afraid. I do apologise.'

A confused chattering of *I thought he was with you,* began among the guests. Clare unzipped her purse, plucked out the notes inside, around two hundred dollars' worth, and shoved them at the woman. Then the three of them made a run for it, Jack and Samson laughing and barking as they sped away. Back on the street, Jack's sticky hand sneaked into hers. The same damned question niggled again. What had she got herself into?

CHAPTER 5

Clare woke to Jack jumping on the bed. She had a vague memory of him doing the same thing earlier on when it was barely light, and of her pulling the pillow over her head and going back to sleep. Clare groaned. Sunday morning, but not like any Sunday morning she could remember. She was used to suiting herself, waking in her own time, at her own pace. She sniffed. There was a sickly, sweet odour in the air. Clare glanced at the clock on her bedside table. Why couldn't she see the time? She raised herself up on one elbow. A large tumbler was in the way, brimming with something that looked suspiciously like urine. What on earth?

Jack bounced off the bed, picked up the glass in both hands and offered it to her, slopping its pale contents over the doona. She recoiled and sniffed again. Wine, stale wine. He'd been in the fridge. 'Jack, no.' What if he'd been drinking it himself? She imagined Kim's reproachful face as they pumped Jack's stomach in the emergency room.

Clare prepared to tell him off, but something in his expression puzzled her, gave her pause. It was an expression she'd not seen on his face before. Eager, hopeful ... shyly proud. Clare was trained to get into people's heads, discover their deepest motivations. How else could you portray them sympathetically to a magistrate? Everyone had a reason for what they did. The trick was to pick it. And then it hit her – Jack wasn't being naughty. He wanted to please her by bringing her the wine. Heaven knows she'd swilled enough of the stuff last night. Another evening of drinking alone, she thought ruefully. How was a four-year-old supposed to know that a beverage she'd enjoyed so much last night, would be repulsive to her in the morning? It was touching really. Thank heavens she hadn't scolded him.

Clare took a sip, trying not to screw up her face. 'Thanks, Jack.' He flashed a swift smile and scampered from the room. Clare fell back on the pillow, still tired. Her tongue was thick and furry. She hadn't brushed her teeth last night. Neither had Jack. Jack didn't even have a toothbrush. What sort of a foster mother was she? With an immense effort she threw off the doona. The room smelled like a bar. She glanced at herself in the mirror. Lank, tangled hair that needed washing. Dark rings beneath bloodshot eyes. Her white T-shirt had a big brown stain down the front, courtesy of last night's tub of chocolate ice-cream. Lovely.

Clare emerged from her bedroom to find Jack asleep on the couch in front of cartoons. It was funny how he could just fall asleep like that. One minute a bundle of energy, the next minute, dead to the world. By the looks of things he'd been up half the night. There were no books left on the shelf. Instead they were strewn over the floor, together with a mangled loaf of bread, its soft middle scooped out. Crumbs everywhere. Biro and lipstick scribbles on the wall. A lidless tub of melted ice-cream on a chair. Double rows of spice jars marched like little soldiers along the artificial turf of Samson's doggy loo, flanking a procession of Pokémon toys.

No serious damage. You couldn't really blame the kid, she thought, considering there wasn't much for him to play with. She'd have to fix that, buy some toys. Put things up high. Fit some childproof locks. Samson whined from his crate. Normally on Sunday she took him on a morning walk to the park. She thought back to the chaos of yesterday. No, the park was off limits for the time being. Anyway, with Jack flaked out on the sofa, she couldn't really leave the flat at all. How on earth did full-time parents manage? She was stuck at home unless she woke him up, and that might be disastrous. As Dad used to say, best to let sleeping dogs lie. Samson would need to use his inside toilet this morning.

Clare cleared away the spice jars, and the toys, and the tiny mirrored elephant with the raised trunk that stood in pride of place on top of the wooden wee post. She dumped them in a sink of hot, soapy water. She fetched the key to the padlock and released Samson from his crate. The dog bounded obediently to the patch of fake grass. He didn't squat like a puppy any more to empty his bladder. Instead he lifted his leg, half-missing the fake tree trunk and leaving a mustard coloured spray pattern on the wall. Oh dear. She'd bought the Supersize Pooch model, but the poky contraption looked like it was designed more for a poodle than for a German shepherd.

Samson trotted into the kitchen and fetched his lead from the hook. Clare shook her head. 'Not this morning.' She poured herself a coffee and sat down in a chair by the window. Samson cocked his head and inspected her face, confirming she was serious. Then he leaped for the treadmill, evenly positioning his great paws, quivering a little with anticipation. He gave a soft whimper. Clare put her forefinger to her lips. 'Shh … not now. You'll wake Jack.' Samson trotted to the sideboard, stood on his hind legs and picked up the remote control in his mouth. He dumped it in Clare's lap. She hadn't realised dogs were so clever.

'Okay, just on slow.'

The dog repositioned himself with a joyful wag of his tail. The treadmill beeped twice and ground into action. Clare kept a close eye on Jack, but he didn't stir. Samson watched her as he padded along the rubber belt, ears pricked, his eyes pleading. She knew that look. He whined again. He'd bark soon if he didn't get his way. She sped up the treadmill until Samson was galloping along, and wondered suddenly what her grandfather would make of it. She recalled a timeless scene – driving down the winding lane to Merriang as a child, sitting high and proud beside Grandad in the sulky, as he cracked the carriage whip above Baron's broad back. Currawong's energetic pair of dalmatians, Pongo and Perdita, leading the way to town, tails aloft, getting all the gossip with their twitching noses. By comparison, Samson here, toiling away on a stainless steel treadmill in a second-floor apartment was a sad and sorry sight. She felt a rush of sympathy for him. Helga was right - this was no life for a dog.

A knock came at the door and Samson leaped from the treadmill in a flurry of barking. His voice was growing deeper and louder every day. What if it was Mr Jacobs, the secretary of the building's body corporate? Strata management had given her permission to keep a dog. Luckily they hadn't asked about the breed. Samson must be pretty close to breaking the *peaceful enjoyment* noise provision by now, and it was Sunday morning for Christ's sake. Why couldn't he just shut up?

Clare opened the door. It wasn't Mr Jacobs. Worse than that, it was Adam. Clare shook her head in disbelief. How could it be Adam? The first time in the entire twelve months of their relationship that he'd dropped by unannounced, and she just happened to look a wreck. And the place was a mess; utterly trashed. It wasn't fair.

Samson growled and Adam backed up a fraction.

'I'll put him away.' Clare grabbed Samson's collar and dragged him off to his crate.

'Feeling better?' Adam asked from the doorway. 'You missed a real treat on Friday.' He flashed his handsome smile, but she didn't respond. 'I tried to ring' he said, 'but your phone's turned off.'

He searched her face with his piercing grey eyes. Sunday morning, and Adam was still the picture of style. White oxford shirt with rolled-up sleeves exposing smooth, tanned forearms. Her favourite Borrelli boot-leg jeans, the ones with the hand-stitched, twisted seams. A razor-straight part in his, dark flicked-back hair. His mouth was straight too, and the bridge of his nose. Everything about him was sharply defined.

Clare, by contrast, was a frump. She needed to shower, to change, to wash her hair. She needed to make Adam go away and come back in half an hour. She needed for him not to go into the lounge room and expect to sit down on the couch. Clare ducked into the bathroom and dragged a brush through her hair. Not that it would help much. Combed greasy didn't look much better than tangled greasy. She spared herself by not looking in the mirror.

Jack ran in and clamped onto her leg.

'Clare?' Adam's voice was uncertain, but he'd obviously moved from the doorway into the lounge room. 'Clare? Who's the kid?' She froze, as if she might thereby evade detection, '...and what happened to the couch?'

Clare looked down at Jack's anxious, upturned face and gave him what she hoped was a reassuring smile. Dogs could sense your mood, that's what Helga said. Maybe kids could, too? She didn't want Jack to think there was anything wrong. And anyway, was there anything wrong? Not really. Her vanity was taking a bit of a hit, that was all. Clare took a deep breath, picked Jack up and went into the lounge room.

Adam stared at them, a confused expression on his face. 'The dog was bad enough, Clare. But a kid? And who demolished the apartment? Were you robbed?'

'This is Jack,' she said, pushing the little boy forward. 'He's the son of a client who's-' She'd been about to say *who's done a runner*. 'A client who's unable to look after him this weekend.'

'Isn't that a bit ... unorthodox?' said Adam. He knew very well that it was. He was a barrister, a rising star. Clare couldn't imagine what he must think about her getting so personally involved with a client. It was about as unprofessional as you could get.

'There were no disability placements available,' she said. 'You can't put such a little boy into a residential unit. He'd be eaten alive.'

She realised her mistake at once.

'Disability?' said Adam. He leaned close and peered at Jack, like he was a bug under a microscope. 'What the hell's wrong with him then?'

Jack spat in his face. Adam recoiled and plucked a tissue from the box on the shelf. 'Dirty little bugger,' he said, wiping his cheek. 'He could have AIDS or anything.'

'Would you please not talk about Jack like that,' said Clare. 'He's not deaf.'

'Okay then. He's not deaf, so what is he? What's wrong with him,' asked Adam again, this time from a safe distance.

Jack ran to the couch and hid beneath Samson's blanket. 'They say he's autistic,' said Clare. 'But I think they're wrong.' She could hear the defiant tilt in her voice.

Adam indicated the ruin all around. 'The flat looks like this and you think they're wrong. *You* do. You — who've had so much experience with children.'

She hated it when he got sarcastic like this.

'Didn't you tell me just last week that you couldn't stand kids? That you didn't have a clue about them? And now you're a f**king expert?'

She wished he wouldn't swear like that in front of Jack. 'This is different,' she said. 'There was nobody else. Jesus, Adam. It's just for a weekend.'

'So that's why you couldn't come on Friday' said Adam. 'You weren't sick at all, were you?' She didn't deny it. He snorted. 'Not much of a relationship if we can't be honest with each other.' It was the first thing he'd said that she agreed with.

They stared at each other in silence for a few moments. Adam frowned then said, 'Sorry. Can we start again?' He slipped an arm around her waist, kissed her cheek, her ear, the nape of her neck. Clare yielded a little. What did she expect? He'd had no more to do with children than she had. No nieces, no nephews. She loved him for his dry wit, his brilliant mind, his ambition, not for his parenting skills 'I've missed you,' he said.

She'd missed him too. It was a whole month since she'd spent a weekend at his South Bank apartment, a month since Samson had moved in. She loved Adam's place, with its panoramic views of the tranquil Brisbane river. You could see the botanical gardens from the balcony, the golden glow of Brisbane's CBD at night. The riverfront restaurant precinct was a short stroll away, Southbank just a two-minute ferry ride. Clare looked at Samson, whining in his crate. Helga or no Helga, she needed to find a good kennel where he could spend his weekends.

Adam kissed her mouth with searching lips. Clare waited for the hot, insistent pull of him to kick in, the delicious hunger for more. But the kiss was a fizzer. Nothing. Well, how was she supposed to feel romantic with Jack peeking from the couch and with Samson keeping up an indignant whine? She pulled away. Adam threw up his hands.

'Lisa brought down the house with her performance in Giselle" he said pointedly. 'Thanks so much for asking.'

'If I'd told you about Jack, you wouldn't have understood.'

'No,' he said. 'I wouldn't have. The reasons we don't get involved with our clients is first-year law stuff. This – ' he gestured around the apartment – 'This ... situation you've got yourself into. It has conflict of interest written all over it.'

Clare was suddenly weary. He was right, of course. She'd been a fool, but a willing one. And she still was.

Adam ran his hand across the tear in the back of the couch, a stricken expression on his face. Then he peered at Jack again. 'Roderick must be ropeable.'.

'He's not happy,' she said. 'But he didn't go off at me like you just did. Christ, Adam, it's only temporary.'

'Fine,' said Adam. 'It's clear I won't be able to talk any sense into you.' He looked at the shambles all around and grimaced. 'Call me when you get yourself sorted.' He turned to go, paused when he reached the door, and came back into the lounge. He kissed her on top of her head. 'Spend next weekend at my place,' he whispered. 'Put the dog in a kennel, find somewhere else for the kid if, God forbid, he's still here, and come home with me on Friday. Okay?'

She nodded and watched him leave. As soon as he'd gone, Jack released Samson from the crate. The two of them started a rowdy game of chasey, racing round and round the beleaguered couch. Clare slumped down among its dishevelled cushions. She glanced at the clock. Time to get ready for Helga's doggy obedience class. What a shame there wasn't one for kids too.

. . .

Clare arrived at Centennial Reserve, a huge expanse of well-kept parks and playing fields. She was on time for once, and sat Jack down on a shady bench with a good view of the class. 'Stay,' she said, without much hope. Then she joined the line of dogs and owners. Samson and Clare were in the *beginner basics* class, but several grades of training were taking place simultaneously. Next door were the agility dogs. They were doing some sort of trial, and had quite an audience. Their arena looked just like a children's playground, complete with colourful equipment, and Jack couldn't seem to take his eyes off it. Neither could Clare.

She watched a dog prance down the course beside his owner. A pitch-black German shepherd – a grown up version of Samson. Before long he was leaping over obstacles and into tyres, shooting through brightly striped tunnels and balancing on boardwalks. He teetered on a seesaw, scaled walls and finished by weaving between a line of purple poles at breakneck speed. So clever. Clare wanted to applaud.

She was less enthusiastic about the next performance. It started off well enough. A graceful standard poodle, sailing over jumps and bounding into stripy tunnels. 'Be mindful of your dog's mood. Always watch his ears,' boomed Helga. But Clare was too busy watching the neighbouring arena to pay much attention to Samson's ears. Samson tugged on his lead just as a ripple of laughter rose from the crowd.

Oh no — please, no. Jack had escaped his bench and was crawling into the tunnel after the poodle. Samson plunged forward and Clare was so distracted that she dropped the lead. He took off after Jack. Here we go again, she thought.

The crowd cheered and clapped as they were all put through their paces. First the poodle and its handler, both trying to ignore the odd turn of events. Then Jack, crawling and seesawing and climbing the equipment with surprising alacrity, copying the poodle's every move. Then Samson, fearlessly pursuing Jack over and under and through every obstacle. And finally Clare, bringing up the rear, calling ineffectually to her charges.

How humiliating. Helga sent them all packing.

Clare had found a dog friendly café on the far side of the park, ordered ice creams and milk shakes, and sat down to lick her wounds. But for some reason, the embarrassment wasn't as bad as she'd expected. Maybe she was just getting used to it. Clare slurped the last of her milkshake, making Jack giggle. Clare hadn't had a milkshake since she was a kid. She'd forgotten how delicious they were. Grandma used to make the best malted shakes, with creamy milk fresh from Angel, their jersey house cow. Angel gave twenty litres of foaming white milk a day, more than enough for her calf and the household combined. Clare had loved Angel's little calves, honey coloured with pretty dished faces. They had the longest, blondest lashes imaginable, framing the biggest, brownest eyes. Just like Bambi. Jack would love them too.

Clare shook her head, chasing away the idea. What was with her? Why was she thinking about the farm so much? Jack let Samson lick his ice-cream, but Clare was prepared for it. She had a second one ready, gave it to Jack, and allowed him to share the first with the dog. It worked a treat. From now on, rather than scold Jack for giving his food to Samson, she'd have something he was allowed to share.

Another little boy arrived with his mother, and started playing with Matchbox cars at a nearby table. Jack stared and got off his chair. 'Sit, Jack,' said Clare. After a moment's indecision, he sat back down and quietly ate his ice-cream. Yes! Clare could hardly believe it. She felt a surge of triumph. Maybe she was finally getting a handle on the kid. It had been a hell of a day, and it was still only lunchtime. But now, sitting in the sun with a surprisingly compliant child and a tired, happy dog, smiling at the other mothers, watching Jack's delight as sparrows stole crumbs from beneath the tables – right now, all seemed well with the world.

Come on Jacky,' she said. 'You've been good. Let's go through the car wash.'

CHAPTER 6

The weekend with Adam never eventuated. It was three weeks now, since Jack had turned Clare's life upside down, and there was still no sign of Taylor Brown. Jolly Jumbucks didn't do weekends. They didn't even do late nights. They closed, in fact, at six o'clock.

Jack hadn't settled well into their kindergarten program. Despite the cheerful sign out the front, proclaiming the place to be *A Worry Free Home Away From Home*, Clare spent her workdays rigid with anxiety, fearing that every phone call might be from the dreaded centre manager. And unfortunately, a lot of them were. Jack was soiling himself. Jack had thrown yet another tantrum. Jack had hurled his food, and everybody else's, at the Happy Elves - the ridiculous name they gave the mostly teenage kindergarten assistants. Jack had bitten another child. Jack was hoarding all the toys. He'd made them into a giant pile and then perched in defiance on top of them, in some sort of heroic last stand. He was screaming and spitting and snapping at anybody who came near.

Adam was no support, although he had calmed down about her having Jack. There'd been some mid-week lunches, and one stolen afternoon at his place, but he didn't visit her flat any more. Adam said it was because he didn't want to upset Jack. 'Don't worry about me,' he'd say. 'I'm snowed under with work at the moment anyway. We'll wait until you find somewhere for the boy.'

The weeks dragged on. At first she was grateful for Adam's patience, then surprised and in the end even a little suspicious of it. He still rang her most nights after Jack went to bed. She used to love his phone calls, full of wonderful stories about triumphs and mistakes in the court room. Lately though, any talk of mistakes left her cringing. Clare had made more mistakes in the last three weeks than she had in her entire legal career. And on top of that, she'd been late for work nearly every day.

Dropping Jack off at child care was a long, drawn-out process. Painful too. Jack clung to her, wailing at the top of his lungs, holding on with surprising strength. When the centre staff intervened, Jack transformed from a clingy child into a violent ball of rage. Clare hadn't yet managed to get away in under half an hour. At work she'd missed a few deadlines, prepared a few substandard briefs that she knew wouldn't pass muster, and then stayed up all night redrafting. In between everything else, she was reading an assortment of child psychology and parenting books, as well as keeping up with case law. Once, the grey light of morning had crept through the window blind before she was through. And there was no catching a quick sleep between sunrise and eight o'clock any more. Jack always woke at the crack of dawn and rattled Samson's crate to make him bark. Clare couldn't risk that. So she had to get up, no matter how tired she was.

Inexplicably, the little boy was a delight in the early morning: cooperative, cute, endearing even. Jack loved getting dressed in the new clothes that she'd bought him. He inspected himself in the mirror, seemingly fascinated by his different reflections. He loved his bowl of cocoa pops, followed by rounds of buttery vegemite toast. Clare was following suit -so much quicker and easier to make them both the same breakfast. Tasty too, and only temporary. So what about Adam's organic berries and yoghurt.

It was after breakfast when the trouble began. Jack didn't want to leave the flat. He'd been okay on day one. Not too bad on day two, but by day three he'd figured it out. Leaving the flat in the morning meant going to child care. So after breakfast Jack hid under the bed, or climbed into the bathtub, or wedged himself beneath the couch. When Clare finally extracted him, which of course she had to do, he'd throw the mother of all tantrums. He'd wet himself, necessitating a change of clothes. But how to dress a kicking, screaming four-year-old? Samson would hide in his crate and Clare felt like joining him. Heaven knows what the neighbours thought. She was exhausted before she even left the apartment.

FRIDAY MORNING. Roderick poked his head in. 'Clare - my office.'

What now? Clare sighed and followed him down the hall.

He gestured for her to sit down. 'Coffee?'

She nodded and he put on the jug. It must be very bad news if he was making her coffee. 'I've heard from Taylor. She wants to know how her son is.'

'That's marvellous,' said Clare.

'She called him Jack by the way.'

'That's what I told Kim.'

'Yes,' said Roderick. 'You did.' He was being unusually reticent.

'Where is Taylor?' asked Clare.

'Living in Ipswich with a new partner. Some sort of boarding house. She didn't say exactly.'

'What about her court date? It's next week. Do you think she'll turn up?'

Roderick poured her a coffee, then sat on the desk and nursed his own. 'She said she would.' He seemed deep in thought.

'Shall I represent her then?' asked Clare. 'Jack will be over the moon. When does Taylor want to collect him?'

'That's the thing.' He gazed out the window for a moment before turning to look at her. 'She doesn't.'

Clare looked blank. She must have heard him wrong. 'What do you mean, she doesn't?' Clare waited for Roderick to explain, but he only shrugged. 'You mean she doesn't want her own child?'

'Taylor's in a difficult position,' he said. 'There's her new boyfriend, for starters. Belts her apparently, and a junkie to boot. I'm afraid that under his influence Taylor has lapsed from the methadone program.' Roderick took a sip from his mug. 'She's actively using again, Clare. The girl has enough sense to know she can't look after her son right now.'

'Where does she think Jack is?' asked Clare. 'Does she even care?'

Roderick gave her a reproachful look. 'Of course she cares. If Taylor didn't voluntarily surrender the child at this stage, the department would be under an obligation to take him from her. She knows that.' He downed the rest of his coffee in one gulp. 'And as to your other question, Taylor believes her child is in a caring foster home. Which is the case, isn't it?'

'But I thought that you didn't approve?' said Clare. 'That you thought it was stupid and unprofessional to take Jack on?'

'I did, I did,' he said. 'But I've changed my mind. Don't forget, my young Sam's the same age as Jack. Nobody wants to see a child that young go into a residential unit. You have a good heart, Clare, a fearless heart, and you've already saved Jack from great harm. You're not afraid to put yourself on the line. The least we can do is back you.' He smiled. 'If you must know, we've all been very moved and humbled by what you've done.'

Clare processed his words. That was all very well, very flattering. But it still left the little issue of Jack.

There was a knock at the door and Veronica came in without waiting for an invitation. She looked at Clare then back to Roderick. 'More problems?' she said with a smile.

Clare glared at her. Why couldn't anybody else see the woman for what she was?

'Whatever it is Ronnie, it can wait,' said Roderick. 'I'm not quite finished here.'

Veronica cast Clare a pitying glance and withdrew. She probably thought Roderick was chewing her out for something. If only she'd barged in a few seconds earlier in time to hear all the compliments.

'I assume you're prepared to keep the child until a more suitable placement is found?' said Roderick.

Clare didn't know what to say. Taylor loved Jack. Clare didn't know exactly how she knew it. She just knew it. And Jack loved his mother. Clare had always believed that Taylor would return for her son sooner rather than later. That her leaving had been some kind of aberration, some kind of desperate, last-ditch measure to cope with an impossible living situation. Taylor would come to her senses, and then Clare could refer her and Jack to the variety of excellent support services linked to the legal aid centre: crisis accommodation, counselling and health care. If Taylor had an abusive partner, there were refuges and domestic violence outreach workers. If she wanted help to manage Jack, Clare could make parenting classes and child psychologists available. If she needed to get back on track with her methadone program, Clare could help there too. There was so much she was ready to do, that she wanted to do, for Jack and Taylor. And now?

'Truth is, I'm having a tough time of it.' Clare disliked the tone of defeat in her voice. 'Jack hates being in child care. It was bad enough for the poor kid when his mother disappeared. Now it feels like I'm traumatising him all over again every morning when I leave It makes me late, distracts me, hurts him ... '

Roderick popped a half-empty packet of Tim Tams onto the table. 'Have one,' he said. 'Go on.'

She extracted a chocolate biscuit. He was being so amenable. For some reason it made her nervous. 'You have some time off owing, Clare,' he said. 'God knows you've only taken one holiday in three years. You've always staffed our Christmas skeleton roster. You're never sick.' What was he saying? 'Take some leave, Clare, until they find somewhere else for Jack. It shouldn't take long. A week or two...'

'So you don't want me...?'

Roderick held up his hand. 'There'll be none of that. I want you working here more than you know. But will it kill you to take a break when you're owed it?'

Clare thought the suggestion through, trying to put aside the idea that this was just a nice way to get rid of her. But Roderick was as straight as they came. She could trust him. 'How's Kim going with finding Jack a new home?'

'She's been a bit vague,' said Roderick. 'Apparently they're expecting a disability placement to open up soon.'

'He doesn't need a disability placement,' said Clare. 'There'd be so many more options available if they looked in the pool of general foster carers.'

'Clare,' said Roderick in a soothing voice that got her back up straightaway. 'We lose our objectivity when we get too close.' What was it with the royal *we*? 'You said yourself, not ten minutes ago, that Jack has some very challenging behaviours.'

'He's four years old,' she said, 'and he's just lost his mother. What do you expect?'

Roderick tapped his finger on the desktop. 'Does he speak?'

'Of course he does. I already told you that.'

'The average four-year-old asks over four hundred questions a day,' said Roderick. 'I know our Sam does. What did Jack ask you today? Or yesterday? What did he say?'

Clare was about to launch into her answer. About how Jack always asked for strawberry ice-cream because he liked it better than vanilla or chocolate. About how he wanted her to read *The Poky Little Puppy* before bed. About how he complained when she switched the television over from cartoons to the news at seven o'clock. 'I want cartoons,' he'd said just last night. But when she thought about it, when she *really* thought about it, she realised that Jack had said no such thing. Clare even surprised herself with this revelation. She knew strawberry was his favourite flavour because he gave chocolate or vanilla to Samson. She always read him *The Poky Little Puppy* before bed because he threw the other books on the floor. He asked her not to switch channels by running off with the remote control.

She wracked her brain to come up with examples of him speaking. 'Jack tells me when visitors come,' she said at last. But that wasn't strictly true either. What Jack actually did was rush to the door with

Samson and bark. It was a game, Clare knew that. A copying game. But she dared not tell Roderick that the only verbal communication the child had made during his fortnight's stay, apart from screaming, was to make animal noises.

It appeared Roderick could read her mind. 'File notes say the boy is completely non-verbal,' he said. 'Taylor's been getting a payment available only to parents of disabled children."

'You've got to be kidding me,' said Clare. 'That payment's far more generous than the regular single parent benefit. Can't you see what's happened? She's gone along with a misdiagnosis to get more money.'

'Wherever the truth lies,' said Roderick, 'Jack is a special case, wouldn't you agree?' Clare had to nod. 'And finding him a suitable placement will take time.' She nodded again, begrudgingly. 'Well, Clare, the offer's there. Take a break until this matter is resolved.'

Clare considered his words. Maybe he was right. She did need a holiday. She was sleep-deprived, strung-out. She'd lost weight. What a luxury it would be to forget about work for a while. And how good for Jack? No day care. He could stay home all day with her and Samson. They could take drives to the beach or into the country. She could let them both off the leash. By the time the child had a new placement, he'd be calmer, more settled. More able to cope.

'I'll think about it,' she said. 'I'll seriously think about it.'

'Capital.' Roderick was beaming. A genuine, open, inclusive smile. The sort that made you want to be around him. 'Just in case, I'll send somebody in and you can bring them up to speed on your cases. Ronnie perhaps?'

'No,' said Clare quickly. 'Not Veronica. She was just telling me yesterday how snowed under she is.'

Roderick looked surprised. 'Really? I thought her workload was a touch on the light side. Much lighter than yours, Clare. I'd better look into that.' He fixed her with encouraging eyes. 'Our extra funding is in. That young bloke Davis starts next week, so we won't be down a solicitor. It's the best possible time for you to take leave.'

As Roderick talked, Clare found she'd made her decision. A weight seemed to lift from he, and she smiled. 'Relax boss. You've convinced me.'

'That's more like it,' he said, sounding pleased with himself. 'I reckon Isaac's our man. He's in court this morning, but I'll send him round to you when he gets back. Now, get out of here.'

'You'll let me know when there's any news?' said Clare.

Roderick nodded. 'And don't worry about Taylor . . . I'll represent her myself.'

CLARE RETURNED TO HER OFFICE. She was lighter, happier than she'd been. Roderick's praise had left a warm residual glow, and everything about her decision felt right. She launched into her day with renewed enthusiasm, pulling out manila folders, going through the most important points that she needed to brief Isaac about. Clare liked Isaac. He was competent and compassionate. She trusted that he'd act in her clients' best interests while she was away.

The phone rang - Roderick again. 'Do me a favour, Clare? The annual Bar Association lunch is on today. I'm supposed to go, but you know how I hate those functions.'

Clare knew all about the lunch. Adam had promised ages ago to take her and she'd been really looking forward to it. That lunch was one of the high points of Brisbane's legal calendar, a supreme networking opportunity. A place to be seen. But then on Monday Adam had cancelled on her. Apparently he had an appearance that day at Dalby court; an assault or something. Dalby was way out west, not too far from Currawong Creek, her grandfather's place. Odd, how little reminders of Grandad kept popping up. Clare hadn't even known that Adam worked the country court circuit, but she supposed a young barrister couldn't refuse briefs - not even a rising star like Adam. He could afford to miss the lunch. As Paul Dunbar's junior, his career was right on track. But for Clare it had been a definite disappointment.

'Take my place today, will you?' asked Roderick. 'They'll bang on a slap-up meal, and you'll have the chance to sound out Justice Cameron before you take that break. He's had his eye on you.'

'Really?' said Clare. 'Don't you normally send Ted to these things?'

'I don't want to send Ted,' he said. 'I want to send you.'

Clare experienced a shiver of excitement and pride. 'Thanks, Rod,' she said. 'I'd love to go. You can count on me.'

CHAPTER 7

Brisbane's Riverview Hotel. The concierge wore a gold braided uniform. Clare told him her name and he ticked it off the list, directing her to the first floor. She made straight for the ladies room. Good, it was empty. She inspected herself in the full-length mirror. For once she approved. The fact that she'd dropped a kilo or two meant her business suit fitted like a glove. Better than it ever had. She looked sexy even, in a sensible, corporate sort of way. Stress must be good for her.

Clare smiled at her reflection, inspected her hair, her make-up, her teeth. Her dark suit contrasted with her blonde bob. The look was serious, but stylish. And for the first time in days she wasn't thinking about Jack. But of course, that wasn't true, was it? She had to think about him, in order to congratulate herself for not thinking about him. Clare shook her head. Today was a career-building exercise, no room for foolishness. She exited the gleaming marble bathroom and followed the signs to the hotel's Grand Ballroom. Tables were already filling up with guests. Impeccably clad waiters dispensed warm bread rolls and jugs of water, bobbing with ice cubes and lemon slices.

The man at the door led her to a table set for six, positioned near the front of the room. Clare couldn't believe her luck. Justice Cameron was at the very next table. It was too perfect. Clare pulled out her chair to sit down and the judge turned around.

'Just the person I wanted to see.' Justice Cameron spoke in a low voice to the man beside him, and he swung around too and beamed at her. It was Paul Dunbar. She'd never actually met him before, but she recognised him at once. Paul Dunbar was the city's most notable criminal barrister, and its most flamboyant as well. He wore a purple shirt, a polka-dotted bow tie and sported a magnificent handlebar moustache, a la Merv Hughes. The moustache, in combination with his massive bald head, made Dunbar look somewhat like a walrus.

'Frank and I were just talking about you, Ms Mitchell,' Dunbar said. 'Discussing your dazzling advocacy.' He twirled his moustache between thumb and forefinger. 'There's been a lot of talk in Chambers about the Fenwick case. Bringing the teacher in like that, at the last minute? You practically turned the tables on the rules of evidence.' He slapped his broad thigh. 'Had the jury eating right out of your hand. I hear the prosecutor went so red at the *not guilty* verdict that he popped a vein. That's the way to nail a trial,' he said. 'With a bit of panache.' His sweeping arm gesture resulted in a firm clout to the head of the judge. 'Ha,' said Dunbar. 'Take that, Frank Cameron. For all the trouble you've caused me in your estimable court.'

'Thank you, Mr Dunbar,' she stammered.

'Call me Paul, please.'

Clare felt herself flush as red as the aforementioned prosecutor. She *had* pulled off a coup in the Fenwick trial. Roderick had almost not let her have the case. If their client hadn't been so emotionally attached to her, he would have farmed it out to one of his pet barristers. But the girl wouldn't have testified for anybody else. She only trusted Clare. Clare spent many hours overtime, settling her, reassuring her, even going to her house when her nerve threatened to fail. That was crossing the line between counsel and client, but it had paid off. The girl ended up being an astonishingly compelling witness. Such a standout victory in a high profile case was bound to attract attention, but she'd never imagined somebody like Paul Dunbar would sit up and take notice. She wished that Veronica had been there to hear Paul Dunbar praise her like that.

'Your Roderick and I go way back,' said Paul. 'At law school together, we were. Best friends for years.'

Clare already knew that. Roderick had given Veronica her job at Fortitude Valley Legal Aid as a favour to Paul. The two always helped each other out with career paths for their protégés. Paul got to his feet and sat down on the vacant chair beside Clare. 'You have ambitions then, Ms Mitchell? Ambitions to go to the bar?'

'Well, yes,' she said. Too softly. She had to be more assertive. 'Yes,' she said again, this time owning the word.

Paul took a fat wallet from his pocket and extracted a business card. 'Call me,' he said, 'if you'd be interested in working together. I'd enjoy a dynamo like you as my reader.'

Clare took the card and stared at it dumbly.

Paul looked right, then left, then lowered his voice to a conspiratorial whisper. 'Truth is, the person I've lined up to read with me next year isn't quite ready …' He trailed off, but the implication was plain enough. Clare almost felt sorry for Veronica.

A waiter placed two bottles of wine on the table, and Paul helped himself to the red. He poured himself a generous glass and another for Clare. She was stunned by the sudden turn of events. It had had the feel of a set-up. A splendid set-up, certainly, but a set-up just the same. Roderick, being so solicitous, giving her time off, insisting she take his place at the lunch. This had been planned. By Paul and Roderick, and maybe by Justice Cameron as well. They'd talked it over, maybe many times. Over drinks, or in chambers, or at the Counsellor's Club. It was overwhelming. Clare was thrilled right down to her toes. She knew she had a goofy grin on her face. Hardly becoming. She tried to arrange her face into some semblance of decorum.

Paul looked her up and down. 'You're pleased then?' Her mouth was suddenly too dry to speak. 'Don't try to hide it,' he said. 'Passion makes the difference between an outstanding advocate and a merely adequate one.' He heaved a great belly laugh, as if at a hilarious, private joke. 'Oh, it will get you into trouble at times, there's no doubt. But without it? Without that ability to reach deep and yank the emotional guts out of a jury? Without that, a barrister can never achieve true brilliance.'

Justice Cameron rose from his chair and caught Clare's eye. 'That passion he's talking about? It doesn't just work on juries. He's ripped my guts out in court more than once. Nobody sums up a case like Paul here. Now if you don't mind, I have someone to see.'

Clare said goodbye and turned her attention back to Paul. 'I just want to clarify - you're offering to take me on as your reader next year?'

Paul plucked an old-fashioned fountain pen from his pocket, scribbled the proposal onto a napkin, and presented it to her with a flourish.

Clare could have kissed it. This was proof of merit, proof of a life lived with passion. If only Adam could have been here. He'd said much the same thing, that it was her passion that set her apart from his previous girlfriends. For all Veronica's good looks and style, she had about as much passion as a snail. No, that wasn't true. Clare had watched a documentary on snail's mating habits. She'd seen them writhing together in a copulation that could last for hours. Veronica didn't even have as much passion as a snail.

Clare was basking in a soft, warm glow when Paul excused himself. He gave his moustache a few dramatic twirls. 'Once more unto the breach, dear friends,' he proclaimed to the room in general, and then charged off to talk to a man at the bar.

Three other people sat down at the table. Clare didn't know them and, in any case, they immediately became engrossed in private conversation. Left to her own devices she had a quiet moment to digest her news. Going to the bar with a man like Paul Dunbar as her mentor. Something her father had dreamed of for her, and now she couldn't tell him. It was a bitter pill. She could tell Adam though. She wanted to ring him then and there. Tell him they'd be working in the same chambers next year. She looked around the rapidly filling room. Was there time to duck out? No, better not. She might miss something.

Clare buttered a bread roll and was nibbling at it absentmindedly, when someone sat down beside her. She stared in disbelief. Adam. He'd come after all. He'd made an effort to rush back from Dalby. He'd understood how important this lunch was to her. For a moment she wondered how he knew she'd be there. Of course, Roderick. Roderick had told Adam where she was and he'd come to surprise her. Maybe he already knew about her news. All of Clare's doubts about him melted away. He'd just proved how much he cared, and warmth rushed through her.

But when she looked into his eyes, Clare didn't like what she saw there. His face, it was all wrong. She'd expected him to seem smugly satisfied that he'd surprised her - that was his usual way. But instead he looked uncomfortable, guilty even. Clare slipped her hand into his. 'Adam, what's wrong?'

Now he was positively squirming. A woman came up behind them. She leaned over the back of Adam's chair, a hand on each shoulder, and gave him a long, lingering kiss, low on his cheek. Veronica slipped into the seat beside him. Clare snatched her hand away from his. Veronica studied them both and comprehension dawned in her eyes. The only gratifying thing about the whole, appalling situation was that she looked as stunned as Clare felt.

They both turned to glare at Adam. He played it very cool, greeting Clare. 'It's good you made it,' he said, a perfect smile on his face.

No thanks to you. The room grew hot and airless. Her leg cramped. Perspiration trickled down her neck, inside her shirt. Clare wanted to scream, but instead she put on a smile as forced as his own, gaining confidence from Veronica's dumbfounded expression. For once it wouldn't be *her* left standing on the back foot. 'How nice to see you,' she said sweetly.

Adam turned his attention to Veronica. Clare strained her ears, listening to their furious whispers. Adam spoke in a low murmur, but

Veronica was unable to keep the strident tone from her voice. *'What's she doing here?... hand on your arm ... must have known ... deliberate humiliation ...'* Adam lapsed into sullen silence. Clare was all too familiar with this particular defence strategy, and it was gratifying to think it wasn't reserved especially for her.

What should she do? Leave? This was her first impulse. Take the high road? She could stay, hide how gutted she really was and outlast them. She didn't want to fight with Adam in public. She should leave, shouldn't she? But how would that look to Paul Dunbar? And by staying, at least she got to see what happened next.

Adam turned back to her, and embarked on a far-fetched explanation of how he came to be at the Bar Association lunch, instead of at the Dalby Court House. Clare briefly closed her eyes. She wasn't listening to his words, rather she was listening to the meaning behind the words. Did he really think he could explain his way out of this? She wiped her forehead with a napkin and glanced at Veronica. Did he take them both for fools?

Adam finally gave up talking and sat between the two of them, staring into middle distance. A waiter served the soup.

Clare's decision to say nothing was weakening, and the desire to make Adam suffer was growing hot and insistent. Was Veronica aware of their twelve-month liaison? Possibly not. No, almost certainly not. Clare was a particularly private person. Roderick may not even have known about her and Adam. Debbie knew, of course, but Veronica would never deign to chat to a secretary. If she didn't know the full extent of their relationship, if her anger was based only on a hunch ... then it wouldn't take much for Adam to talk himself out of trouble and back into Veronica's good books. He would get away with it.

But before she could formulate a plan, Veronica leaned across in front of Adam, and fixed Clare with anguished, perfectly plucked brows. 'Are you screwing him?'

Clare took a bottomless breath and her opinion of Veronica went up a few notches. This was a woman who knew how to cut through the bullshit.

'Yes,' said Clare, 'For about a year, now.' She threw Adam a long, accusing stare. He dropped his head to his hands and the table went quiet. The other people didn't know where to look. She tried to imagine Veronica naked with Adam, but mercifully the image wouldn't come.

Clare's phone rang, making her jump. For a moment she wondered who might be calling, but she should have known. Jolly Jumbucks, of course. This time Jack had surpassed himself. He'd bunkered in beneath the stairs and held the entire staff at bay for fifteen minutes with a cache of fire extinguishers he'd discovered there. Clare found herself impressed that Jack had figured out how to use the devices. Then again, they weren't that complicated. All you had to do was pull the pin, rather like a hand grenade, then press the lever.

She imagined a blizzard of foam, burying the Happy Elves in soft white drifts. This was it, surely. Jack's last chance at Jolly Jumbucks, gone. No matter. She didn't need them any more.

Clare sat back, took a long, objective look at Adam, then stood to leave, praying her legs would not betray her. She stepped away from the table, paused and stepped back. She leaned down, brought her mouth close to Veronica's cheek, as if for a kiss. 'He's a good lay at first,' she said in a loud stage whisper. 'But he wears off.' Then she excused herself to the room in general, and walked out with head held high.

CLARE PICKED a delighted Jack up from Jolly Jumbucks, barely hearing the manager's long-winded account of the boy's wrongdoings, and why he wasn't welcome any more. She had a far warmer reception from Helga. 'You should collect Samson early more often. It would do you both the world of good.'

Clare drove in silence, numb, like she'd been cut with a very sharp knife and was waiting for the pain to set in. By contrast, the two in the back were in high spirits. She drove them beyond the city limits, found a stretch of bushland and set them free. Jack ran along a river, splashed after fish in the shallows, threw sticks, skipped stones. Nobody here to report them for anti-social behaviour. No signs saying keep that dog on a leash or stay off those gardens or don't climb the trees. Not a sign in sight. Not another person in sight, for that matter. Just them and the bush. Jack spotted some horses in a paddock and took off down the slope to investigate, with Samson at his heels. But for once their impetuous bolt didn't cause her stomach to lurch in fright. Out here, there were no roads, no shops, no stranger-danger. Clare could let them go. She sat down on a stump to watch.

It was a pearl of an afternoon. From her perch on the hillside she had a spectacular view across to Moreton Bay, a shining, azure crescent in the distance, merging with a deep blue sky. Somewhere a currawong called. Paddocks stretched out along the river flats below. Jack ran to the fence with Samson and put an outstretched arm through the wire. A horse grazing nearby raised its head, stared at them for a few moments, then ambled over. Clare stood up in readiness to sprint down the hill if Samson went in for the chase. But dog and horse simply touched friendly noses. Good on you, Samson. Clare was proud of him.

Jack amused himself by tugging at long grass on his side of the fence and collecting green bunches to give to the horse. It accepted these offerings with a gracious, bowed head and whiffling lips. Half an hour later, Jack still hadn't budged from the fence. When it was time to go, Clare had a battle to tear him away, and he really cried. Not yelled. Not his usual angry screams, that sounded more like a roaring animal than a child. No, he cried, with real tears. It was a breakthrough, she knew that.

CLARE STRETCHED out on the couch and flicked on the television. Her strategy had been to tire the pair out, and it had worked like a charm. Jack was asleep. Asleep in his own room for once. Samson was asleep too, curled up at the foot of Jack's bed, and it was only seven o'clock.

Clare's phone rang. It was Debbie. 'I can't believe it.' Her voice was high and excited. 'What Adam did, I mean. I've heard all about it.'

Clare sighed. Of course she had. Who knew why? Who knew how? But Debbie had the uncanniest nose for gossip. She launched into a protracted appraisal of Clare's relationship with Adam, founded on nothing, apparently, but the odd snippet or two of news that Clare had carelessly let slip at work. And the once or twice that Debbie had met Adam at the office. Hardly a sound basis for judgement. It was surprising then, how accurate Debbie's assessment actually was. 'Ooh, you just can't trust blokes like him.' How right she was. 'I could tell the minute I saw him,' Debbie said on the phone. 'It's the eyes that give them away, every time. Kind of shifty.'

Clare tactfully refrained from reminding Debbie that she'd swooned over Adam's grey eyes just last week. They'd been *dreamy* then. Now they were shifty. Clare smiled. They agreed on that much, at least.

Clare fobbed Debbie off as kindly as she could, and tossed the phone in the direction of the coffee table. It slid along the smoked glass top and onto the floor. Exhaustion washed over her, and she left it where it fell. There was a nature documentary on the telly. A weasel chasing a rabbit. Clare always cringed at moments like these. She decided she was barracking for the rabbit this time. She didn't always barrack for the prey animal. It depended on the day she'd had. She never did if pictures of the predator's hungry young were shown prior to the hunt.

This rabbit didn't have much going for it. A rough crevice in a cliff served as a temporary hiding place, but it wouldn't fool the hungry weasel for long. And worst of all, it was a dead end. The weasel sniffed out the refuge and prowled about for a few moments, sizing things up. Then it dived for the rabbit. Clare jumped. Jeez, were her nerves ever shot! But to her surprise and delight the rabbit flung itself skywards, somersaulted in mid-air and scampered to freedom, having cheated death by inches. The thwarted weasel seemed to shrink in embarrassment, as if it knew that the cameras were upon it. Clare made up her mind then and there to never be the rabbit again.

The documentary ended and advertising took over the screen. Clare's eyes glazed over. Her gaze wandered to the painting on the wall above the television. A pair of harnessed clydesdales stepped out with power and grace. The figure of a man wearing overalls, her grandfather, followed behind them, treading the furrows made by the hand-held plough. An old farmhouse with a wide verandah stood in the background. Clare had owned the painting for many years - so many years that she'd ceased to really see it. *Days of Gold* had followed her around all through her student days , from shared houses to cramped flats, to this wall right here. She almost hadn't hung it. The painting's warm, earthy tones hardly went with twenty-first century minimalism. Clare looked at it, as if for the first time. Mum wasn't a bad artist. She'd captured the spirit of the great horses in the angle of their erect ears, in their arching necks and straining shoulders. She'd caught the care in Grandad's lined face.

Clare's phone rang. She retrieved it from the floor and checked the caller ID. Adam. Clare switched it off. If she never heard Adam's voice again, it would still be too soon. Her afternoon in the country with Jack and Samson, watching the river flats and the horses, had done something towards healing her heart. Some small thing. Just as well she'd found out about Adam before she got in any deeper. Now she just wanted to forget about him, to escape the memories, to get away from Brisbane.

Maybe there was a way. Clare went into the bedroom. After Dad's funeral her brother Ryan had helped pack up the house. They'd put most of what was worth keeping into storage, but she had retrieved a few items.

Clare found the step-ladder and heaved down a crate from the top of the wardrobe. There, beneath dad's car manuals, lay a taped-up box marked *Currawong Creek*. She was almost too scared to open it. Clare fetched herself a glass of wine and perched it on her dressing table. Then she broke the seal and removed the objects from the box one by one. She laid them on the bed. Photos of beautiful clydesdale horses wearing championship sashes. Some baby clothes tied with lace. Mum's old school reports. Memories tumbled back thick and fast. A black and white currawong feather. The cracker for a stock whip. Some large nuts in a little box. Bigger than Brazil nuts, but Clare couldn't remember their name. She lifted out two brown paper packages with cancelled stamps. Posted to her father's address, but both still unopened. One was marked *for Ryan Mitchell*. The other was for Clare.

She broke the seal with an unsteady hand. Inside was a letter from her grandfather.

My dearest Clare,

I am writing to let you know that Grandma passed away last week. I'm sure your father has told you. It's been a very sad time, but don't worry about me. I'm holding up okay. Grandma always loved you and your brother very, very much. Right up until the end, she would talk so proudly of you both. Here are some small things she wanted you to have. If you ever have time to come to Currawong Clare Bear, I would be so happy to see you.

All my love,

Grandad XXOO

The letter was dated seven years ago. In a panic Clare leafed through what was left in the box. More unopened mail for her and Ryan. She tore an envelope and pulled out a card. It had a Dalmatian dog on the front and *Now You're 14* in glittery writing. A twenty dollar note fluttered out when she opened it. *Happy Birthday Clare* it said. *From your loving grandparents.* There were dozens of letters. Dozens of letters that her father had kept from his children.

A wave of heartache threatened to drown her. Clare knuckled the tears from her eyes and looked inside the package from her grandfather. A locket with a photo of her and grandma inside. An opal ring. A kitchen journal that looked vaguely familiar. It was filled with hand written recipes and pressed flowers. In an instant she was a child again, scouring the paddocks of Currawong Creek with Grandma, searching for pretty leaves and blossoms. Clare gazed at the faded flowers, held between pages of recipes for salmon bake, savoury mince, pavlova and scones. Here was a sprig of coolabah blossom, still retaining its creamy colour. She thought of the sad little coolabah tree growing outside her window at work, and choked back sobs.

Clare scrabbled around in the box until she found what she was looking for. Her father's small green address book. She flipped through it until she found her grandfather's number. With trembling fingers she punched it into her phone.

'Grandad? It's me, Clare.'

CHAPTER 8

Jack hit the little girl sitting next to him on the head with the whip. She burst out crying. 'Come on, sweetie,' said Clare, dragging Jack out of the stagecoach by his arm. 'Sorry,' she called, as a man holding a camera stormed over. She hurried Jack away. So much for the happy snap.

When the department gave her permission to take Jack on a holiday, Kim had asked for a photographic record of the trip. Something Jack could share with Taylor when he saw her. They'd reached Toowoomba, an hour and a half west of Brisbane, and the Cobb & Co Museum had seemed like the perfect stopover. It would set them in the mood for Currawong.

The museum housed over fifty horse-drawn vehicles, including sturdy drays and farm wagons of the sort pulled by Grandad's clydesdales. They told the story of European settlement on the Darling Downs. The original Cobb and Co coaches, including the last coach which ran from Yuleba to Surat in 1924, were the pride of the collection. Clare had given Samson a quick walk, a drink of water and put him back in the car. Then she'd taken Jack's hand and headed for the entrance to the museum. The visit had been a disaster from the minute they passed through the gate.

Jack had made a beeline for a stand where a wizened old saddler with a bushy white beard was giving a leatherwork demonstration. He was plaiting what looked like the thong of a whip. Jack had clambered up a wall display of belts and bridles, toppling the whole thing to the ground. Then he'd snatched a stock whip and run off.

The old man barely looked up from his task, but his lips cracked into a thin smile. 'You need a kelpie to round up that one, love.'

Clare stared after Jack. Damn. She'd have a fight getting that whip off him. 'I'll buy it,' she said. Thank goodness she could still see Jack in the distance, climbing up onto a dray. No Samson to keep tabs on him now.

The saddler put down his work, taking his time and extended his arm. 'I'm Sid.'

Clare shook his hand impatiently.

'That young feller of yours, he's picked a good 'un,' said the man, in a slow drawl. 'Six-foot, twelve-strand kangaroo. For its weight, roo hide's the strongest leather in the world.' He lit a hand-rolled cigarette and continued. 'A whip's like a chain, love. The more links in a chain, the smoother it runs. Likewise, the more strands a thong has the more supple it moves.'

'That's very interesting, Sid,' said Clare, trying to keep one eye on Jack. 'How much do I owe you?'

But Sid would not be hurried. He stood up and fished a whip from among the leather goods scattered in the dust. 'Now this little number,' he said, shaking it, coiling it and offering it to Clare, 'is the right size for your boy. Red hide, three-foot, four-plait. It's cowhide, better for beginners. Heavier than roo, puts more weight into the belly of the whip. Makes it easy to crack.' The man demonstrated by cracking it loudly, three times in succession. 'Hear that? That's a mini sonic boom.' Sid cracked it once more for good measure. Jack turned and looked in their direction. Then he came pelting back. The man waited for him to arrive, then put on a bit of a show. A crowd gathered around. Jack was mesmerised, eyes large as Frisbees.

Sid held out the smaller whip to the boy. 'Want to swap, snowy?'

They made the exchange, then Sid gave Jack an impromptu whip cracking lesson.

After five minutes, Jack made his whip ring out like a rifle shot. Then again, with a grin as wide as his face. Sid was grinning too. He kneeled down and showed Jack the parts of his whip. 'You've got the handle, and the flick. The flick gives the whip shape and speed. And this long plaited lash part? That's called the thong.' He pressed each part as he described it into the palm of Jack's hand. 'This slotted leather loop is the fall. It connects to the cracker. That's the bit at the end that goes bang.'

Jack was fascinated. Clare hadn't seen him listen like that before. Afterwards, he set about practising his whip cracking, causing people to give him a wide berth. She gave Sid a grateful smile and helped him put right the display stand. Then she paid him for the whip. 'Much obliged,' he said, and returned to plaiting his leather.

'Come on, Jack,' she said hopefully. 'Let's look at something else.' But the visit was all downhill from there. She tried taking him to the toilet, but instead he pulled down his pants and peed up against a carriage wheel in front of everybody. He brandished the lash and threw his drink bottle at a boy in the café. Clare had hoped for some nice photos of Jack in the charming children's area, *The Coach Stop.* Here kids could play in a pint-sized general store or take a ride on a full-size replica horse, or even dress up and pretend to ride a Cobb and Co coach through the outback. But every time she tried to take the shot, Jack was frowning or belting somebody with the stock whip.

'I give up,' she said, and they headed for the car park.

Jack and Samson greeted each other like long lost friends and chased each other in ever widening circles. Samson bailed up a young couple, barking and jumping. Oh no, now Jack was barking too. Clare raced off to retrieve them, burning with embarrassment. She apologised and bundled her wayward charges back into the car. It seemed like she'd apologised more times in the last month than she had in her entire life.

Samson had taken a chunk out of the back seat upholstery. Of course he had. The dog panted and grinned at her, as if to say *that'll teach you to leave me behind*. Clare took off down the road, wheels spinning on gravel. Samson laid his head on Jack's knee and the pair promptly fell asleep as if nothing had happened. She could use a very strong coffee right about now, but she dare not stop at a shop. She dare not leave the car. Whatever had possessed her to embark on a four-hour road trip with those two?

Clare settled in for the drive. It took some time to escape Toowoomba's sprawling outskirts and catch her first glimpse of Gowrie Mountain. This distinctive, flat-topped hill was a perfectly preserved extinct volcano. She'd explored its lofty slopes with her grandfather as a child. He'd shown her the funnel-shaped opening of the crater. The great hole where molten lava erupted long ago to fill the valley below.

Childhood memories crowded in thick and fast, and Clare's anxiety slipped away along with the miles. This was easy driving. Up until now, Warrego Highway had required all of her concentration. It had been raining as she approached the eastern face of the Great Dividing Range. Parts of the road had recently been washed away and the crumbling bitumen and potholes had kept her on constant alert. The rich, volcanic farmlands of the Lockyer Valley were known as Brisbane's salad bowl, its fertile hinterland. But Clare had found it hard to admire the scenery. Some years ago, dozens of people had perished here. A tropical cyclone combined with a deep rain trough had sent a deadly, seven-metre wall of water surging through the valley. An inland tsunami. She'd shivered a little as the windscreen wipers worked harder. The sense of foreboding didn't lift until they'd left the floor of the basin and started the steep climb up to Toowoomba.

Now they were waving goodbye to the town and heading for Dalby, following the railway line. Clare turned on the radio. Static, apart from a country music station. It would do. Simple chords and *he done me wrong* lyrics suited her mood. Signs warned drivers to beware of road trains: monstrous trucks hauling equally monstrous trailers, some bound for Darwin more than three thousand kilometres away. Paddocks grew bigger and bigger, stretching away to the horizon.

The sun came out to celebrate the first day of spring. Driving to Currawong was like going back in time. Clare hadn't seen these black soil plains since childhood, but they felt familiar. The landscape was dominated by rolling hills, patchworked with lush green pasture and spring crops. Local dirt roads intersected the highway. They stretched away into the distance, crisscrossing bushy ridges and winding creeks. Roads with evocative names like Jumbuck Way, Stagecoach Track and one with a simple signpost saying Stock Route. Tumbledown wool sheds and rusted machinery lay scattered in paddocks, remnants from a bygone era of exploration and settlement. They passed water tanks and farmhouses and silos, big and small. Proud windmills stood dotted across the farmlands, raising the life-giving waters of the Great Artesian Basin. It comforted Clare to see their silhouettes. She loved the bottle trees too, with their signature swollen trunks and dense, evergreen crowns. Cattle dozed in their shade. The Downs retained its solid, well-remembered sense of place.

There was one feature of the landscape though, that she didn't remember. In some paddocks, haphazard arrangements of odd machinery squatted on squares of bulldozed ground. They weren't connected to the iconic windmills and bore heads. In fact the two never appeared within cooee of each other. Irrigation systems, perhaps? She'd never seen anything like them before, but things must have modernised out of sight in the last sixteen years. Some were no more than ugly collections of pumps and wheels and gauges. Others had storage tanks and tall, thin chimneys like giant flues, with pale flames peeking from the top. Solar panels mounted on stands, seemingly attached to nothing, powering who knew what? Pipes appeared and disappeared into nowhere, and strange dams of dark red water had been scoured into ground made bare for hundreds of metres around. Stout, steel-panelled fences guarded these installations. More than sufficient to keep out the odd, inquisitive cow or kangaroo who didn't heed the yellow hazard signs. The occasional outline of taller towers loomed on the horizon, well off the road, like oil rigs in the desert. Except this wasn't the desert. This was the finest agricultural land in the continent. What was so much industrial equipment doing in this peaceful, rural place?

A crop-dusting plane flew low overhead. She would have liked to show it to Jack, but he wasn't awake. An hour passed. Approaching Dalby now, and still Jack and Samson slept. Clare amused herself by trying to identify crops along the road. She could pick the wheat and corn. The paddocks of baby sunflowers. By summer their iconic, dinner-plate blooms would stand metres tall, bright faces following the sun across the sky. Fresh shorn sheep and fat cattle grazed beside swathes of sorghum. Or was it barley? Did they even grow sorghum at this time of year?

There was a time when she would have known. Once she could pick them all: chickpeas, mung beans, millet, soy – crops of all kinds. Grandad had taught her and Ryan their various growth habits and seed row widths. If the Lockyer Valley was Brisbane's salad bowl, the Darling Downs was a prime food bowl for the whole of Australia. It had been great fun, riding in Grandad's old truck, trying to pick out all the different crops and types of trees. Clare suddenly missed Ryan. He'd followed in Dad's footsteps, joined the army straight from school and married young. Their communications had grown less and less personal, their visits farther apart, and now she rarely saw him. His fault or hers? She supposed they were equally to blame. After all, she hadn't told Ryan about Jack, or about this trip to see their grandfather after so many years.

Clare slowed as she came into Dalby, and glanced into the back seat. Two terrors still asleep. She could have died for a coffee, but stopping might wake them. They passed the racecourse and approached a bridge surrounded by parklands. It all flooded back. A day in Dalby with her mother and grandparents - a picnic in the park. Playing chasey with Ryan round an engraved bluestone pillar. The memory was clear as a Condamine bell. Grandma's voice, explaining to them about the monument, a tribute to Cactoblastis, the humble caterpillar that had eradicated a plague of prickly pear in the 1920s.

Such happy days. Days of sunny summer holidays and intact families. Days of Mum with Dad, with all of them, and no concept of change that might lurk around corners. Of the gut wrenching gap Mum would soon leave in all their lives. It hit Clare then, a confusion of past and present loneliness, leaving her close to tears. Her mother was gone, and her father. Grandma too. Ryan as good as gone … and Adam. Now she returned alone to Currawong, to her grandfather. Her family had shrunk, through death and abandonment, to this one old man.

They crossed the bridge that spanned the swollen waters of Myall Creek, on its collision course with the Condamine River south-west of town. The Condamine drained the northern Darling Downs into the mighty Murray-Darling basin. The river gave its name to Condamine bells. Or bullfrog bells, as Grandad used to call them. He had quite a collection of the classic, square-mouthed cow bells, all strung up in the cart shed. Clare used to love running beneath them with a big stick, setting them pealing like it was her own, humble cathedral. Would they still be there, she wondered? Would she get to teach Jack that old game?

Dalby was a thriving country town with wide streets and plenty of pubs. Clare turned right across railway lines on its outskirts, leaving the Warrego Highway and heading north on the Bunya Road. An hour's driving and she'd be at Currawong Creek, turning into its century-old cast-iron gates. Sunshine gates, Grandad called them. Clare had loved to swing on those gates. She could see the word *SUNSHINE* wrought on the centre strut. And what was written above it? That's right - H. V. McKay. She'd chanted the name, over and over, as she played a complicated swinging game devised with Ryan. It had involved counting the number of swings you could do, in the time it took the windmill blades to turn ten times. It all depended on determination and wind speed. Fancy remembering that. Grandma had said they were called Sunshine gates because of the McKay machinery company, which had made cultivators, swingle trees and horse yokes in the 1880s. They were famous for their Sunshine brand of harvesters and gates. But Grandad always said his gates were named for the sunshine itself, for the happiness they brought into the lives of people who entered through them. Clare had never doubted him for a minute.

It was a rough road to Merriang. The landscape grew hilly and wild. A pair of eagles spiralled high in the sky, causing her to crane her neck for a better view. Scatterings of gum trees turned into patches of forest: Myall, Cyprus and Wilga. She slowed down to negotiate a deep floodway, one of dozens that crossed the road. Clare was thankful that Jack and Samson slept through it all. She wanted time to herself, time to think about seeing her grandfather again. How would he look, she wondered, after all this time? Her memory was of a lean, tanned man with smiling eyes. An old man, though he'd only been in his fifties. She didn't have a clue what he might look like at seventy. It frightened her to think of him as aged and frail.

Soon the Bunya Mountains loomed in the windscreen. They rose abruptly from the surrounding flood plain, dominating the landscape. Someone stirred in the back seat. Clare glanced behind to see Jack yawning, eyes still sleepy. She pulled the car well off the road and let the pair of them loose. Samson bounded about in circles and Jack chased after him, or sometimes vice versa. A simple game, but one of which they never seemed to tire. Clare smiled. It suited her well enough. All she had to do was sit on a tree stump and watch. It really was astounding how good Samson was with Jack. The dog seemed to have in mind an invisible safety zone, outside of which the boy was not allowed to stray. If he tried, Samson lured him back with engaging moves, bowing low on his forelegs, tail raised and wagging – an irresistible invitation to play. Sometimes he used his body to physically shepherd Jack home.

Clare checked her phone. Two thirty - they'd be there by three. What perfect timing. Jack was usually on his best behaviour just after a sleep. Though Jack's golden time, for what it was worth, wouldn't last long. They'd better get a move on. With Samson's help she bundled Jack back in the car. She tried calling Grandad again, but had to leave a message. Oh well. She'd see him in person soon enough. Her foot was heavy on the throttle as they flew through the little town of Merriang. Past the general store, the pub, the post office. Not far now.

The road to her grandfather's place was officially and inexplicably named Railway Road. Inexplicably, because the nearest railway was eighty kilometres away. Grandad had removed the road sign long ago, together with one marking it as a scenic route. *The last thing I need are a bunch of bloody tourists taking pictures,* he'd said. Grandad replaced the old sign with one of his own, renaming the road to Currawong *Clydesdale Way*. And that's how it had stayed. On a few occasions council workers had reinstalled the correct sign, but it had received short shrift. And now, all these years later, it was still Clydesdale Way that Clare turned the car into.

The road aimed them straight at Bunya's peaks. The view of them left her mouth dry and her body breathless. Clare shrugged off the irrational, mounting fear that she wouldn't be able to find Currawong, that she might not recognise the driveway. That she'd have to turn around and go home. She had no idea why this thought unsettled her so. It had been such a long time. She had every excuse, sixteen years of excuses. But to miss the turnoff would be like saying her childhood hadn't mattered. It would be like saying the happy times weren't worth remembering. Only the dreadful days after Mum left.

Clare shivered. She hadn't expected the visit to affect her this deeply. It was turning a self-possessed professional woman into someone she didn't recognise and wasn't sure she liked. Of course she'd know the turn off. What could have possibly changed, way out here?

CHAPTER 9

Twin Bunya pine trees marked the gateway, just as she remembered. Clare was sick with anticipation as Jack began to yell. 'Almost there,' she said. Samson whined at the sound of her voice — a voice strained and thick with emotion. The Sunshine gates were closed. The old *Currawong Creek* sign hung on the rail, with the same weathered image of a draft horse etched into its timbers. Beside it, however, hung two new signs. One read *Merriang Veterinary Surgery*. That was different – and a disagreeable reminder that time hadn't stood still.

The second sign, however, was much more troubling. A yellow triangle proclaimed *Warning Notice* in bold red letters. It went on to say *All common law rights to enter are expressly withdrawn. Admittance by invitation only to any persons and entities. Otherwise trespass applies.* The last bit was the most disturbing of all. *HCA 1991 171 CLR 635 F.C. 91/004.* Clare frowned. Why on earth would Grandad be citing a Full Bench decision of the High Court on his gatepost? It was bizarre.

Clare opened the gates and drove in, drinking in the view. Framed by the dramatic backdrop of the Bunya Mountains, the old farmhouse still looked like something from a pioneer movie. Things may have grown a little more dilapidated. The fences more sagging, the track more rutted than she remembered. But this was without doubt the cherished holiday home of her childhood. There was Grandma's garden ... and the cart shed ... and the training paddock - its driving course marked out with rusty forty-four-gallon drums. Jack spotted a pair of clydesdales dozing in the yards beside the shed. He squealed with delight and banged on the car window. More horses grazed beyond the yards, on the green pine-sprinkled slopes that rose towards the mountains. Here was something Clare hadn't fully remembered – Currawong's breathtaking beauty.

A little choke caught in Clare's throat, as an aristocratic pair of dalmatians trotted down the drive to meet them. Pongo and Perdita? No, of course not. The playmates of her youth would be long gone. It wasn't them, but Clare was delighted by that sweet, foolish notion.

'Samson - shush.' He was barking in her ear, attention fixed on a row of three ugly demountable rooms perched in a paddock to the left. They looked like they'd accidentally fallen off a truck and someone would be back for them any minute. A roughly graded square of gravel lay out the front, with a battered jeep parked there. A lonely-looking crow sat atop a home-made sign, that rather grandly pronounced this to be the *Merriang Veterinary Clinic - Client Car Park.*

It would be nice to walk up to the house – let the dogs all get to know each other on the way. Clare parked beside the jeep under the shade of a coolabah tree, a tree she remembered climbing with Ryan when it wasn't so tall. Compared to her weedy carpark specimen back in Brisbane, this coolabah was in robust good health. Tall and spreading, its shimmering canopy fragrant with the scent of eucalyptus. She climbed from the car and stretched muscles grown stiff from the long drive.

A clydesdale horse in an adjoining paddock raised its head and nickered to her. Then it plodded across to hang its massive neck over the fence for a pat. She gingerly stroked its broad, white blaze, having not touched a horse since that last day at the farm. Clare pressed her face to its nose. She'd read that people loved or hated certain smells because of the context in which they'd first encountered them. She was sure she loved the old-fashioned scent of lavender because it reminded her of Grandma's garden. Clare breathed in the horse's familiar, comforting smell and knew she'd come home.

Samson was barking louder now. She turned to see Jack's little hand waving out the back window. The dalmatians were standing nearby, noses raised, curiously sniffing the air. They looked friendly enough. It was the other dog that bothered her. A big blue heeler, crouched between her and the car. Where on earth had it come from? She stared at the dog as a rumbling growl rose in its throat. Samson stopped barking and the dalmatians turned around, as if to watch the show. The dog dropped down on its belly, like a lion about to launch an attack. 'Good boy,' she said, trying to smile. 'Good dog.' Did its hackles rise or was it her imagination?

Clare didn't like heelers. One had bitten her last year, launching itself from the darkness one night when she was walking with Adam. It had ripped through jeans, through skin, through muscle, and left her lame for weeks. This dog looked just like that one.

According to Helga, dogs perceived eye contact as a challenge. Clare wrenched her gaze away and waited a moment. When she looked back at the dog, it commando-crawled closer and growled louder. Clare screamed. A small scream, true – not much more than a squeal — but it was enough to set the dog off. It rushed at her, barking wildly, tail lashing from side to side.

Clare climbed the tree. She didn't quite know how she did it. One minute she was standing on the ground, rigid with fear. Next minute she was astride a broad branch, peering down like a possum with the heeler leaping and snapping below. There was little danger of falling. She was wrapped round that trunk so tight, she might as well have been welded on. Getting down, on the other hand, might present some problems.

Clare took the risk of reaching into her pocket for her phone. A bull ant chose the same moment to crawl over her fingers. She screamed again - a proper scream this time - and flung her arm out, propelling the ant and her brand new iPhone into mid-air. She groaned as she watched the phone spin in the sunlight, then plummet to the ground. Where had it landed? There, near that stick. Its sparkly case, studded with tiny Swarovski crystals, glinted in the light. The case was a present from Adam. Hand-stitched Tuscan leather with a waterproof, polycarbonate core, designed for extreme impact protection. His taste for high-end goods had paid off this time.

The heeler stopped its insane barking, turned around ... sniffed the ground. Clare held her breath. Maybe it was leaving? No, it seemed instead to be searching for something, scratching around in the leaf litter. A horrible thought struck her. Please no — not her phone. Then he had it. Damn Adam! Damn his glittery, leather case, which had turned her new iPhone into a highly visible chew toy.

The dog picked it up and trotted back to the base of the tree. He lay down, tail wagging. 'Drop it,' yelled Clare. 'Drop it, you stupid dog.' Then a sickening crunching sound.

The heeler spat out the phone and redoubled his efforts to snatch her from her perch, growling and jumping. The dalmatians trotted over to join in the chorus, and Samson too from the car - all barking at the top of their lungs. Clare looked hopefully at the modest little clinic. If someone was inside, surely they'd hear the racket? 'Help,' she shouted. 'Help ... help.'

A man's head appeared out of the window. 'Red,' he called, barely making himself heard above the commotion. 'Get here.' The heeler spun around and galloped off, its feet raising tiny plumes of dust.

Clare took a relieved gulp of air and almost lost her balance. The dalmatians kept on barking, but their hearts didn't seem to be in it any more. She could hear Jack yelling, his hand still waving out the open window like a pale, fluttering bird. Any minute now the man would come out. What would she say? She must look pretty silly, sitting halfway up a tree. No, she mustn't think like that. The heeler belonged to the man in the building, that much was obvious. He'd left a vicious dog at large ... let it rush a visitor. When the other heeler had bitten her, she'd been unable to identify its owner. This time would be different. This time, the owner would have to take responsibility for his negligence.

Minutes ticked by. Where was he, anyway? Why hadn't he come out? The dalmatians gave up and trotted back up the drive to the house. Not much chance of Grandad hearing her. He'd been a bit deaf even when she was a child.

Clare tried to assess just how high up she really was. How the hell had she climbed so far? Must be four metres at least. She'd break a leg if she tried to climb down. There was nothing for it but to wait for the idiot to come out. Would he have a ladder? He'd need a ladder to get her down. Probably not much call for one in a vet clinic. He'd have to go up to the house and borrow one. The sting of impending tears pricked the back of her eyes. Clare sniffed them back. This was not how she'd wanted to meet Grandad.

Clare waited and waited. Every now and then a loud thud came from the demountable, and an occasional shout. What on earth was happening in there? Jack had settled into a harsh singsong wail. She could see him rocking in rhythm with his own cries, slamming his seat back and forth. Thank God the car was in the shade, and the window was open. He wouldn't be too hot. Would he?

Clare had promised Taylor to keep Jack safe. Taylor didn't know about the promise, of course, but that didn't matter. Clare had made it just the same, and she always kept her promises. It was a habit she'd cultivated to differentiate herself from her mother. Her mother's promises were like autumn leaves – bright and beautiful in the beginning, but fading to nothing in the end. Just a rotting mess to be trodden underfoot or swept away. Clare's promises weren't like that. Or were they? She'd hauled Jack out to the middle of nowhere and left him stranded in a car. That wasn't keeping him safe.

Beads of sweat formed on Clare's forehead. She wiped them away with the back of her hand and squinted into the blinding sunshine. No more yelling or barking came from the car now. It was disturbingly quiet. Each second seemed to take an hour. To play a waiting game in this heat was to play a very dangerous game indeed. Clare manoeuvred herself into a new position. A precarious position, but from here she might be able to reach the next branch with her foot. She looked down again. Not so much of a branch, really. More of a twig. It was curious how the branches she'd scaled in panic on her way up looked far too flimsy to bear her weight on the way down.

Clare took a deep breath. Hugging the trunk, she lowered her body, extended her right leg and fumbled for a foothold. Clare wasn't much of a physical risk-taker. She'd made some brilliant gambles in court and they'd paid off, but they were always carefully calculated. More importantly they didn't pose actual danger to life or limb.

Clare didn't like heights. She didn't bungy jump or parachute or hang glide. The older she grew, the more cautious she'd become. But the urgency of Jack's need outweighed her fear. Her foot found purchase and she gingerly lowered herself onto the branch below. So far so good. The bough felt sturdy enough underfoot.

Clare found herself a metre closer to the ground than before. She sized up the next branch with more confidence, and steeled herself to step off, to make that leap of faith. It was then she felt the tickle on her wrist. A spider the size of a saucer crawled onto her forearm. Clare willed herself to hang on regardless, but it was no use. Her reflexes weren't listening to her brain, and suddenly she was hurtling towards the ground. She closed her eyes.

Clare landed hard. The momentum of the fall slammed her head forward into a stump. Stabbing pain ricocheted round her body as the wind was knocked out of her. She fought for air, fought against the suffocating horror of empty lungs. Blood ran from her nose and lip. She tasted it on her tongue.

When Clare could breathe again, she struggled to her feet and stumbled to the car. She wrenched open the doors and stood panting and apologising to Jack and Samson. For once, the dog didn't erupt from the car in an explosion of energy. He just looked at her with those deep brown eyes, his velvet brow wrinkled in concern. Jack too, was uncharacteristically quiet — large-eyed and staring. Heat exhaustion perhaps?

Then Clare caught her reflection in the car window. Her blood-smeared face. Her tangled hair and intense, wild eyes. So that was it. They were scared of her. Clare tried to smile, but it hurt her face. She smoothed her hair into some sort of order, combed out leaves and twigs with her fingers. A small spider abseiled from her forehead to her nose on a thread of silk. She cast it away with a flick of her fingers. Jack opened his eyes a little wider. Was she shaking? Clare steadied herself, though her legs felt like straw, and tried the smile again. 'It's all right,' she said. 'I'm here now.' It seemed to work. Samson's ears relaxed and Jack gave a familiar protest yell. The dog's huge tongue swept over the boy's face and he burst into laughter. Good, they were okay.

Clare wasn't so sure about herself. Her ankle ached. She'd skinned her hands and knees. She had a fat lip. Was her nose broken? She pinched it gently and wiggled it a little, but she couldn't tell. The last time she'd felt this sore was after falling off a bolting Smudge in this very paddock. For some reason the thought cheered her up.

With a little encouragement, Jack and Samson tumbled from the car and embarked on their inevitable game of chasey. Her previous concern for their welfare was morphing into anger at the man in the vet clinic. What if she'd broken her leg in the fall? What if she'd been knocked out, or worse? What if she'd been unable to rescue Jack from the car? The possibilities didn't bear thinking about.

Clare stalked towards the clinic, Jack and Sampson romping along after her. She spread arms in a protective gesture designed to keep them behind her, and took hold of Samson's trailing lead. The heeler was still around somewhere, and the thought gave her a chill. Only the strength of her outrage made her bold enough to open the door.

An urgent voice sang out. 'Quick, get in here – and close that door.'

Just as she suspected. The heeler must be outside somewhere, ready to attack. She grabbed Jack by the hand and pushed inside, slamming the door after her.

AN EXTRAORDINARY SIGHT CONFRONTED HER. Waiting room chairs lay scattered and upturned. Shelves stood dragged away from walls, their contents spilled to the floor. No wonder the man hadn't come to her aid. He was struggling in the corner, wrestling with a snake – a python, to judge by its enormous size. The creature's length was wrapped around his body. 'Grab its tail,' he yelled. 'Grab its tail!'

Was he mad? Clare stood statue still, trying to make sense of the scene. But before she could manage to, Jack had darted forward and wrapped both hands around the snake's twitching tail.

'That's right,' said the man. 'Now hang on while I get his front.' He dived for the reptile's head, which had escaped his hold and was snaking out towards the window ledge. Its purple tongue flicked in and out, tasting the air. Samson started barking. Clare tied him to a cupboard and wished she could do the same to Jack.

'Jacky,' yelled Clare. 'Come away!' He ignored her. Instead he hugged the creature tighter to his body, while the tip of its prehensile tail twined around his wrist.

The man grasped the snake's neck, and brought its head up next to his own. Reptile and man regarded each other for a moment. Then in an awful, mesmerising dance, that involved passing the snake's head rhythmically from hand to hand and around his back, he unwound the snake from his torso. Clare hated herself for thinking it, but his actions were oddly sexy.

Finishing his dance, the man's tanned face cracked into a smile. 'I'm Dan, by the way. Dan Lord, the new vet. Help me get her into the surgery, will you?'

'Are you insane?' said Clare. 'Aren't you going to take it outside?'

'Not a chance,' Dan said. 'Not when I went to so much trouble to catch her.'

'You caught it?' said Clare. 'I thought it caught you.'

Jack was doing a surprisingly good job, helping manoeuvre the snake through the door and onto a stainless steel table. Dan wrestled its head into a rubber funnel attached to a plastic tube. The tube was in turn attached to some sort of machine. 'Press that button,' the vet said, looking straight at Clare and pointing to a red switch. The snake flipped, almost knocking Jack over. Clare was paralysed with fear. Dan raised his voice a notch. 'If you want me to put this snake to sleep, you'd better bloody well press that button. That red one.'

Clare hesitated for a moment longer, then pressed it. She felt unaccountably sorry for the snake.

'Will it be quick?' asked Clare. 'And painless?'

'Relatively so. I'm using Isoflurane.' Dan adjusted the tube. 'It's gold standard for anaesthetising reptiles and there's no oesophageal or tracheal irritation. That's the problem with most of these gases.'

Clare was touched. How many people would care enough to humanely put down a snake? She waited with bated breath. For a little while, nothing happened. Jack still hung on, and the snake seemed as recalcitrant and active as ever. 'It can take a few minutes. She doesn't breathe as fast as a mammal.' The vet flashed Clare a killer smile. 'Won't be long now.' He was really quite good-looking, in a rough and ready sort of way. Sandy blond hair worn in a no-nonsense, almost military, buzz cut. Rugged tanned features. The material of his blue scrubs strained across broad shoulders and outlined the arch of his upper back.

The snake sagged in the middle. 'Get that wooden board in the corner and lay it on the table.' Clare obliged, and he laid the front third of the snake across it. The vet gently disengaged Jack's arms from their death grip. 'Good job,' he said. Jack beamed with pride. The snake looked lifeless.

'Why the board?' asked Clare.

'Metal tables suck heat from reptiles and she's weak enough already. Wood will keep her that little bit warmer.'

Weak? The snake was more than weak. It was dead, wasn't it? Why would you want to keep a dead snake warm?

Jack was watching the man's every move with rapt attention. Clare had never seen him so focused. It had certainly been an adventure for him. The thought that it might not have turned out as well as it did made Clare shudder. Dan scrubbed forearms and hands, pulled on surgical gloves, then stopped and stared at Clare as if seeing her for the first time. 'Something's happened to your face,' he said. 'It's all puffed up and bleeding. You'd better let me look at that afterwards.'

CLARE FELT her nose and ignored his comment. Jack was patting the snake. It was good for children to learn about life and death through animals. For her it had been Grandma's chickens. Collecting eggs one morning, she'd found a hen lying quite still in the nest box. It took some time for Grandma to convince her that it wasn't just asleep. For the first time she'd seen what *dead* looked like. Clare overcame an instinctive reluctance to touch the snake. She stroked its body, surprised by the skin's dry silken texture. Its scales, reflected in the light, took on a transparent violet glow, dazzling in its brilliance.

Dan followed her gaze. 'Beautiful, isn't she? Gets her name from that purple sheen. *Amethystine python,* although most people call them scrub pythons. Not nearly as poetic.'

'It's enormous. How long do you think?' asked Clare.

The vet sized up the reptile. 'Four metres, maybe? But she's just a tiddler. I've seen ones up north go eight and a half.'

Jack gave the python a shake.

'Sorry, darling. It won't wake up,' she told the little boy in a consoling voice.

'That's right, mate,' said Dan. 'It won't, thanks to this little beauty.' He inserted a thin tube into the snake's mouth and tied it in place. 'This goes down her trachea,' he said. 'It's what she'll breathe through. I'm running oxygen and isoflurane down it so she'll stay asleep, like your mum said. But don't worry. She's going to be fine afterwards. Now, let's get her x-rayed.' The vet wheeled the table across the room, positioned it beneath the arm of a tall, grey machine, and heaved the prone reptile onto her back.

'You mean the snake's not dead?' asked Clare.

'I should hope not,' said Dan cheerfully.

'I thought you were ...' Clare stopped, unwilling to admit her mistake, but Dan didn't appear to be listening. Jack was still stroking the snake. She sprang for him and gathered the child protectively in her arms. Her reward was a head-butt in the face. Jack squirmed free and returned to the snake's side.

Dan glanced up. 'She's completely harmless' he said, then added with a grin, 'Right now.' Clare didn't know how to respond. She became curious about the procedure this strange man was performing. His hands expertly massaged the reptile's belly as if feeling for something. His large fingers were surprisingly tender, as they made their way down the body, probing gently as they went. 'Aha.' He disinfected a section of pale belly scales, then made a short incision. By now Clare was as fascinated as Jack.

'Don't worry,' said Dan. 'She can't feel a thing.' He mopped away a small amount of blood. 'There's the problem.' The final slice of the scalpel revealed three dimpled spheres lined up along the reptile's gut. What were they? Eggs? With a pair of tongs Dan eased one of the objects out. It wasn't an egg at all. It was a golf ball.

'How in heaven's name?' said Clare.

'Old Mick used them as decoy eggs in the hen house. They encourage the new pullets to lay in their nest boxes. Those chickens weren't the only ones fooled. Madam here thought she was onto a good thing.'

Mick. Clare's grandfather.

Dan eased out a second ball. 'This morning Mick found the nest empty, and her in the corner with a bellyache. He put two and two together and called me.' Dan took out the final ball and lined it up beside the others. They were covered in mucous and blood. The sight made Clare sick.

Dan prepared to suture the wound. 'Come on, Jack,' she said. 'Time to go.' The boy shook his head violently.

'Hold on. I'll be with you in a minute.' Dan indicated Samson. 'He's a fine-looking dog. What seems to be the problem?'

For a moment Clare didn't understand. 'I'm not here as a client-'

'Snake,' said Jack.

Clare caught her breath. Had she imagined it?

'A special kind of snake,' said Dan. 'A python.'

'Python,' said Jack.

'That's right. You've got a smart kid here.'

'He spoke,' whispered Clare, mainly to herself. 'Jack spoke.'

Dan tied off the stitches and eased the tube from the snake's throat. 'So you're Jack,' he said, giving him a warm smile. 'And what's your mum's name?'

'I'm Clare,' she said, still stunned that Jack had spoken.

'Clare ... Mick's granddaughter? I didn't know you had a son.'

She nodded. The nod was for the first bit. It was a nod for, *Yes, I'm Mick's granddaughter*, not for, *Yes, I have a son*. She opened her mouth to clear up the misunderstanding, but Dan was talking again. 'The old man's been waiting for you all day. Never seen him so excited. You didn't have to stop in and say hello to me first.' Clare sighed. Dan really was exasperating. He coiled the sleeping snake into a pet crate, then swung Jack into the air. The little boy giggled with glee. 'I'll come up to the house with you two. Update Mick on his snake.'

She should say no. She should tell him to take his ugly portable buildings and his snakes and his vicious dogs and leave her alone. Maybe it was the shock of Jack speaking, or maybe she had concussion from falling out of the tree, but for whatever reason, she allowed Dan to carry Jack out the door.

CHAPTER 10

Time had stood still. The cream and green cupboards, the matching enamel stove, the battered timber table top – all just as they had once been. Clare might have been eleven-years-old again. The funny thing was that she couldn't have recalled a single thing about that kitchen if you'd asked her an hour earlier. But now? Now she recognised each tiny detail.

'Mick,' called Dan, still holding Jack aloft. 'Got something for you.'

Her grandfather emerged from the hallway. Unlike the kitchen, he had changed. The few strands on his head were white now. His clothes hung loose on a skinny frame and the years showed on his lined face. But he still stood tall, unstooped, and when he saw Clare, his smile was as warm as ever.

'Well, look at you,' he said, taking her in, not seeming to notice her dishevelled hair and bruised face. 'My little Clare all grown up and quite a beauty, wouldn't you say so Dan?'

For some ridiculous reason, Clare found herself waiting on Dan's response. She turned her head away a fraction in embarrassment.

'That I would, Mick,' came the answer. 'That I would.'

Clare bit her lip. The man had some hide.

. . .

MICK STRODE over and embraced Clare, holding her for the longest time.

Clare blinked back tears. What a precious sensation, to be encircled in her grandfather's protective arms. It was a feeling to hold on to. 'I'm sorry about your dad,' he said.

She felt a shaft of shame. *'And I'm sorry about Grandma,'* she wanted to say. *'I'm sorry for not being here, for not caring enough,'* but the words were like a weight she couldn't lift.

'And who have we here?' asked Mick.

'This is Jack,' said Clare. 'The little boy I was telling you about.'

Comprehension dawned on Dan's face. 'So he's not yours then?'

'I'm his temporary foster parent.'

'I'll bet that's quite a story.' Dan's smile broadened. 'She's got a dog too, Mick. He's outside. A black German shepherd pup.'

'Well, bring him in,' said her grandfather. 'The more the merrier.'

Dan put Jack down. 'I'll fetch him.' The little boy followed Dan out the door, ignoring Clare's call. 'He's fine with me,' said Dan. 'We'll be back in a jiffy'.

Clare hesitated, then nodded and let Jack go. She was too worn out to argue. Truthfully it was a relief to abdicate responsibility, even if it was just for a minute, even if it was to that insensitive idiot.

Being alone with her grandfather left Clare a little tongue-tied. It had been easier with Dan there, helping the conversation along, but now she felt the gulf of years between them. What to do? What to say? They were strangers.

Mick put an ancient kettle on the cast iron range and indicated for her to sit. Clare sensed an awkwardness in him too. He fussed about the kitchen while they waited for the others to come back. Clare was on to her second cup of Grandad's strong, sweet tea, when Samson poked his head in the door. She froze. The blue heeler was right behind him, a deep growl in its throat. She jumped to her feet, tipping over her chair and retreating against the wall.

'Don't mind Red,' said Mick, with a chuckle. 'He's daft. Growling's his way of saying hello.'

Grandad sounded like the daft one. The dog advanced, a snarl on its lips. Clare edged around the wall towards the hallway. Thank god Jack was still outside.

Mick gave her a bemused look. 'That snarl? ... that's just him smiling. I told you he was daft. People get the wrong idea.' As if to prove Grandad's point, the heeler jumped up and licked his hand, still making the rumbling sound. 'See? He's like a cat purring.'

Clare began to relax. Had she really got it so wrong? The heeler turned his attention to her now and she steeled herself to stand still. He licked her toes where they poked through her sandals, making her flinch. He looked up and whined. She tried to imagine his bare-toothed snarl as a grin. 'Hello, boy,' she said hesitantly, smothering a squeal as the heeler jumped up for a pat.

Grandad was rummaging round in a cupboard. 'There are biscuits somewhere.'

Samson and Jack tumbled inside and played chasey around the kitchen table. The heeler joined in the fun, growling and snarling and wagging his tail. Clare composed herself and sat down just as Dan came in. He took a seat beside her and watched the game, shaking his head. 'Red sure is one, crazy mixed-up dog.' He glanced up, laughing, and caught her watching him. She flushed a little, hoping it didn't show. 'Let me take a look at those cuts to your face,' he said.

She shook her head.

'What happened?' he asked. 'You come a cropper off a horse?'

She nodded. Anything to avoid admitting that she'd climbed a tree to escape his stupid, smiling dog, and had promptly fallen out of it.

Grandad produced a packet of Iced VoVos, offered one to Jack, and shook the rest onto a plate. Clare took one and examined it. Pink fondant icing atop a wheat biscuit, a strip of strawberry jam running down the middle, and the entire thing dusted with coconut. She turned it over. The back still bore the fancy moulded design that she remembered from childhood. A memory of sharing these same biscuits around this same table hit her so powerfully that Clare half-expected Grandma to walk in the door.

'You were right about the python,' said Dan, helping himself to a biscuit. 'I just cut three golf balls from her belly. Had a hard time holding her, but these two were a big help.' He stood up and dusted crumbs off his shirt. 'Better get back to it. You coming to the meeting tonight, Mick?'

'Planned to,' said Mick, 'but I wouldn't miss the first evening with my granddaughter, not even for the cakes.'

'Righto,' said Dan. 'I'll fill you in tomorrow. Never know your luck — I might bring you back a lamington.' He waved an expansive goodbye, and left with Red trotting at his heels.

'What's it about?' asked Clare. 'This meeting?'

'Nothing for you to worry about.' Samson sat at his feet, squirming and smiling as Grandad rubbed his ears. 'How about I find this scoundrel of yours a bone and the lad some toys, eh?' His face, alight with pleasure, already looked ten years younger.

Why had she left it so long between visits? They'd lost too many years - years that should have been filled with love, and family, and a sense of belonging. All of it sacrificed to her father's bitterness, and the altar of her own ambition.

Mick emerged a few minutes later with a huge cardboard carton. He put it on the kitchen floor and called Jack over from where he was watching flies buzz at the window. Clare drew in a quick breath. Here was a treasure trove of memories: a wind up jack-in-the-box that used to frighten her, a fleet of hand-carved trucks, a wooden skittle set. Jack started gathering together the Matchbox cars.

Samson picked up a worn rag doll in his mouth. It wore a purple dress that Clare remembered Grandma knitting. Mick took an enormous marrowbone from the fridge and offered it to Samson. 'This'll suit you better.' He rescued the doll, and Samson took the bone into the corner. Clare watched the boy and the dog, both of them relaxed and happy in a way that just didn't happen back at her apartment – like they'd broken free of something.

Clare gazed around the kitchen. Sixteen years of memories held in its walls and she didn't know what they were. She could guess. Grandma cooking her famous roasts. Grandad dancing her around the table. Card games and flower pressing. Writing and wrapping all those unopened cards and presents. Grandad taking over the cooking as Grandma got sick. Boiled eggs and cups of tea. Chicken soup and toast. Clare could guess, but she didn't know. She wanted to ask her grandfather about it, but she couldn't. Not yet. Not when she looked at the door and realised just how long it had been since Grandma had walked through it.

'Do you ever hear from Mum?' she asked.

He gave her a heavy-hearted smile. 'Not often, love. She's all caught up in her own world. No time for her old dad.' Or her children, thought Clare. But who was she to judge? She'd been just as bad, abandoning Mick for all these years … and Grandma. That was unforgiveable. She was suddenly horrified to think she'd never see her again, as if the dreadful finality of her grandmother's death had only just hit home. Guilty tears pricked at her eyes, but all that she could see in Grandad's eyes was love.

CLARE SPENT a magical afternoon showing Jack around. They pushed each other on the tyre swing in the garden. They played the giant xylophone of Condamine bells in the cart shed until her ears rang. They collected eggs from the chook house and picked the first broad beans of spring. They climbed on the haystack and practised whip cracking. The little boy was entranced by each activity. 'That's a fine stockwhip,' Grandad said, when he came to find them. Clare told him an edited version of their day at the Cobb & Co museum. It turned out he knew the saddler. 'I thought it was one of Sid's.'

Grandad and Jack took the horses some carrots, while Clare returned to the house to make up Ryan's old bed in the verandah room. When she opened the curtains, spectacular orange trumpets of winter-flowering flame creeper crowded against the rusted fly wire.

Childhood memories lay in ambush around every corner. Memories that made her ache with both sadness and happiness.

Later Clare helped Grandad prepare the roast: a plump leg of lamb nestled among potatoes and carrots, pumpkins and parsnips. She could already taste the rich, dark gravy made in the pan. Clare prepared fruit for the pie. The kitchen was redolent with the aroma of hearty country cooking. Quite a contrast to her own, where the microwave was the only appliance to get a regular workout.

After dinner Clare stood at the bedroom door while Grandad read Jack a tattered copy of *Where the Wild Things Are*. The little boy dropped off to sleep, clutching his stock whip, before the sun had fully set behind the mountains. She smiled as her grandfather kissed Jack's cheek and closed the curtains. Samson hopped onto the foot of the bed and turned beseeching brown eyes on Clare.

'Leave him,' said Grandad. 'The lad has a right to his dog.'

He turned out the lamp and followed Clare back down the hall. She'd only been at Currawong for a few hours, but already the distractions of Brisbane and the pain of her recent breakup seemed a world away.

She helped Grandad tidy the kitchen and do the dishes, mulling over the events of the afternoon. Her thoughts kept returning to the remarkable way Jack had responded since he'd been at the farm, and of how he'd actually spoken. If you didn't know any better, Jack would have almost seemed like a normal little boy today. Grandad pulled an old Scrabble set from a bookshelf. 'I won't be quite so easy to beat these days,' she teased.

'We'll see,' he said. The tension between them was slipping away.

To her surprise, Grandad trounced her - twice. 'I'm done,' she said, standing up. 'You're too good for me.'

He gave her a heartfelt hug. 'It's a great joy having you here, Clare.'

'It's a great joy being here,' she said, smiling at the pet name she'd forgotten about. 'I've missed you, missed this place. Funny thing is, I didn't even realise how much until today.' She reached for his hand. 'Goodnight, Grandad.'

'Goodnight, love.'

Clare tiptoed down the hall and looked in on Jack. Moonlight streamed through a crack in the curtains, spotlighting his pillow. The little boy looked serene, his features relaxed in sleep. Samson stretched and thumped his tail. 'Goodnight, you two.'

She slipped into her room, slipped into her old bed. The moon sailed high outside her window, bathing the familiar space in a soft light. The giant bunya pine, standing guard in the yard, cast a reassuring silhouette against the luminous sky. Clare drifted off to sleep, overcome by the strangest notion – the notion that returning to Currawong might be the wisest decision she'd ever made.

CHAPTER 11

Grandad placed a steaming plate of scrambled eggs before her. Jack was already shovelling great spoonfuls into his mouth, while Samson sat beside him, wolfing up the inevitable spills. A knock came at the door. 'It'll be Dan,' said Grandad, with a chuckle. 'That boy can smell breakfast a mile off.'

Clare ran her fingers hurriedly through her hair. She hadn't expected to see anybody so early.

Dan came in and sat down beside Jack. Clare looked warily around. Friendly or not, she was still not a great fan of Red, but there was no sign of him. Soon they were all hoeing into the biggest breakfast Clare could remember. Piles of buttered toast. Bacon, tomato and grilled mushrooms the size of her hand.

'Mick grows them in bags of compost under the house,' said Dan, taking a second helping. 'Bloody beautiful, they are.'

Clare imagined how horrified Adam would be at the cholesterol-laden spread, and then took another slice of bacon.

Dan was playing spider fingers with Jack in between mouthfuls, threatening to pounce whenever the little boy reached for his spoon, generating a storm of giggles.

'How was the meeting?' asked Grandad.

'Got a bit out of hand at the end,' said Dan. 'A few blokes turned up that were on Pyramid's side. Reckoned we were just scaremongering, trying to spoil things for them.' He reached across for more toast, brushing against Clare's arm in the process. She was acutely aware of his touch; the warmth of his skin. 'Pyramid offers generous compensation for each well per year, as well as an up-front fee. If you host say, twenty wells, that's big money. Can't blame people for being tempted.'

'No, I suppose you can't,' said Grandad with a sigh. 'The almighty dollar always wins out in the end, eh?'

'Maybe,' said Dan, tousling Jack's hair, and pushing his chair back from the table. 'And maybe not. Look at Pete Porter. He makes a good income from his wells, but he'd get rid of them in a heartbeat, given half the chance. Those for Pyramid were outnumbered ten to one by the rest of us. It's not hard to see which way the tide of community opinion is running.' He washed up his plate, gave Clare a nod and left.

'What wells?' asked Clare.

'Coal seam gas wells,' said Grandad. 'Pyramid Energy reckons the biggest field in Australia lies right under Merriang. They've taken out exploration licenses for the whole region.'

'Natural gas?' asked Clare.

'There's nothing natural about it.'

'And what ... they want to put wells here at Currawong Creek?' He nodded.

'Is that what the sign on the gate's all about?'

'Yep.' There was a grim set to his jaw. The subject was apparently closed. 'Thought I'd take the young fellow yabbying.' He stood and collected up the empty plates, scraping the scraps into the chook bucket. 'And don't worry, love. I remember you've got a soft spot for the little snappers. We'll let them go afterwards. What do you say, Jack? Do you want to catch some yabbies? Maybe we'll dig out that old aquarium and you can keep a few as pets, just like your mum used to do.'

'I'm not his mother,' corrected Clare.

'Course you're not,' said Mick, taking some steak from the fridge and cutting a few tiny slivers. 'My mistake.' The little boy bounced from his chair and grabbed Mick's arm. Clare studied him as he tried to drag her grandfather outside.

Should she let them go? 'Jack ...' She stopped, not wanting to say too much while the little boy was listening. 'He runs away,' she said at last, 'and tantrums ... unless he's with Samson.'

'The dog looks after him then?'

She nodded. 'And Grandad, Jack can't speak - except he did, once, with me, and then again yesterday with Dan.'

Mick looked at her without surprise, his expression matter of fact. 'I expect the lad will talk when he's good and ready,' was all he said, and the pair headed for the door.

'I'll join you in a bit,' she called after them. 'Watch Jack around the dam, won't you?' Clare fetched her laptop and checked without much hope for internet access. Nothing. Dan must have Wi-Fi. Surely you couldn't run a modern vet clinic without it?

Through the window, she saw her grandfather make his way across the yard, bucket in hand, while Jack and Samson chased each other in a wide arc around him. Pongo and Perdita trotted ahead. Apparently the same names had been used for different dogs in the family for fifty years. Ever since Grandma read Dodie Smith's classic novel, *101 Dalmatians*, there'd been a Perdita and Pongo at Currawong. Tradition played no part in the life Clare knew in Brisbane. She was oddly appreciative of finding it alive and well out here at the family farm.

Clare packed up her laptop and made her way down the drive to the clinic, where a couple of cars were parked. A short girl with three border collies stood by the surgery door, along with a red-faced man sporting a comb-over. He was holding two buckets labelled *Henry's Honey*.

'Hello,' said Clare.

'Hello,' said the girl shyly. Clare waited nearby, shifting from foot to foot. The man nodded a greeting, then proceeded to cast odd glances her way, as if he didn't quite approve of her being there. At last the door swung open. Dan turned the little sign in the window from *Closed* to *Open*, then stared past the others to Clare. He smiled, crinkling the little laugh lines at the corners of his mouth.

'Here you go,' said the man, offering the buckets.

Dan looked puzzled. 'What's this, Henry?'

'Thought it might do as a trade for what's left on my bill,' he said and marched inside, followed by the girl, the border collies and finally Clare.

The room was still a mess from the previous day. Shelves were once more in place against the walls, but their contents had been jammed back in haphazard piles. Stacks of books, brochures and journals spilled from the reception desk, almost burying the ancient computer. The collies roamed about the room, poking curious noses under cupboards and onto shelves. Their girl made no attempt to control them. Instead she waited patiently beside a sign saying *All dogs to be on a leash*. Maybe the snake wasn't entirely to blame for yesterday's mayhem after all. It could just be the natural state of affairs around here. Clare moved closer to the desk and discovered a wireless modem behind a box of horse worming paste. Good, that solved her communications problem.

'What am I supposed to do with all this honey?' asked Dan,

'There's loads you can do with honey, besides eat it of course,' said Henry. 'Use it as a facial, hair conditioner, antiseptic, and my missus swears by it for treating rough elbows.' He turned to leave.

'Wait,' said Dan. 'I don't think ...'

Henry held up his hand. 'No need to thank me doc,' and with that he ducked out the door. An old gentleman arrived next, with a bald cockatoo wearing a little knitted jumper. Clare wondered if he was going to try and trade it as well.

The *If I Could Talk to the Animals* tune rang out, and Dan found his phone under a box of catnip. Who did he think he was? Dr Doolittle? She shook her head in disgust. How on earth did the clinic even function? She'd never seen anything so unprofessional in her life. Perhaps it would be better to come back later.

As Clare turned to go, a hand touched her arm. She looked up into Dan's clear blue eyes. Summer sky blue. 'Can I help you?'

'I want to get online.'

Dan's hand remained on her arm. It was rough-skinned like a farmer, and long-fingered like an artist. 'Be my guest. There's no password,' he said and disappeared into the consulting room with the collie girl.

The cocky spread its bald wings and said, *'Hello stranger.'* Clare laughed and said hello back. It answered her with a wolf whistle and a little dance.

'Buddy's always been a flirt,' the old man said fondly. The bird nuzzled his cheek.

Dan emerged from the consulting room, followed by the girl and her dogs. 'All up to date now,' he said. 'That C5 vaccination covers Canine Cough as well, so they'll be right to go into kennels in a couple of weeks.'

'Can I have two tick collars as well, please?' asked the girl.

Dan looked around at the cluttered shelves. 'Now where did I put them?'

Clare spotted a box labelled *Excel Tick Control Collars* behind a stack of dog toys. She retrieved the box, placed it in a more prominent position, then took out two packets and handed them over. Dan looked impressed. The girl paid the account and he turned his attention to Mr Cockatoo man.

'Paddy, if you'd like to come in ...'

'I'll not be dragging this out,' the man said in a thick Irish brogue. 'Do you have those test results?' Dan nodded. 'And you wouldn't go beating around the bush with me, would you doc?'

Dan's expression softened. 'I think we both knew, Paddy, but the test confirmed it. Buddy has PFBD ... psittacine beak and feather disease.'

The old man scratched the bird's neck and it bounced with pleasure. 'There's no cure, is there now?' Dan shook his head. The man's face had crumpled alarmingly. 'My wife Betty, bless her heart, found Buddy here as a wee nestling, the week we lost our son Patrick to the pneumonia. In the middle of our back paddock, Buddy was, with never a tree in sight. I think a crow must have dropped him, but Betty said he'd fallen from heaven. She nursed him day and night till he was well. I used to tease her - tell her she loved that bird more than me.'

Buddy bobbed his head and called out, 'Betty, Betty, Betty.' They all smiled.

'That was forty years ago now, if it was a day.' Clare was enthralled. 'Betty was a church-going woman, so she was. One morning she told me that God had spoken to her in a dream. *I will lend you this magic bird,* he'd said to her, *for you to love while he lives and mourn when he dies.'* Paddy's voice held a world of sadness. 'She said the Lord gave us Buddy to comfort us after Patrick.'

A chill fell on the room, and it dawned on Clare that something awful was about to happen. She felt the prickle of tears behind her nose. 'And comfort us he did, for all those years, and then kept me company when I lost Betty. He's been a great joy, Buddy has - my truest friend.'

'I can give you a cream ...' began Dan.

Paddy shook his head. 'No, no ... he wants to fly, you see. He tries so hard, I can't bear to see him always disappointed ... and he'll get sicker, won't he? I've read enough to know.'

Dan pressed his lips together and followed Paddy into the consulting room. Clare gulped and tried to compose herself. Thank goodness there were no other clients. The silence screamed as she waited for Dan to finish, waited for it to be over. At last they emerged. Paddy carried a small bundle wrapped in a towel. Clare began to cry. The old man put a wrinkled hand on her shoulder. 'Thanks for your tears, lass,' he said solemnly, and then he was gone.

'Hey, now,' said Dan. 'I thought you were a tough city lawyer. It was the kindest thing.'

'There's nothing kind about taking away a lonely old man's best friend,' managed Clare between sobs.

'No,' Dan said. 'I suppose not.' He boiled the electric kettle in the corner and poured her a cup of coffee. 'Stay and use the internet.' Dan grabbed what looked like an old-fashioned doctor's bag from behind the counter. 'You have the place to yourself.'

Clare said goodbye and tried to pull herself together, but the old man's face haunted her. How utterly bereft he must be. Now she was alone, Clare could no longer sniff back the tears. She laid her head on the desk and wept like a child.

When she was finally spent, Clare washed her face at the sink and peered in the mirror. Swollen, bloodshot eyes peered back. She looked as bad as she felt. Clare gulped down the lukewarm coffee and opened her laptop. No emails from work of course. That felt very strange. In fact there were hardly any emails at all, at least nothing personal. Clare checked Facebook. She hadn't been on the site for a long while and wasn't up to date with anything. She'd been so preoccupied lately. Between Dad's illness, her work and Adam, she'd allowed friendships to take a back seat. The embarrassing truth was that nobody seemed to have missed her.

She pushed aside the emptiness of that thought, made another coffee and googled coal seam gas on the Darling Downs. Dozens of websites popped up and she combed through the opposing views. It was a hot-button issue, no two ways about it, but Clare's legal training obliged her to put aside the hype and concentrate on facts. The first fact required no research. Under Queensland law, all resources below ground were the property of the state. Providing miners had the correct permits, farmers could not refuse them access to private land, no matter how many High Court decisions they quoted on their front gates.

Coal seam gas, she discovered, was just natural gas – mainly methane – extracted from coal seams deep below the ground. It was a low carbon energy source, producing half the greenhouse gas emissions of coal. As Dan had mentioned that morning, there was an upfront advance to landholders with wells, followed by annual payments. Companies were legally obliged to make good any damage caused, and surrounding land could still be used for cropping and grazing.

For the first time Clare considered how Grandad might be travelling financially. From what she remembered, his clydesdales used to give demonstrations at agricultural shows and were hired out for gypsy caravan holidays. He sold yearlings, stood stallions at stud, broke in horses to harness and ran a few steers. How much of that, she wondered, was he still capable of? He was old now. His back remained straight, but he was thin and so much frailer than she remembered. In some lights there was an odd translucency to his skin, as if his tan disguised an underlying pallor. The property too showed signs of neglect. Sagging fences. Stands of lantana and other weeds that Clare couldn't identify. The house could use a coat of paint. It might well be worth having a few ugly gas plants at Currawong Creek if it meant Grandad could take it easy.

The waiting room phone rang. Clare hesitated for a moment before answering it.

'Thank goodness the doc's come to his senses and hired an assistant,' said the caller. 'You have a job in front of you, my girl, trying to organise that one. Anyway, let him know Mrs Potts has an egg-bound budgie.'

Clare took down the message. 'When can you bring it in?'

'Oh, I don't drive, dear. Doctor Dan comes to me. It's so much easier that way.'

Easier for who? thought Clare, but dutifully noted the woman's phone number. She packed up her laptop and escaped the clinic before the phone could ring again.

Clare walked back up to the house, but there was nobody there. How was Jack getting on, she wondered? Maybe she shouldn't have let him go off like that with Grandad. She went to find them, heading down through the veggie patch towards the dam. Past the old tyre swing in the garden. Her mother used to tell her wonderful stories while pushing her on that swing. Stories of strong independent princesses. Princesses who won battles and slew dragons, without a Prince Charming in sight. Past the stack of old bricks that Ryan had piled up by the tool shed long ago. She couldn't believe it was still there. He'd named it *The Stone Table*. They used it to play *The Lion, the Witch and the Wardrobe* games. He'd been Aslan and she'd been Jadis, the evil White Witch. They'd reenacted scenes from the book. She'd regularly tried to sacrifice him on the bricks, with varying degrees of success. Past their old cubby. It wasn't in too bad a shape. Maybe she'd fix it up for Jack.

Clare detoured down a grassy track that led to Currawong Creek. It opened onto a familiar expanse of winding water, more of a river really. Here were the red gums, bunya pines and reedy shallows of memory. This was the scene she'd recalled back at Koala Park. Back on that awful day when she'd lost Jack and they'd retreated from the reserve in disgrace.

The sound of laughter drew her back up the path. Grandad, Jack and the dogs were returning from the dam. 'The yabbies weren't biting, but we haven't come back empty-handed. Show her, Jack.' Jack proudly showed Clare their bucket. It was filled with enormous eggs. 'I finally found their nest, with the help of your shepherd pup,' said Grandad, fondling Samson's head. 'There'll be goose egg omelettes for breakfast tomorrow.'

They put the eggs in the kitchen and sat out on the verandah with cups of tea. Samson was helping Jack collect sticks. The little boy assessed each one carefully, then either discarded it or added it to his pile. 'What's the difference?' Clare said. 'They're all the same. A stick's a stick.'

'To you maybe,' said Grandad. He nodded when Jack balanced another stick on his pile, as if he agreed with the choice. A breeze blew out of nowhere and Grandad turned his head to meet it, staring into the distance and sniffing the wind. 'Storm on the way.' Clare studied his weathered face in profile. They'd lost so much time. In some ways Grandad was as big a mystery to her as Jack was.

CHAPTER 12

A week now at Currawong Creek, and Clare could feel the cares and anxieties of Brisbane slipping from her like an outgrown skin. She yawned and cleared away her dishes. Jack and Samson had already headed out with Grandad, leaving Clare to enjoy a lazy breakfast. No phone, no email, no need to do anything at all in particular. She'd been spending her days playing with Jack, or weeding Grandma's veggie patch or exploring the house and sheds. Sometimes she simply sat in the garden, reading a book selected from Grandma's well-thumbed *Collection of Modern Classics*. Jane Austen, Charles Dickens, Sir Arthur Conan Doyle - the dusty hallway bookshelves were stacked high with all sorts of gems. A copy of *Treasure Island* that Grandad used to read, putting on a silly pirate voice. Mum's *Golden Treasury of Poetry*, its spine mended with packing tape. A photo album. On the cover was a shot of Clare riding Smudge. Mum stood proudly by her side, holding the pony's reins. Clare had flipped slowly through the old pictures, stroking each page, closing her eyes to help summon memories. Here at Currawong, the past wasn't gone. The present was crowded with it.

Clare found Jack and her grandfather seated on picnic chairs by the dam, throwing bread to a gaggle of grey geese, and drinking lemonade. The day was picture-perfect. Water sparkling like diamonds. The sun sailed in a blue sky between islands of cotton-wool clouds. The morning air had a special clarity that seemed to bring the Bunya mountains close enough to touch.

A lone horse in the adjacent paddock trotted over to the fence to say hello. He was of a monstrous size, with an arched crest and proud, high-stepping gait. 'Is that your stallion?' asked Clare. 'He looks a bit like Rastus.' Jack moved towards the fence and Clare protectively blocked his way.

'Well picked,' said Grandad. 'That's Goliath. Last stallion standing at Currawong Creek. Same bloodlines as Rastus and just as gentle. He'll do your boy no harm.'

'Aren't some stallions dangerous?' asked Clare.

Grandad stood up stiffly and went over to stroke the horse's nose. 'Any stallion worth his salt is bound to be high-couraged,' he said. 'But Goliath hasn't a mean bone in his body. He'd do almost anything for me without the slightest argument.'

Jack darted past Clare, ran to the fence and joined in patting the horse. 'The lad's not scared,' said Grandad. 'He's got the knack, you see. Not everybody does. I've seen grown men try to hide their fear of stallions with a show of bravado - a loud voice, and perhaps a whip for defence. They may trick others, they may even trick themselves, but they'll never deceive a horse. That stallion decides that since the man has no confidence in himself, there must be something wrong with the man, and stallions don't suffer fools lightly. That's when they get dangerous.' Clare edged forward and willed herself to be brave. Goliath nuzzled her cheek with utmost gentleness, while Grandad beamed at them both.

Back at the dam, two yabbies sat in the bucket. She'd forgotten how beautiful they were – flawless satin shells, dappled with soft beige, and brandishing electric blue claws. Jack was entranced by the little crayfish. He'd been at Currawong for just a week, but his attention span already seemed to have stretched. Grandad took Jack's hand and moved him a little way down the bank, then threw a baited string in the water. 'Hold this,' he said. Jack did as he was asked. Amazing.

Samson sat down next to him, ears cocked forward, watching the rippled surface as intently as any human yabby hunter. Grandad returned to Clare wearing a thoughtful expression. 'What's the lad's story?'

It was a relief to pour it all out. Not just about Jack, but everything else that had happened since the day Taylor Brown turned up at the office. How could Clare have predicted the profound effect Jack's arrival would have had on her life?

'That's some story,' said Grandad. 'Did he break your heart, this Adam feller?'

Clare was floored by the question. A broken heart was such an old-fashioned, sentimental concept.

'Yes,' she said at last. 'I suppose he did.'

Grandad leaned across and kissed her cheek. 'He never deserved you then, love. I can promise you. You're well out of it.'

How good it was to be affirmed like that? Since Dad died, there was nobody who cared enough to say such things. Clare suddenly missed her mother. She turned and wrapped her arms around her grandfather's bony shoulders.

He held her very tight for a moment, then pointed to Jack. 'The pup's been a help there?'

Clare nodded. 'Without Samson I probably would have given up on Jack. You have no idea what he's been like because, for some reason, he's all of a sudden on his best behaviour. But the kid was expelled from kindergarten for God's sake.' Her grandfather chuckled. 'It wasn't funny,' said Clare.

He moved to Jack's line and, with infinite slowness, began to haul it in. 'No, I guess it wasn't.'

A little kingfisher landed on the pump house to their left. It was a colourful bird, with a cobalt blue back, buff-orange breast and violet streaks along its flanks. In a flash it dived into the dam at their feet, and carried away the squirming yabby off Grandad's string. 'Good luck to you,' Mick said. 'At least the little snappers will make someone a good supper.' He re-baited the line and threw it back into the water. 'If I were you,' he said, 'I'd ask Dan about the lad. Dan has a certificate in equine therapy, or some such thing. Worked with kids back home in the Hunter Valley.'

'He doesn't seem very responsible,' she said. 'I don't want Jack getting hurt.'

'I'm telling you, love, Dan ran groups at *Riding For The Disabled.* Worked wonders with those children apparently.' Really? Clare considered her grandfather's words. Dan might be a blockhead, but he did have a way with Jack.

'It won't hurt you to talk to him,' urged Grandad.

'I will,' she said, cutting herself a piece of string. 'Just as soon as he's back from his rounds.' She checked the watch Grandad had given her. It was her grandmother's and she loved it. Plus it was the only way to tell the time now her iPhone was defunct. Still early. She held up the string to check its length, and Grandad gave it an approving nod.

'Now,' she said. 'I just need some bait.'

CHAPTER 13

'Gee up,' Dan told the grey mare. 'I have someone for you to meet.' He led Fleur down the hill to where Mick and the little boy stood beside the stockyard with Clare. There was straw in Clare's hair. She must have been collecting eggs, fossicking through the hay shed where Mick's hens stubbornly continued to lay, instead of in their nest boxes in the chook house. The tousled look suited Clare – her windswept, shoulder-length bob both messy and stylish at the same time. He couldn't help thinking it was how she'd look straight out of bed.

'This is Fleur,' said Dan, bringing the big horse to a halt. She nickered a greeting. Age had not detracted from the mare's natural air of nobility and she arched her snow-white neck as proudly as if she was back in the show ring.

'What is she?' asked Clare. 'Not a clydesdale.'

'Fleur's a percheron,' said Mick. 'A draft breed originally from France. They're used a lot over outback station mares to put size and strength into stock horses. Add a bit of toughness.'

Fleur stood just sixteen hands, on the short size for a draft horse, but she was quality through and through: short-coupled, strong of top line and straight of bone. Her legs were clean and free from feather and her eye was kind.

'She's a nice sort of mare,' said Dan.

'Supreme Champion at Royal Sydney Show three years in a row.' Mick's voice swelled with pride. 'One of her foals is the drum horse for Victoria police. The national vaulting team has two more.' He stroked her neck. 'This old girl's done well by me, but her breeding days are over. Sent her off to Macca's new stallion two years in a row and she never came in season. Wouldn't have a bar off him.' He chuckled. 'Reckon she's telling me she's done.'

'Haven't you got something smaller?' Clare was trying to hold Jack back from climbing into the yard.

'Sorry, love,' said Mick. 'Fleur's the smallest horse at Currawong. But she's gentle as the day is long, is Fleur. I trust her and Dan with your lad, love, and I'd tell you if I didn't.'

Clare did not look convinced. 'Jack's not going to ride her,' said Dan. 'Not if you don't want him to.'

'What exactly will you be doing then?'

'I have a diploma in Equine Facilitated Learning.' Dan threaded a piece of long grass around his fingers as he talked. He noticed Clare watching his hands. 'There's plenty of clinical evidence that being around horses changes our brainwave patterns, calms them down. Horses can help kids to stop fixating on negative events in their past. EFL works particularly well for kids with autism - kids who find it hard to communicate. Can we see how Jack likes it?'

It was already pretty clear how Jack was going to like it. Clare was struggling to hold him back.

She nodded and let him through. 'How does just being with a horse do all that?'

Jack approached and stroked Fleur's shoulder. The mare bent her giant head in greeting.

'Horses mirror people,' said Dan. 'Reflect back their emotions. Don't let her size fool you; at heart Fleur's a prey animal so she wants to feel safe. If Jack is fearful, she'll be fearful. That's the challenge: in order to get Fleur to cooperate, Jack must first overcome any fears himself. Horses are good at picking up on human emotions, so he'll have to modify his own behaviour in order to get the horse to cooperate. He has to be calm and reasonable to put her at ease. This teaches him that his behaviour affects others. It's a great communication aid.' Clare looked a bit happier. 'That's the theory anyway. There's a mystical side to it that I swear no theory will ever explain. Shall we give it a try?'

Clare nodded, though he could tell she wasn't convinced. 'Calm and reasonable? I'd try anything for calm and reasonable. Although, I admit, just being at Currawong has already worked wonders.' She smiled at Jack, who was hugging Fleur's front leg. 'Good luck, Jacky.' She blew him a kiss.

'You're going to help me work with Fleur today, all right?' Dan said to Jack.

The boy nodded, eyes shining.

'Now hold this rope in your right hand, which is this hand, and stand there by her shoulder.' He positioned Jack correctly. Fleur stood steady as a rock. 'Before we start, I want you to say hello to your horse, okay?' Jack nodded. 'I want you to say *Hi Fleur*.'

'Hi Fleur,' said Jack softly. He didn't quite get the L, but it was a good attempt. Dan heard Clare's sudden intake of breath.

'Say, *How you doing?*'

'How you doing?' said Jack, with a bit more confidence.

'Good. Now gather up the rope — that's how you're going to lead her.' The boy was following his instructions to a tee. 'Now I want you to say *walk on* and then we're going into that big yard over there.'

'Walk on,' said Jack.

'Say it like you mean it,' called Mick.

'Walk on,' Jack said more firmly. For the next ten minutes he led Fleur around the ménage, learning how to change direction, halt her, even to back her up. It was quite a sight - the mighty mare and the tiny boy, acting in concert. It always amazed Dan to see the natural affinity kids had with horses. Clare was taking photos from the wings. In no time Jack had Fleur circling him on a lunging rein: the horse, the whip and the rope making sides of a perfect triangle.

'Let him jump her,' said Mick. 'Give the lad a real thrill.'

Clare was looking worried again. Mick came into the yard and began to set up cavaletti – low jumps made of crossover end pieces and a centre pole. 'Just the one,' said Dan. 'But make it two poles high.' He took the rope from Jack's hands. 'You're going to watch me and then do what I do. Okay?'

'Okay,' replied the boy.

'You're going to step over this and then Fleur's going to follow you.' Dan led the mare over the cavaletti and gave the rope back to Jack. 'Do you think you can do that?'

Jack nodded and copied Dan, struggling a little to get over the low jump. Fleur followed obediently, stepping over the poles. Everybody clapped and Jack grinned from ear to ear. Dan swapped the lead rope for a lunge rein. 'Now what I want you to do is ask Fleur to walk in a circle … that's the way. This whip you're holding isn't to hit her with, it just makes your arm longer.'

Fleur encountered the cavaletti at the perimeter of the circle and dutifully stepped over. 'Great,' said Dan, a protective hand on Jack's shoulder. 'Now, let's ask her to trot. Just raise your whip and say *trot on* in a loud voice.'

'Trot on,' said Jack.

'A bit louder.'

'Trot on!'

The mare broke into a cadenced trot. This time when she came to the jump, she gathered herself as if in slow motion, rose up on her powerful hindquarters and made a great leap, towering over not just Jack, but Dan as well. It was a truly magnificent sight. The ground trembled at her landing and Jack's eyes were saucer-wide. A look of pure joy and astonishment lit up his face, as cheers rose from the sidelines.

'Well done,' Dan said. 'That was fantastic, but it's enough for one day. I want you to lower the whip and ask Fleur to stand up.'

'Stand up,' said Jack, and the great mare came to a graceful halt. She swung around to face them, ears pricked as if asking, *what now?*

'Go and say thank you. Tell her she's a good girl.'

'I've got carrots,' called Clare, slipping through the rails. 'Offer them on the flat of your hand. That's right.'

'Good girl,' said Jack. 'Good girl.'

Fleur lowered her head, graciously taking the titbit with gentle lips. Jack threw his arms as far as they could reach around her neck in a fierce hug. Dan patted the little boy on the back. This had gone better than he could have imagined. He'd even impressed himself.

'I'm speechless,' said Clare. 'How was that even possible?'

'I tell you, this stuff really works,' said Dan. 'There's nothing better than to bring a child like this together with a horse like that - and just watch the magic happen.'

'I don't know how to thank you,' said Clare. 'That was truly amazing.'

Dan thought quickly. What did he have to lose? 'Let me take you to dinner at the pub tonight,' he said. 'That's if Mick's okay to watch Jack?'

'Go on, you two,' Mick said. 'I'm happy to mind the lad.'

What a break. Mick approved. It would have been a major obstacle otherwise.

Now for Clare ... she took her time answering. 'Okay, you're on.' She held his gaze for a long moment.

Dan grinned, picked another blade of grass and threaded it between his fingers. On first meeting Clare had seemed so uptight. She'd reminded him of the professional girls he'd met back in Sydney, caught up in their appearance and their careers; searching for their next step up the ladder. Not his type at all. But he'd misjudged her. This girl had a heart, taking on a little kid like Jack. That set her apart for a start. And of course the fact that she was drop dead gorgeous didn't hurt any.

Mick was looking at him. Dan turned his head, and tried to stop thinking about what Clare's skin might feel like. Better not rush this. He'd made that mistake before. Clare was all class, and Mick's granddaughter to boot. Take it slow, he told himself. Take it slow. 'Pick you up around seven?' She nodded and Dan led Fleur away, impatient for the evening to come.

. . .

Clare finished her rather gelatinous chocolate mousse and took a deep, contented breath. She'd almost had too much to drink. It was a bad habit she'd got into. Lawyers drank a lot; it was embedded in the culture. Wine with lunch, beers after work, a tokay or two in chambers. Adam always seemed to be swigging back scotch, and he kept a case of French sparkling wine at his place, just for her. She couldn't remember a time she'd been to bed with him when she was completely sober. But she didn't want to think about Adam now. Her grandfather barely drank, and she'd been aiming for an alcohol-free few weeks, but tonight the temptation had been too much. She was already onto her third wine. Dan was becoming more fascinating by the minute.

'Have you considered the possibility that Jack's not autistic?' asked Dan.

Her mouth went dry. Finally somebody agreed with her. She told Dan about the string of professionals confirming the boy's autism. She told him how, at the beginning, she'd disbelieved the diagnosis. She told him about the nightmare few weeks with Jack in Brisbane, and how she was beginning to believe she'd imagined Jack's first few words – until today. She told him about Taylor Brown, and her addiction, and about the stolen bull terrier puppy, and how she knew that Taylor really loved Jack, but that she didn't want him back.

'Jack's lucky to have you,' Dan said.

Clare wasn't good at receiving praise. Instead of accepting the compliment, she was inclined to argue the point.

'Lucky? Since I've had him he's been kicked out of child care, got lost, been locked alone in a car and now I'm sending him into yards with giant horses.'

'Locked alone in a car?' asked Dan. 'When was that?'

Clare finished her wine and asked for another one. Dan went to the bar and returned with a riesling and a beer. He was drinking light. She launched into the falling-out-of-the-tree story.

Dan looked genuinely horrified. 'I had no idea.'

'That was the problem,' she said.

They both burst out laughing. A droplet of beer shone on his lower lip and she wanted to dab it away. He wiped a finger around his dessert bowl like a kid and sucked it.

'Is your waiting room always so chaotic?' she asked.

'Afraid so,' he said. 'I've got no experience at all running my own practice. Used to work for a big clinic in the Hunter Valley. They took care of everything, but I wanted to go out on my own. Merriang was all I could afford, but it's a start. There's plenty of work.'

'Well, you can't go on like you are,' she said boldly. 'The place is a total shemozzle.'

He spread his arms wide. 'Guilty as charged, your Honour.'

Clare sipped her wine. 'Why did you ask me if I thought Jack might not be autistic?'

'He doesn't fit the profile,' said Dan. 'He makes good eye contact, he listens, he can focus on a task. He can certainly form attachments, at least with animals. Look at him and Samson.'

'He head bangs,' said Clare. 'He bites, he rages, he can't make friends, he won't talk.'

'Ah,' said Dan, brandishing his beer. '*Won't* is the operative word here, not *can't*, wouldn't you say?' He looked very handsome when his eyes lit up like that. Full of life, pulsing with energy. She wanted to kiss him. 'Have you heard of selective mutism?' Clare shook her head. 'It's an anxiety disorder, different to autism. Kids *can* talk, but for some reason they don't.'

'Wouldn't the paediatricians and psychologists have picked that up?' said Clare.

'Apparently not. They say Jack has no language, right?' She nodded. 'But we know that's not true. You, me, Mick - we've all heard him talk. What does his mother say?'

'Taylor used to say he could speak, but it seems like nobody believed her. They put her on a higher welfare payment because of Jack's disability, so I think she gave up trying to convince people.'

'Maybe. The problem can worsen until the child never speaks to anyone at all, even to close family members. Whatever the case, Jack's been misdiagnosed, pure and simple.'

It all made perfect sense. 'What causes selective mutism?' asked Clare. 'And how come you know so much about it?'

'Lots of things can cause it,' said Dan. 'But from what you've told me of Jack, trauma's the most likely culprit. You say he's been in care before?'

'More than once,' said Clare, 'and he's only four years old.'

'That could do it. Repeated separation trauma. A teenage mother with addiction problems, and he's probably suffered at the hands of her boyfriends as well. You said there'd been domestic violence?' She nodded. 'It's a wonder he can speak at all.'

All the pieces seemed to fit. How could so many professionals have missed it? 'And the other part of my question. How come you know about selective mutism?'

'A crash course in child psychology as part of my EFL diploma.'

'You've no idea how good it feels to hear all this.' The riesling and the relief and the proximity to Dan all combined in a thoroughly delicious way. Clare relaxed into the evening. Conversation flowed as easily as the wine. She told stories about Jack and Samson in Brisbane that made him laugh. They swapped jokes. Dan opened about his life. Never married. No kids. Divorced parents. A sister somewhere. His hand rested near hers on the table, close enough that she could almost feel it.

He reached across and covered her fingers with his own. An aching tug of desire ambushed her. Suddenly she couldn't breathe, couldn't think. 'Clare, I was wondering ...'

She wanted him to take her to bed, then and there. She wanted him beside her, wanted his unfamiliar flesh to erase all trace of Adam. His eyes locked onto hers, and he gently stroked her wrist with his thumb. The sensation was electric. 'If Mick doesn't mind ...'

'Yes?' she urged. 'Go on.'

'Could you help out for a few hours in the clinic tomorrow?'

Clare slumped a little, and offered him a weak smile.

'Oh,' she found herself saying. 'Okay.' She felt heat climbing her cheeks, and the night spiralled around her. How drunk was she exactly? And how had she read him so wrong?

Dan's phone rang. 'It's Mick. Jack's acting up. I suppose we'd better go.'

Clare nodded, hoping her disappointment didn't show. There was nothing in Dan's voice to match the path his thumb had made across her wrist.

CHAPTER 14

Sun streamed through the window. Clare looked at the time and groaned. She must have forgotten to set her alarm. She dragged herself from bed and into the shower. Why had she ever agreed to help Dan out today? Why had she drunk so much, might be a better question? Last night Dan had seemed irresistible. The *beer goggles* effect no doubt. Still, she'd promised, and it was just this once.

In the kitchen Grandad presented her with an omelette. 'Sorry,' she said. 'Don't have time,' Clare drained her mug of tea and downed a couple of headache tablets.

'Good luck, love,' said Grandad.

She waved goodbye to Jack, who was dipping toast soldiers into his soft-boiled egg.

Clare walked down to the clinic while lazy kookaburras chortled a belated dawn chorus. A car was parked out front. She opened the door and cautiously edged inside, on the look-out for snakes and biting dogs.

Dan emerged from the consulting room in faded blue scrubs. Maybe they were a size too small, maybe they'd shrunk, but for whatever reason they were too tight a fit. They emphasised his narrow hips and broad shoulders. They emphasised the bulge at his crotch.

A young woman in a revealing halter-neck top was standing at the counter, holding a shivering teacup chihuahua. 'What can I do for you, Dallas?' asked Dan.

'Tiny has a rash.' The little dog dived in between the woman's ample breasts and peeked out nervously. 'Would you take a look?' She made no effort to extract her pet. 'Don't be scared. He won't bite.'

What an outrageous flirt! Dan was looking everywhere except at Tiny.

Clare stepped forward. 'Here, let me help,' She removed the chihuahua and presented it to Dan, answering his grin with one of her own.

'Who are you?' asked Dallas, clearly peeved.

'This is Clare,' said Dan. 'She's helping out in the surgery.'

Dallas looked Clare up and down. Dan mouthed a silent *thank you* behind her back and examined the dog. 'Flea dermatitis,' he said, parting the little dog's fur. 'I can give you a spot on treatment for that.'

The door opened and a man entered with a pair of kelpies.

'Never mind.' Dallas snatched Tiny from Dan's arms. 'I'll buy it at the produce store. *They* won't charge through the nose.' She swept out as a fat woman came in with a little pink pig and set it down on the floor. It proceeded to run around the room squealing, pursued by the barking kelpies. The piglet sought refuge under a cupboard.

Dan looked perplexed. 'Is it sick, Martha?'

'Not at all, Doc. It's in lieu of payment.' she said. 'What with milk prices down, we're a bit short this month. Thought a nice piglet might do the trick instead. He'll grow into a fine, fat porker for you.'

Clare helped the man haul off the kelpies, while Dan retrieved the piglet. 'Thanks Martha, but...'

'No worries, Dan,' said Martha. It was hard to hear over the screaming pig and barking dogs.

Another man came in with two bleating lambs. Dan gave Clare a helpless look.

She took a deep breath and pushed her way through the throng to stand behind the counter. She'd seen Debbie take control of an unruly waiting room back at the legal aid centre plenty of times. How hard could it be?

'Everyone with animals requiring treatment, please take a seat.' Dan gave her an encouraging smile and tried to hand the piglet back to Martha, who dodged and frowned.

'From now on,' Clare added, 'this clinic will be conducted on a cash or account basis only.'

Everybody started talking at once. 'Is this true, Dan?'...'Who is this woman?'...'But you took six geese from Bob Barker just last week.'

'Quiet!' called Dan. 'She's absolutely right. As of today, terms of trade are strictly cash or account.'

'And who is she? 'asked Martha, pointing an accusing finger.

'Clare is my new assistant,' announced Dan, with only the slightest waver in his voice. 'And what she says, goes.' Martha glared, but this time she accepted the piglet back when Dan offered it to her.

People looked a little stunned and began filing out. In the end, only the man with the kelpies remained. Dan heaved a great sigh and positioned a chair behind the counter for Clare. 'You're a godsend,' he whispered, before escorting his client into the consulting room.

A steady trickle of patients arrived throughout the morning. A tabby cat needing stitches. A diabetic pug. An angora goat with impacted baby teeth. This was more fun than she'd expected.

When the last client said goodbye, Clare was almost sorry her shift was over.

Dan washed up and made two mugs of coffee. 'You were magnificent, you do know that?'

'Was I?'

'This last month I've been paid in everything from duck eggs to tractor tyres.' He shook his head. 'See that painting?' A framed portrait of a heeler hung above the counter. 'That's Red, painted in settlement of an account for an alpaca caesarean.'

A familiar snarl sat on the lips of the dog in the painting.

'It's a good likeness.' Clare sipped her coffee. 'Why did you do it?' she asked. 'Accept payment in kind, I mean?'

Dan laughed and shrugged. 'Guess I'm a soft touch. Felt sorry for one old codger and word spread like wildfire.'

'Well, enough's enough,' she said. 'From now on it's cold, hard cash ... and don't give anybody an account who's not good for it.'

'Right,' he said with a boyish smile. Clare looked at him sideways. Charming, but not very convincing. Dan was too kind for his own good. She had to admit though, it was refreshing after the dog eat dog world of Brisbane petty crime. Maybe she'd work at the surgery for a few more days — help him to stick to his guns.

CHAPTER 15

Dan topped up the teapot while Mick plonked a dish of pancakes down in the middle of the kitchen table. 'Eat up.' Dan put a pancake on his plate, and another one on Jack's. Where was Clare? He'd hoped they could walk down to the clinic together.

It was a week since Clare had started doing mornings at the surgery. Two hours, that's all it was, roughly from nine until eleven, but already she'd brought a degree of order to what was formerly chaos.

So far Jack hadn't been a problem. There was nothing the little boy enjoyed more than spending time with the horses, so Mick took him along on his morning paddock rounds. When Mick was done, or Jack had had enough, the pair would come by the clinic. Mick would always take Jack into the room serving as the hospital ward. Here lived the inpatients, and animals recovering from surgery. You never quite knew what you'd find. Cats and dogs were commonplace, but there were more unusual patients as well. Cleo the scrub python was still there. Being cold-blooded, reptiles were slow to heal, and it would be at least another week before her stitches came out. There was a barn owl with a broken wing, a flying fox with barbed-wire fence injuries and a koala with chlamydia, all waiting for pick up by local wildlife carers. When Jack had finished looking around, Clare would finish up and head back to the house with Jack and Mick.

It had been a wonderful, if frustrating, week. Dan was falling hard for Clare. It seemed he couldn't properly think about anything else. She moved about the clinic, blonde hair neatly pinned up, exposing the long sweep of her graceful neck, the ridge of her clavicle, the curve of her throat. They'd be discussing the best time for Mrs Madden to bring in her sick peacock, when he was really imagining the taste of her polished skin. He sometimes stole little brushes against her. Once he got so distracted by the soft swell of breasts peeking from her open-necked shirt, that he forgot about the syringe he was holding and stabbed himself in the hand. At least he'd be immune to cat flu now.

There'd been no repeat of that night at the pub, when Clare's smile had been so full of promise. The memory of her hand in his wouldn't let him go, yet no similar opportunity had since presented itself. The following night Mick had some kind of turn. He insisted he was fine, and went about his daily chores the next morning, but Clare didn't want him to worry about babysitting Jack at night any more.

'What sort of a turn?' he asked her.

Clare furrowed her perfect brow for a second. 'He got up from the table and sort of lost his balance. Said he was seeing double. It was a minute or so before he was right, and then he complained of being tired. It's not like Grandad to get tired, is it? And I imagine it's even more unusual for him to complain about it.'

'That's true enough,' Dan said. 'Mick's no whinger.'

Since then, Clare had insisted her grandfather have early nights. The old man had argued no end about it, but Dan could see that deep down he was pleased that she cared. Now Clare was no longer free to go out in the evening. He could go to her for dinner, of course, cadge an invitation. But when he'd leased the site for the clinic, Mick had included breakfast in the deal. Dan had been up at the house for his morning meal almost every day for six months now. It might be a bit of a stretch turning up for dinner as well.

Then there were his living arrangements. Dan lodged with

Bonnie Black, a young widow in town. Her interfering mother, Blanche, stayed over so often that she might as well have lived there too. Dan had moved in to discover that Blanche had appropriated the spacious spare room, and that he'd been relegated to the verandah.

It was fully enclosed with insect screens, but mosquitoes still managed to get in. Dan had patched up any obvious holes. He'd tried everything: repellent, insect spray, mosquito coils left to burn all night. Nothing worked. If anything his efforts seemed to attract them, and he was forced to sleep with a sheet pulled over his head, listening to the frustrated drone of the little bloodsuckers, inches from his ear. Occasionally they dive-bombed him, inserting their proboscis right through the thin linen, and he would be covered with itchy red welts by morning. On top of that, there were the cane toads. God knows how they got in, but each morning he'd find at least a couple of the ugly creatures somewhere.

Once he'd woken up to one beside him on his pillow, like something from the Princess and the Frog fairy tale. But even if he was looking for a prince, he wouldn't be kissing this frog. The skin of *Bufo marinus* oozed a poison that irritated skin and burned the eyes. Dan hadn't heard of deaths in humans, but their venom was potent enough to kill dogs and cats, along with any unfortunate wildlife that consumed it. Quolls, goannas, dingoes – he'd seen them all succumb to this toxic invader. What would Clare think of waking up next to a cane toad? Even if she was free, and a romantic pub dinner led to something more, he couldn't bring her home.

Clare came into the kitchen and sat down beside him. She reached for the golden syrup with a slim, lightly-tanned arm. Her singlet top exposed the delicious curve of neck and shoulder, the sheen of her skin, damp from the kitchen's clammy heat. He imagined how her breasts might look, minus their flimsy wrapper.

'If you don't like my pancakes, just say so,' said Mick. The old man's words brought Dan back to earth with a crunch, and he heaped up his plate. 'Don't do me any favours,' snorted Mick. He drained his tea and thumped the mug in the sink. 'Come on, Jack,' he said. 'We've got horses to feed.' The little boy scrambled from his chair and raced out the door after him.

'What's got into Mick?' asked Dan. He had an uneasy suspicion that the old man somehow knew of his daydreams.

'He hasn't been sleeping —' began Clare.

Dan's phone rang. A new client, Willow Moore, was apparently waiting for him down at the clinic. 'Minnie's in labour,' said an urgent voice, 'and I think a pup's stuck. She's been trying for hours, but nothing's happening.'

'Be right there,' said Dan.

Clare pushed back her chair. 'I'll go change.'

Dan sprinted down the hill. A tattooed young man dressed like a Goth waited beside an ancient mini minor. A tearful teenage girl, dressed all in black and carrying a shoebox, rushed to the clinic door as he approached. Dan fumbled in his haste to turn the key. As soon as he stepped inside he could tell something was wrong. A few pamphlets lay on the floor. A tin of cat food had rolled beneath a shelf and the broom had fallen over. The door to the hospital ward stood wide open. Damn, he must have forgotten to check it last night. He hurried in to see what creature might have escaped.

Cleo. The scrub python's cage was empty, and the box that had contained Ginger, a geriatric guinea pig, was on its side. He'd been in overnight with pneumonia. The prognosis had been poor, even with saline, antibiotics and a steroid injection. Dan searched in vain through the spilled straw. No rodent.

Dan returned to the waiting room, keeping one eye peeled for the wayward snake. Willow stood clutching the shoe box, her facial piercings glistening with tears. 'Where's the patient?' he asked. A tortured squeal came from the box. Willow offered it to him with trembling hands. Inside was a distressed piebald rat. Dan heaved a great sigh. It was going to be one of those days.

Dan gently took the rat from Willow. It was a warm morning but Minnie felt cold, a sure sign of shock. Her breathing was rapid and shallow, and her ears and mucous membranes were pale. Blood oozed from beneath her tail, and every now and then she squealed in pain.

He fetched a heating pad and laid the little creature on the examination table.

'Blade said you'll just do a caesarean and then she'll be fine,' said Willow, her expression hopeful.

'Did he just?' Dan looked up to see the Goth boy in the doorway. Curse Blade for raising such unrealistic expectations. Rat caesareans were notoriously difficult, and he didn't have the right small-scale implements. On top of that, it wasn't feasible to deliver the young and then repair the uterus. A full hysterectomy would be necessary, meaning Minnie wouldn't be able to produce milk even if the babies could be saved. Without a foster mother, her pinkies would not survive.

'I'd like to try something first —' began Dan, then froze. Cleo was gliding along the floor behind the unsuspecting Willow, a telltale guinea-pig-sized bulge in her body. She slid behind the bags of dog food in the corner. He took a deep breath. On the bright side, at least he knew where she was. 'Oxytocin injections can stimulate a tired uterus to contract,' he said, trying hard to concentrate. 'First I'll x-ray Minnie to check there's no extra-large pup stuck in the birth canal, otherwise strong labour could rupture her uterus.' Willow crossed her legs and turned white. 'Perhaps you should wait outside,' said Dan. The girl nodded and left. Dan quickly x-rayed the rat, keeping one eye on the corner. Good. They were normal-sized pinkies, well positioned, and only five of them. Now to take a guess at dosage.

Clare came in looking cool and collected. Dan saw a flash of flickering tongue and pale scales as the snake slid across the room and disappeared behind the filing cabinet. He tried to remain calm. Should he tell Clare? No, he just couldn't do it. He'd scare her again for starters, and look like a complete incompetent to boot.

Clare pointed to Minnie. 'What's that?'

'Pet rat in labour.'

Clare made a face. 'Don't take too long. You've got a Mr Baker with his bassets at nine for vaccinations.'

Dan groaned. Brian Baker always insisted on having Dan express his dogs' anal glands, whether it was needed or not. 'Better out than in,' he'd say in a satisfied voice, then head for his car, offering no help at all. With most dogs it was a simple enough exercise, but not with Brian's bassets. They howled and leaped and growled, making the procedure downright dangerous for everyone involved. On top of that, Brian's bassets were simply the smelliest dogs in the world. The place always stank to high heaven after their visits. Clare couldn't be there for that. She'd never be able to think of him in a romantic way again. He'd have to find a way to get rid her.

Dan injected Minnie with the oxytocin, feeling a twinge of sympathy for the tiny rodent and hoping her exhausted frame could withstand the strain of renewed contractions. He placed her and the heating pad in a box, took it to the hospital ward and then went to talk to Clare. He'd taken a few steps when he returned and fastened a lid on the box, just in case Cleo had designs on Minnie for breakfast.

Clare was behind the counter entering treatment notes into the computer. 'You should set some time aside to catch up on these,' she said in a chastising tone. 'There's quite a backlog.'

'Never mind that,' he said. 'I was thinking, since it's such a lovely day ... Why not take Jack for a drive in the Bunya Mountains?' I can manage here.'

She shot him a puzzled look. 'It's such a busy morning. Are you sure?'

'Absolutely. Go enjoy yourself.'

Clare went through the appointment list. 'You've got the Baker bassets, some crazy man who thinks his wife is poisoning their siamese cat, a boxer with toothache, a newfoundland with indigestion, a kitten with a rash, a litter of puppies for vaccinations, a lame goose, and there are bound to be walk-ins.'

He looked out the window. Oh no — Brian Baker was pulling up with his dog trailer. Dan dashed for the door and waylaid him as he was unloading his hounds.

'Sorry, I'm flat out right now,' said Dan. 'Tricky labour. An emergency caesarean might be all that can save the pups. Can we do this tomorrow?'

'Course we can, Doc,' said Brian, juggling a tangle of excited basset hounds. 'Course we can.' He chuckled. 'Don't suppose you vets know what will land on your doorstep next, eh?'

'Got it in one, mate.' This was going to be simpler than he thought.

A voice from behind startled him. It was Willow. 'How's Minnie?'

'She's had an injection to restart her labour,' he said, hoping the girl wouldn't somehow put her foot in it. 'Come and we'll check on her now.' Willow nodded, her expression taut with nerves, and started to follow him back to the clinic.

'Don't worry, love,' Brian called out after her. 'The Doc here will save them pups, and their mum too.'

Willow gave him a grateful smile. 'I hope so. Minnie's my favourite rat.'

CHAPTER 16

Clare went back to entering patient notes on the computer, trying to ignore the tattooed teenage boy sneering at her from across the room. Where was Dan? And why would he want her to leave on such a busy morning? He was acting very strangely, even for Dan.

She hadn't been so confused about a man for a long time, maybe never. Clare thought back to her early days with Adam. His dazzling advocacy had been the talk of Brisbane's legal set, and she'd been more than a little star-struck when the hot-shot young barrister had asked her out. Feeling flattered wasn't a good way to start off though. It had set the pattern for their whole relationship. Her trying to impress, feeling not-quite-good-enough. Him acting superior.

Dan was very different. Adam always looked for an angle and Dan took people as he found them. Adam earned top dollar and Dan was paid in piglets. Adam had a killer streak and Dan saved the lives of snakes and pregnant rats. He was rough and ready, true, but she had to admit he did exude a sort of raw, unconscious sexuality. Clare suddenly imagined him pulling her in close, in tight, and kissing her with hard, searching lips.

A soft, scraping sound in the corner interrupted her daydream.

She peered under the shelves. Was that something moving?

Dan and the pierced girl came back in and headed straight for the ward. A man with a bevy of basset hounds burst in after them. That must be Brian Baker, their first appointment for the day. Clare couldn't stop staring. She'd heard of people growing to look like their animals, but in this case the resemblance was astonishing. Brian had his dogs' same sagging cheeks and long face. His nose was large and shiny and his lids drooped over red, rheumy eyes. His expression, however, wasn't hangdog like his bassets. It was angry.

'I won't be fobbed off, Doc,' said Brian. 'Not for a bleeding rat.' Pierced girl burst into tears and Brian looked abashed. 'Sorry love, but they're vermin. What do you want to go around saving vermin for? It's bloody crazy. I just spent a fortune at my place exterminating the little buggers.' Brian noticed Clare, seeming surprised to see her. He looked to the crying girl and then back to Clare, took off his hat and wrung it between his hands. 'No offence meant, mind.'

The girl cried harder, and his face softened. 'It really is your pet then is it, this rat?'

'I love her.' The words were little more than a sob, but they lent the girl a delicate vulnerability. Beneath the piercings, she suddenly looked about twelve

'You do, do you?' asked Brian in astonishment. 'You love this rat?'

Willow nodded, choking back tears. 'Minnie's my heart rat.'

'Well, I'll be.' He plucked a box of tissues from the counter and offered it to her. 'Can't believe I'm saying this,' said Brian, shaking his head, 'but I sure do hope the Doc can help you out, love.'

'Clare?' Dan's voice came from the ward. 'Can I have you, please?'

She found Dan hovering over a shoebox, looking pleased. Clare peeked inside. Two tiny pink babies were squirming and squeaking on the paper towel. Minnie was holding another in disturbingly human-like hands, nibbling at it with little pointy teeth. 'She's not eating it?' asked Clare, horrified.

Dan put a reassuring hand on her shoulder. His touch made her momentarily forget all about the rat. 'She's cleaning it,' said Dan, 'and eating the afterbirth. Rats are devoted mothers.'

A scream and a barking chorus erupted from the waiting room. Willow rocketed in. She'd gone very pale. 'There's a snake!'

Clare glanced at Cleo's cage. Empty.

Dan shoved the shoebox at the panicky girl. 'Here Willow, take Minnie. She needs a midwife.'

Willow became suddenly brave, oohing and aahing over the babies. 'I won't let that big old snake get you.'

Dan grabbed a long pole with a deep hook and emptied out a rubbish bin, then went back into the waiting room. Clare tentatively followed him. Cleo was apparently holed up beneath a cupboard, to go by the basset pack milling around in full cry. The noise was deafening.

'Get them out of here,' yelled Dan. Brian didn't seem to hear him. 'Get them out,' he shouted, louder this time, and pointed to the door. Tattooed Blade helped Brian drag the dogs outside.

Dan expertly hauled the python out. There was a suspicious bulge in her sleek lines. Dan manoeuvred the hook roughly to the middle of her body, lifted her in one smooth motion and deposited her in the bin. Soon Cleo was safely back in her cage.

'Cool,' said Blade, now hovering in the inner doorway. 'I like snakes. What's that bump in it?'

'Ginger, the guinea pig,' said Dan in a strained voice. 'Previously my patient.' He rubbed his forehead. 'Now his six-year-old owner will be traumatised and her mother will probably sue.'

Clare's jaw dropped. She'd seen the weeping, golden-haired girl when Ginger had arrived yesterday morning. *'I don't care what it costs, just fix the bloody thing,'* her mother had said, showing a distinct lack of affection for her daughter's pet, but a healthy respect for her daughter's temper. *'Melody will have a fit if it dies.'*

Dan checked in on Minnie, who was birthing her fourth baby. Blade's sneer had vanished. Instead he wore a broad grin, like a proud father. Even Clare felt a warm glow as Minnie groomed her newborn pups.

'My sister's got guinea pigs,' said Blade. 'What colour was this Ginger? Sort of reddish-brown?' Dan nodded. 'Short haired?' Dan nodded again. A look of comprehension dawned on his face. 'Boy or girl?' asked Blade.

'Boy,' said Dan. 'A large, reddish-brown male guinea pig.'

Blade gave him a sly smile.

'You can't,' said Clare. 'It's completely unprofessional. Completely unethical.'

'I'll be back.' Blade dashed off.

'Please don't look at me like that,' said Dan, before escaping outside. She looked through the window. He was crossing the car park to where Brian was tying his bassets to the side of his trailer. The two men began an animated conversation. What were they saying? They'd been speaking for a minute or two, when Brian burst out laughing - a loud, raucous sound that made Clare jump. For some reason he was pointing to the surgery, bent over with mirth. She ducked out of sight and went to see how the rat count was going.

'Five,' said Willow, her voice bursting with delight. 'I think she's finished.'

Clare had changed her opinion of little Minnie. At first she'd wrinkled up her nose and agreed with Brian. Why would anybody want a rat as a pet? But now she had a sneaking admiration for the new mother. Minnie had arrived near death, exhausted, her frail body wracked with pain. She'd endured the cramping agony of forced labour, without the benefit of pain relief. Clare's cousin had gone through an oxytocin-induced labour with her second child. She said the artificial contractions were infinitely stronger, more frequent and more painful than natural ones.

Yet Minnie had valiantly rallied from her ordeal, and was crouching over her babies to encourage suckling, despite her own weariness. The mother's devotion was inspiring. It gave Clare a whole new appreciation and sympathy for rodents.

Dan had come back inside and was talking to a beaming Willow. 'You have quite a rat there.'

He looked very handsome – the sun catching copper tones in his hair, and a warm smile on his face. Clare's heart missed a beat. Life at Currawong Creek was becoming more interesting by the minute.

CHAPTER 17

Marlene Price produced her credit card to pay the bill, while Melody stroked Ginger -mark two. 'Ginger must like the food here,' the girl said to Clare, hugging the guinea pig close to her cheek. 'He's grown so big and fat.'

Dan held his breath. Would Clare give the game away? She looked uncomfortable, but said nothing.

'Look, Mummy,' said Melody. 'Ginger's all better now.'

Marlene shrank away from the creature with a look of distaste on her perfectly-made-up face. 'Thank goodness for that.' She favoured Dan with a smile. 'I would never have forgiven you, Dan. Not if you'd let my daughter down.'

Dan avoided Clare's eyes. He mumbled something about *just being here to help* and escaped outside with his veterinary bag to where Brian was waiting.

'Thanks for levelling with me, Doc. The rascals do pong a bit when you squeeze their glands.' He presented the first dog for vaccination. 'Wouldn't want to offend the little lady, eh? Might scare her off. You reckon that catching hook of yours would work on women as well as pythons?' Brian was greatly amused by his own joke.

'All done,' said Dan, giving the dog a friendly slap on the rump. 'Next.' Two more cars pulled into the gravel road. 'Won't be long,' called Dan, keeping his tone cheerful.

Clare arrived, looking confused. 'Why aren't you treating the dogs inside?' she asked.

'Easier and quicker out here, love,' said Brian. Dan shot him a grateful glance.

'It's so busy this morning,' said Clare, gesturing to the new arrivals. 'Are you sure you don't need me to stay?'

'Of course he needs you, love,' said Brian 'Tell her, Dan.'

'On second thoughts,' he said, 'I could use a hand.'

Clare smiled, and hurried back to the clinic. Brian winked. 'That one likes you,' he said. 'She's got that lovelorn look in her eye.'

Really? Clare *had* looked pleased when he asked her to stay. He watched her go, her loose hair swaying in time with her hips.

'Put your eyes back in your head, Doc,' said Brian, as he pulled another dog over to be treated. The basset hound jumped up and licked Dan's face with her broad ribbon of a tongue. 'Violet here'll get jealous.'

It was after twelve o'clock before they were done with morning surgery. Mick had dropped by with Jack and seemed in no hurry to leave. Thank goodness the old man was in a better mood today. Jack was making friends with a little boy named Timmy, whose mother, Bronwyn, was getting her six-week-old kelpie pups their first shots.

'I've never seen that,' Clare whispered to Dan, as the kids chased each other round the car park. 'He's normally violent with other children.'

'Well, he's doing fine at the moment.'

They watched the boys collecting gumnuts and making piles on the porch. Jack was examining a particularly large gumnut, obviously a prize. Clare gasped as he added it to Timmy's pile. 'He's sharing,' she said. 'That's impossible.'

'Currawong seems to agree with your boy.' A fancy took him as he watched her sweep a stray lock of hair from her forehead. 'My next job's at a pony stud. Worming, checking broodmares, that sort of thing. Would you and Jack like to come along?'

She gazed at him with cool green eyes. He couldn't see anything remotely lovelorn about them.

'Yes,' said Clare. 'We'll come.' Dan tried to hide his excitement. 'I used to have a pony here at Currawong when I was a kid.' She interrupted Mick's conversation with Bronwyn. 'Smudge. Remember Smudge, grandad?'

'Top little mare,' said Mick. 'Only lost her last year.'

'Really?' said Clare, looking stricken. 'I should have been here … should have said goodbye.'

'No matter,' said Mick. He looked suddenly weary. 'What's done is done.'

'You must bring Jack round some time to play,' said Bronwyn.

'I'd love to,' said Clare. 'Jack doesn't have any friends.'

Bronwyn nodded. 'It's hard when you live in the country. There aren't always kids the same age nearby. It's so great you and Jack have come to stay.'

Dan waited for Clare to protest that indeed she wasn't staying, that in a week or two she'd be back in Brisbane. But instead Clare just looked at Dan and smiled. He loved that smile, the way her cheeks grew round, and dimpled just a fraction. 'Jack likes it here,' she said finally, 'and so do I.'

'Is the Brady stud your last job?' asked Mick. Dan nodded. 'Why not take Clare and Jack for a picnic in the mountains afterwards? You'll be half-way there. I'll make sandwiches, and throw in a packet of bikkies and a bottle of Buderim ginger beer.' He slapped Dan affectionately on the back. The weariness seemed to have passed.

'How about it, Clare?' Dan searched her face and she flashed him that gorgeous smile in answer.

'Let's go pack a feast then, eh?' said Mick. He leaned a little on Clare as the three of them headed up to the house.

Dan watched them go, Clare's slim figure framed by the tall old man and the little boy. He felt the hairs stand up on the back of his neck. Dan didn't know how or why, but he knew with sudden certainty that these three people would utterly change his life.

CHAPTER 18

'The Bunya Mountains are a national park,' said Dan. 'No dogs allowed.'

Clare held her breath. Jack usually panicked at being separated from Samson. This time he just hugged the dog goodbye and climbed in the car.

'He finally trusts that Samson will be here when he gets back,' said Dan.

During the journey Jack sat calmly in his seat and stared out the window. No head banging, no screaming, no hitting himself.

'Look Jacky,' said Dan. 'Kangaroos.' Sure enough a mob of forester kangaroos bounded from the roadside scrub, keeping pace with the car.

'Kang-a-roos,' said Clare, slowly and deliberately. 'Now you say it.'

'Kang-a-roos, kang-a-roos, kang-a-roos,' Jack chanted.

Clare was at once thrilled and exasperated. 'Why does he only talk when no one's watching? It's like having some magical animal that nobody else can see.'

'We're not *nobody*. Neither's Mick,' said Dan. 'We'll vouch for the kid.'

'But you're not in Brisbane, are you?' said Clare. 'You're not in Kim Maguire's office. She's impossible. It would take a miracle for me to convince that woman that Jack can talk.'

'He still has a way to go,' Dan pointed out. 'I've only heard single words so far.'

'Jack can string a sentence together when he wants to. The first thing he said to me was *Daddy's dead*.'

Dan shot her a concerned look. 'Is he?'

'I've no idea.'

They turned into an impressive gateway and drove beneath a wrought-iron arch featuring a pair of prancing ponies. Dan got out to open the gate. It bore a sign identical to the one at Currawong. The yellow triangle proclaiming *Warning Notice* in bold red letters. The one withdrawing common law rights to enter the place. She'd seen the same notice on just about every paddock gate along the way.

'Those signs are useless,' said Clare. 'Freehold titles in Australia provide that all minerals are reserved for the Crown.'

'I'm no lawyer,' said Dan. 'So I won't argue with you. But we have advice that there's a loophole in the law. The Government must prove there are minerals on your land, and they can't do that unless you let them in to do the preliminary exploration. It's worked so far. The coppers in Dalby told me they can come through an open gate regardless of the sign, but can't open one. That's why we always keep our gates closed. They can't even deliver a summons past our signs unless a felony has been committed under the Crimes Act and a warrant issued.'

'What helpful police you have around here,' said Clare, as they drove between neat post-and-rail paddocks.

'That's because they're all on our side.' Dan pulled up in front of a low-slung shed, divided into loose boxes. A pony popped his head over a stable door and Clare did a double-take. It looked just like her Smudge. Jack began banging his head, eager to escape the car. 'Come on, you two,' said Dan. 'There's work to do.'

They were greeted by a cheerful middle-aged woman with kind

eyes and a neat grey bun. 'I'm Anne Brady.' The woman shook Clare's hand. 'And you must be Mick Macleod's granddaughter.'

'This pony,' said Clare, going over to its stall. 'It looks just like one at Currawong when I was little.'

'That's Smudge's grandson, Sparky,' said Anne. 'He's been on lease to a lady out Kingaroy way, but apparently her girl's lost interest.'

Clare stroked Sparky's grey velvet nose. Jack ran over and the pony nibbled his hair. The little boy burst into a fit of joyful giggles. His laugh was infectious and soon everybody was smiling. Clare looked around. More ponies were scattered across the green paddocks: mainly greys, but with a sprinkling of blacks and chestnuts.

'See you've got yourself one of our signs,' said Dan.

'My word,' said Anne. 'Those Pyramid blokes were over at Bert Jordan's place last week, having a friendly chit-chat.'

'Bert let them in?' asked Dan.

'Poor old bugger didn't know any better. Invited them for a cup of tea even. Very charming people, apparently. Looked like farmers. Wore farmers' hats and farmers' shirts.'

'I'll give him a ring,' said Dan, 'Ask him to one of our meetings.' He headed off with his vet bag towards the yards.

'Neville will help you,' Anne called out after him. 'I'll stay and talk with Clare.'

Clare picked some grass and let Jack feed it to the pony. 'What breed is he?' asked Clare.

'Sparky's an Australian pony, same as all the others here.'

'I didn't know Australia had its own breed of pony,' said Clare.

'The studbook was founded way back in 1931,' Anne said. 'All sorts went into the mix: Timor ponies, small Arabians, Welsh mountains – even the odd brumby or two I suspect. We've ended up with a quality, homegrown pony with a sweet character all of its own … and perfect for children, I might add.'

Clare admired Sparky's classic head, his alert ears and large dark eyes. 'He sure is beautiful.'

While Dan wormed the yearlings and checked their teeth, Anne looked out a box of toys for Jack. 'I had these for my grandchildren when they visited from Sydney. It doesn't happen much,' she said with a wistful smile. 'They'll have grown out of them by now anyway.'

Clare sat down with Anne at an outdoor table, while Jack investigated the box. 'Tepig!' he cried, seizing a figurine. Unbelievable. The child only talked in front of people who expected him to. Clare recognised the toy at once: the piggy body, the tall black ears, the yellow nose. But this was no cheap plastic Happy Meal toy. This was sturdy and as big as a grapefruit, its tail painted permanently purple. The joy on Jack's face was a delight to see. He soon ferreted out a variety of other Pokémon toys.

'Take the box home with you,' said Anne.

'I couldn't —' began Clare.

'Please,' she said. 'I can't think of a better place for it.'

Clare looked into Anne's generous, smiling eyes, thinking about how long she'd spent climbing the career ladder, where everything came with strings attached, where there was always a *quid pro quo*. But here was Anne simply giving, with no expectation of anything in return. It didn't matter that it was just a carton of secondhand toys; Clare couldn't have been more moved. Out of the blue, tears came. 'Thank you,' she said. 'You're very kind.'

Anne squeezed Clare's hand, then knelt down on the ground to play with Jack. 'Pokémon,' she said, making a procession through the grass with the toys.

Jack snatched one of them up, ran to Clare and plonked it down on her knee. 'Pokémon,' he said, eyes alight. He climbed up and gave her a bear hug, while she kissed his hair. Could this really be the same child she'd first met in Brisbane? Maybe she wasn't so bad at this mothering caper after all.

'He's adorable,' said Anne. 'Mick never said he had a grandchild.'

Clare was about to say *Jack's not mine,* but a perverse desire kept her silent. A sudden, fierce, hopeless desire for Jack to actually *be* hers. To properly belong. To permanently belong. Dan's arrival rescued her from having to respond.

'All done,' he said, putting his bag in the ute. 'The palomino needs his wolf teeth out before you put a bridle near him, though.'

Jack climbed into the car and Clare placed the carton of toys beside him.

'Score,' said Dan when he saw Jack's loot. He and the little boy high-fived each other.

'When did he learn to do that?' asked Clare in wonder. Jack was certainly full of surprises.

THE BUNYA MOUNTAINS were an island of distinctive, basalt peaks, the remains of ancient volcanoes, cut off from the rest of the Great Dividing Range. They rose abruptly from the surrounding plains, as if dropped intact from some far wilder place. It was a sacred feeling to leave the open farmlands and enter the forest - like stepping into the stillness of a cathedral from a busy street. Narrow winding roads offered mountain panoramas and breathtaking views across the southern plains. Hoop pines and myrtle dominated the lower slopes, but the vegetation changed as they climbed. Soon dome-shaped bunya pines raised their majestic heads above the sub-tropical rainforest canopy. Sunbursts of golden king orchids graced their trunks. It was overwhelming, Clare discovered, to find herself back in this primeval forest; back in the place she'd so loved as a child.

'Bunya pines are living fossils,' said Dan. 'They're found in geological records dating way before the Jurassic.' He glanced at Jack. 'Dinosaurs, Jacky, you like dinosaurs?' The boy grabbed a toy brontosaurus from the box and marched it up and down his car seat. 'Well, dinosaurs just like your Bronte were snacking on these kind of trees two hundred million years ago.' Dan grinned at Clare. 'It's hard to get your head around, isn't it?'

'I had no idea these pines were so old,' said Clare. Until now they'd been simply a symbol of childhood happiness. Now she felt their significance reaching right through the ages, to long before humans existed, to beyond the dawn of history.

Jack began to bang his head on the car seat. 'He needs to wee,' said Clare.

Dan found a safe place to pull over. 'September's not bunya nut season, but I still wouldn't hang around. Their cones are dinosaur-size too, bigger than footballs, and you're a goner if you cop one on the head.'

Clare already knew that. These mountains had been her grandparents' favourite picnic spot. They'd always told her and Ryan that it was a magical place. Back then, Clare had believed them.

She took Jack from the car and looked around. They were deep inside the cool forest here, hidden from sunlight. She gazed up at the ancient trunks, towering one-hundred-and-fifty-feet tall. They remained the dark, mysterious trees of childhood fantasy. This was an Enid Blyton enchanted wood, full of portals and blurred boundaries. A tawny wallaby peered at her from among the ferns, as Jack peed against a rock. Its bright eyes regarded her with primal wisdom. She half-expected it to speak in this charmed place. Something was calling to her, as clear as a clarion bell. Call it intuition, call it magic – call it love. She didn't know what it was, but its impossible message was plain. *Stay* it said. *Stay at Currawong. Stay in the foothills of these magic mountains. With Grandad, with Jack ... with Dan. Let nothing tear you away.*

Jack took her hand. 'Clare,' he said. She shivered as he tugged her towards the car. It was almost as startling as if the wallaby had spoken. She laughed out loud, picked Jack up and spun him around and around in excitement. Dan leaned out the window, a curious look on his face.

'Jack said my name,' called Clare. 'He said my name.' Until that moment she hadn't realised how much she'd longed for that. It was as if Jack had finally claimed her.

She bundled the giggling, wiggling child back in, struggling to clip up the straps of his car seat. Dan leaned over the back seat to help. Sunlight flickered across his features, and Clare unexpectedly found herself kissing him, full on the lips. A kiss like she'd never known, all heat and breath and surprise. A wonder kiss. A Dan kiss.

When she pulled away there was shock and pleasure on his face. With superb comic timing, Jack clapped a hand over his mouth and widened his eyes. It was impossible not to laugh, but when Clare met Dan's gaze, behind his amusement, she saw exactly what she'd hoped to see. Hunger for more.

CHAPTER 19

'There's nothing to talk about,' said Clare, debating whether or not to hang up on Adam.

'Look, I did the wrong thing, and for that I'm sorry. But Veronica just about threw herself at me. I won't apologise for being flesh and blood.'

'I don't want you to apologise, Adam. It doesn't matter any more.'

Clare sat in the hallway alcove, gazing out the dusty window overlooking the yards. She ran her fingers across the heavy handset of the old phone. Her mother had used this same phone to make urgent, whispered calls to someone on that very last visit to Currawong - not to Clare's father. She and Ryan had tried to listen in, tiptoeing down the hallway towards her, but a squeaky floorboard had always given them away.

'When are you coming back to Brisbane?' asked Adam.

'One, it's none of your business, and two, like I said, it doesn't matter.'

'Not to you, maybe.' There was a note of real pain in Adam's voice. 'Paul Dunbar dismissed me. I'm no longer his junior.'

Clare thought she must have misheard him. 'But you're his *golden boy*.'

'Not any more.' There wasn't a trace of pretense in his voice.

She let her fingers slide over the carpet, felt the news in her gut, even after what he'd done. 'Why? What happened?'

'What do you think happened?' He let the question hang. 'Congratulations on your own appointment, by the way. Paul Dunbar's reader – quite a coup. Seems Paul's a bit of a white knight.'

'I don't understand.' The feeling in her stomach was growing stronger.

He spelled it out. 'Paul said that, considering how I'd treated you, it wouldn't be fair expecting you to work alongside me.'

So that was it. Her public denunciation of Adam at the Bar Association lunch. Who would have thought Paul would take her side so strongly? She couldn't help feeling flattered, but she hadn't meant to cause the collapse of Adam's brilliant career. Some short-term embarrassment was all she'd hoped for. The Brisbane legal fraternity was a small world and Paul Dunbar was its shining star. Get on the wrong side of him and it could be a long climb back up the ladder.

'That's dreadful,' she said. 'I'm truly sorry. But what do you expect me to do about it?'

Adam hung silent on the end of the line for the longest time. 'Nothing,' he said, his voice softer now. 'Nothing except listen. The truth is, I still love you, Clare.'

She drew her breath in, watched the squares of sunlight on the carpet, how the old faded pattern disappeared beneath the glare. This was crazy. Adam had never once told her he loved her when they'd been together – outside of the bedroom, that was.

'Let me finish, please Clare. I know I hurt you, and that you probably don't want me back in your life.'

'Got it in one,' she said.

'I deserved that.' Adam had never sounded contrite before. 'But my life's a train wreck right now. I'm asking for your friendship, that's all. For you to keep the lines of communication open. I've hit rock bottom, Clare. I really have, and I miss you. Your warmth, our walks. I even miss you dragging me around those weekend farmer's markets. Where am I supposed to get my organic pomegranate juice now?'

She smiled, relenting a little, tracing her finger over the wallpaper roses the way she did as a child. A friendship with Adam - was it possible?

'Please,' he said. 'Have a heart.'

'Okay. You win ... friends.'

He breathed what sounded like a relieved sigh.

'What are you going to do?' she asked him.

'Go back to corporate law, for now. Even though it's boring as batshit.'

'At least it's a job.'

'If you can call it that.'

Clare didn't respond. She wasn't a fan of self-pity.

'Don't worry,' said Adam. 'I'll bounce back. I'll be downing scotch in the Barrister's Bar before you know it.'

'Of course you will,' she said. 'Look, I've got to go.'

'Goodbye, Clare ... and thanks for listening.'

CHAPTER 20

Sunday morning and something was up. All through breakfast, Dan had looked like the cat that ate the cream. Clare studied Grandad. To go by the grin on his face, he was in on it as well. Clare helped Jack to another sausage. 'Okay, you two. What gives?'

'Never you mind, Clare Bear,' said Grandad. It was the first time he'd used his old pet name for her. Clare felt like she was about ten again. 'You always were too inquisitive for your own good.'

Something about the name caught Jack's fancy. He climbed onto her lap, put his nose against hers and stared into her eyes. 'Clare Bear, Clare Bear, Clare Bear,' he chanted in a deep voice that made her laugh. When Jack went back to his seat, he looked around as if searching for something. The little boy lifted the cloth and peered beneath the table. 'Samsam stole my sausage.'

They all froze. Clare looked first at Dan, then at Grandad. Jack had spoken a complete sentence.

Dan hurried to a bag that sat on the floor in the corner and pulled out a video camera. He aimed it at the little boy. 'What did Samson do, Jacky?'

'Samsam stole my sausage.'

Clare felt the soft swish of Samson's tail. The dog had been hiding under the table all along.

Dan took another sausage and placed it on his own plate near the edge of the table. Samson's nose poked from under the cloth, and in a flash the sausage was gone. Jack pointed and giggled. Dan kept the camera trained on his face. 'What did Samson do just then?' he asked.

Jack was bobbing up and down with excitement. 'He stole *your* sausage.' Grandad did the same thing. Once again the sausage disappeared. Jack's mouth dropped open and his eyes grew large with fun. 'Samsam stole Grandad's sausage.'

Emboldened by the success of his sneak attacks, Samson emerged from underneath the cloth, put his giant paws on the table, and helped himself to the whole plate. Jack was beside himself with delight. 'Samsam stole *everybody's* sausage!'

Clare crouched down and threw her arms around the neck of the surprised dog, in one mighty hug.

Dan was studying the video camera. 'Got it.' He showed Clare the footage of Jack. There it was, captured for anybody to see, audio and all. The little boy's voice sounded clear as a bell. 'Look, Jack,' said Dan.

The child stared at the screen in wonder. He stabbed it with his finger. 'Jack,' he said, his voice small and uncertain. He searched Clare's face for reassurance. Clare released Samson from her arms. The dog jumped boldly up at the table, eyeing off the rounds of toast this time.

'Get out of it,' growled Grandad, and shoved him down. Samson slunk off, realising that for some reason his charmed breakfast-stealing life was over.

'Here's your answer,' said Dan, holding up the camera. 'The department won't be able to argue with this sort of evidence.'

That was true, it was wonderful, but a question still burned in Clare's brain. 'How did you know that would happen? I saw you before. You were pleased before Jack even spoke. And why do you just happen to have a video camera?'

Dan didn't answer her. She looked at Grandad who was showing a sudden interest in his shoes.

'It'll all be clear in a minute,' said Dan, stowing the camera in his bag and slinging it over his shoulder. 'Come on.' He took Clare's hand. 'I have a surprise.' He tousled Jack's snowy head. 'You too.' Dan led them out of the house, past the barn to the stockyards.

Clare couldn't believe her eyes - Smudge. Her old pony was dead, she knew that, but the pretty, dappled-grey imposter standing in the yard was the spitting image.

'Recognise him?' asked Dan. 'It's Sparky. I bought him for Jack.' If Clare hadn't already been keen on Dan, this extraordinary, unexpected gift might well have been the clincher. It was like being a kid again, seeing the pony there. Like having a boundless, bright future stretching before her and not a care in the world. She wanted to climb onto Sparky's back, bury her face in his neck and inhale his warm, equine scent.

'That pony's a dead ringer for Smudge,' said Grandad. 'It's almost like the old girl's come back.' He rubbed his eyes and turned away. Were those tears?

'Come on in, Jacky,' said Dan. He opened the gate with one hand and beckoned the boy inside the yard. His other hand held the camera. He was videotaping the meeting. So that's what the camera had been for.

Jack approached Sparky with care, just like he'd been taught to do. The pony bent his head and snorted softly, inspecting the little boy with his muzzle. Jack flashed Clare a brilliant smile. He stroked the pony's crest, running his tiny fingers through his thick mane. With Fleur, even on tiptoe, he could barely reach her shoulder.

'Sparky certainly is more his size,' said Clare. 'I won't mind Jack riding him.'

'Not so fast,' said Dan. 'Riding's the last thing I'll teach him, not the first. These two need to get to know each other, learn how to connect on the ground. They need to build a relationship. Riding will just be the icing on the cake.'

'You're the expert,' said Clare. 'But if Jack's not riding Sparky, maybe I will. Right now I have an urge to take him for a swim in the dam.'

Dan smiled and gave her the video recorder. Then he took a head collar, showed Jack how to fit it, and snapped on a leading rein.

'Shall we get started?'

The little boy nodded and a sunny smile lit up his face. He looked particularly angelic today. No two ways about it, Dan was a miracle worker. Or maybe it was the horses, or the dogs, or just the space? There was room here at Currawong. Room for Jack to be himself, room for him to grow.

Clare thought back to her cramped apartment, to the television that ruled the lounge room. She thought of Samson and the wretched inside doggy loo with its fake tree. She pictured the treadmill, with Samson running on the spot like a mad thing. Running and running and never getting anywhere. No place for a dog ... or for Jack. Maybe it was no place for her either.

Yet it was merely a matter of time before Samson would be back on the treadmill. Clare's dream job awaited her in Brisbane, in just a few months' time. She was living a fiction here, building a fanciful future upon the shifting sands of an overactive imagination. Or more ridiculous still, built on a delusional encounter with an enchanted forest. She could just imagine Roderick's face when she told him that magic trees had told her to stay here at Currawong – to stay here with Dan and Jack. *Jack isn't your child,* he'd say, and he'd be right. What was the point of giving him a pony? Just like Clare and Samson, he'd soon be back in Brisbane. With his mother. With Taylor.

Where was Taylor, anyway? Roderick had promised to call the minute there was word. An unspeakable hope slipped into Clare's consciousness from where it had been lurking at the edges of her mind. Maybe Taylor would never come back.

CHAPTER 21

'Are you sure you'll be all right?' Clare asked for the tenth time.

'Positive,' snapped Mick. 'Now you get along to that meeting and see if somebody can't talk some sense into you.'

Clare sighed. Her grandfather had been impossible today. They'd argued. She'd been trying to point out the advantages of at least allowing Pyramid Energy to drill some test wells at Currawong. Clare had done her research, even visiting Pyramid's office in Dalby to clarify a few points. Under the *Petroleum and Gas (Production and Safety) Act 2004* and the *Petroleum Act 1923*, the miners held all the cards. Providing they produced a current authority to prospect and had issued a notice of entry, Pyramid had every legal right to enter Currawong. But what Grandad didn't seem to understand was that they also had statutory responsibilities. They had to provide compensation for well heads and minimise environmental impacts. There were strict regulations with respect to fencing, stock and weed control. Surrounding land could still be used for grazing and a duty of care existed for land rehabilitation at the completion of drilling. If Pyramid were coming in anyway, it made more sense to work *with* them than to fight them. And according to the company's landholder liaison officer in Dalby, there was no doubt they were coming in. He'd shown her the map. Currawong and its immediate surrounds were coloured red – an area estimated to be of high production value.

But talking to her grandfather was like talking to a brick wall. 'They'll ruin the place,' he said. 'Pollute the air, the ground, the water, just like at Quimby Downs. Pete Porter's had wells there for two years now. Won't even let his dog drink from the bore any more ... and he's been crook for ages.'

Grandad was going to blame every coincidence on the presence of the wells, that much was obvious. But she hadn't put it to him as bluntly as that. She'd chosen her words very carefully. 'The wells are constantly monitored,' Clare had said, hoping to reassure him. 'Not just by Pyramid, but by external government inspections. I think you're worrying about nothing.'

Grandad had snorted. 'Nothing? Is it nothing that Pete's packed up and gone to live with his daughter in Dalby? He's been my neighbour at Quimby Downs all my life. Best friend a man could ask for. Built the house with his own two hands. Brought up six children, nursed his wife there until she died. Thought the only way he'd leave his land was in a box, same as me. But no – he's gone. Driven out by those bloody gas wells.'

It was no use. He wasn't listening. She'd tried a different tack. 'The compensation payments might actually make it easier for you to stay on at Currawong.'

'I don't want their bloody compensation payments!' He was shouting now. 'I just want to be left alone. Your grandmother would turn in her grave to hear you talk like that.'

He'd glared at her like she was the enemy. That last remark had cut deep. Was this really about the gas wells? A pool of guilt lurking just below the surface bubbled up. For the last sixteen years all she'd done was leave him alone. Was he having a go at her? Clare hated upsetting her grandfather like this, but it was no use him putting his head in the sand. The gas wells were coming whether he liked it or not. 'If I promise to get together the best, most up-to-date information on the pros and cons of what Pyramid's proposing,' said Clare, 'will you at least read it?'

He'd looked suddenly cagey. 'Go along with Dan to the *Shut the Gate* meeting tonight. I'll mind Jack. Keep an open mind and see what you make of it. Do that for me, and I promise to read whatever you want. Deal?'

'Deal,' she'd said. It seemed like a fair arrangement.

IT WAS ALMOST seven o'clock when Dan marched in the door. 'Thought I'd never get away tonight. That Mrs Potts would talk the hind legs off a donkey. Reckon I could recite the pedigree of every one of her budgies by now.'

Jack pulled at Grandad's sleeve and pointed to the top of the kitchen dresser. The old man reached up, took down a board game and set it on the table. 'What do you say?' he asked the little boy.

'Ta,' said Jack, pulling off the lid.

Grandad beamed at Clare, and ruffled the boy's hair. 'He's coming along in leaps and bounds, this one.'

'He certainly is,' said Clare. She kissed her grandfather's cheek. 'Are you sure you wouldn't rather go to the meeting instead?'

He held up his hand.' A deal's a deal. And to tell you the truth, I've been a bit crook today. I'd just as soon stay home and play *Snakes and Ladders* with Jacky.'

'Crook how?' asked Clare. 'What's wrong?'

'I'll live,' he said. 'Get her out of here, will you, Dan? Jack and me are busy.'

'Wait.' She ducked into the bathroom to brush her hair in front of the mirror.

'The lass won't be a minute,' she heard Grandad say. 'Probably putting on her face.'

'If she didn't do a thing,' said Dan, 'she'd still be streets ahead of the rest.'

Grandad chuckled appreciatively and Clare emerged, feeling both embarrassed and pleased. Dan saluted and took hold of her hand in an almost proprietary way. Grandad took in the gesture with a long, considered stare and Clare held her breath until he cracked a smile.

'See you, Jacky,' she said, waving goodbye as Dan pulled her out the door.

THE MEETING WAS at the Merriang Soldiers Memorial Hall on the outskirts of town, a small weatherboard building with a gabled porch like a Californian bungalow. The car park was overflowing, and they had to park up the street.

'It's a good turnout,' said Clare.

'The local MP's coming,' said Dan. 'Gordon McCrae. We hope he'll take our fight to parliament.'

Inside, chairs had been set up facing the stage. A document tray full of fat envelopes stood on a card table by the door. It was labelled CSG *Submissions*. An elderly lady in front of them dropped an envelope into the tray. Basildon Bond, the same elegant brand of stationary her grandmother had used for letters and thank you notes. It was addressed in ink, a graceful, flowing hand. Another man dumped a box file beside the tray. Dan slipped an envelope from his own pocket and added it to the pile.

A teenage girl was playing John Williamson's *True Blue* on a piano in the corner. In proper bush fashion, benches and tables groaned with plates of sandwiches and cakes. An urn bubbled beside the sink in the kitchen.

'We should have brought a plate,' said Clare. 'Why didn't you tell me?'

'I'm not in the habit of bringing one,' said Dan, popping an Anzac biscuit in his mouth. 'I'm in the habit of taking one home.' He ate another biscuit. 'I love these things.'

'Don't,' said Clare, and found a seat. Dan squeezed in beside her. 'Is that another biscuit?' she asked.

'There's always too much food,' he mumbled, his mouth crammed full. 'I'm doing them a favour.'

The piano stopped and a man brought a microphone and stand onto the stage and people began to take their seats. A loud buzz of conversation came from the back of the hall. Clare turned to see what it was about. An unassuming middle-aged man, grey at the temples, had arrived, and was clearly the centre of attention. That must be Gordon McCrae, the MP.

A young man with dreadlocks, who couldn't have been more than twenty-five, thanked everyone for coming, and the crowd greeted him with an enthusiastic round of applause. 'We'll get housekeeping matters out of the way first,' he said, 'and then Gordon will talk about why he's here. He's vowed to take your questions into parliament.' There was a little cheer.

'Who's the hippy?' whispered Clare.

'Gavin Butler, the group convener.'

'He doesn't look like a farmer.'

'He's not,' said Dan. 'Gavin's an artist – a painter. This gas business has led to some strange bedfellows. Farmers and greenies both want to do the right thing by their land. There's more sense in them teaming up than fighting, I guess. And it's not just the greenies. There's both sides of politics here as well.'

Clare was impressed. This kind of community consensus was rare. Only a powerful groundswell of protest would fuel it. Maybe there was more to the gas wells than she'd imagined?

Now Gordon McCrae began to speak. He gave some background about where things stood politically, and the leverage of independents in the current house. The audience listened politely, although there was a grim set to many of the faces. 'There's plenty of power in the cross bench,' he said, 'So let's use it.' A general nod of approval came from the crowd. 'Now, I'd like to hear from you folks who've come along tonight,' said Gordon. 'I've done my own research, discussed it with the bigwigs on both sides of the house. Sat on a parliamentary committee or two on the subject. What I want now is some anecdotal evidence about what it's like out here on the ground. So ... stories please folks.'

One by one people stood and spoke. Clare knew better than to be swayed by emotional rhetoric. There was plenty of that on show. But some accounts were genuinely disturbing: bores losing pressure, groundwater tasting of metal and salt, sick stock and failed crops.

Some people claimed health impacts, too. Reports of nose bleeds, and sore eyes and rashes. How much was truth, she wondered, and how much was paranoia?

After almost two hours, Gavin closed the meeting. The MP stepped down from the stage to enthusiastic applause and cries of 'You tell 'em Gordon,' and 'We're depending on you, mate.' The crowd descended on the refreshments at the back of the hall and Dan joined them. Clare hovered at the edges, observing. Nobody approached her, even though she recognised quite a few people. Anne Brady for instance, and the basset man, Brian Baker. They all seemed too preoccupied to make idle chit-chat with a virtual stranger.

Dan caught her eye and separated himself from the cake table. 'Try these rum balls.' She shook her head. Dan tempted her, holding a chocolate sphere to her lips. She couldn't resist snapping at it. He pulled the sweet away, teasing. Clare got it on the third try and Dan went back for more.

People were still lining up to put their case to Gordon. The relentless fears they held were beginning to unnerve her. She studied the poster of a gas plant beneath storm clouds that was pinned to the wall. The odd machinery squatted, alien and strange, over a familiar patchwork of crops. A sinister image, carefully designed that way. Clare knew all this, but found herself swayed nonetheless. It wouldn't take much for her to embrace their alarm.

Clare caught Dan's eye. He swallowed two dainty sandwiches at once and made his way back to her. 'Can we go?' she asked. Dan nodded and said some swift goodbyes. Then taking her elbow he guided her out the door. How different he was to Adam. Half the time with Adam she'd felt like she was just tagging along, a bit of an afterthought. She hadn't realised quite how unimportant he'd made her feel, until she had Dan for comparison. By contrast, his need for her was plain.

'That was pretty intense,' she said when they were back in the car.

Dan slung his arm around her shoulder and pulled her close. 'You want to see intense?'

He kissed her slow and hard, then cradled her face in his hands.

Butterflies stirred in her stomach, but a curious group of people passing on the footpath caused Clare to pull away. She wished she hadn't. The sky was darkening outside. She could hear Dan shifting in his seat and the sound of their breathing. Why had she moved away? What if she'd put him off?

'The night's still young,' said Clare. 'Shall we go back to your place?' Dan didn't respond.

Oh. Had she been too forward? She tried again.'Grandad won't mind if we don't go straight home.' His hands were on the wheel now, instead of on her. Perhaps he was just overwhelmed. Her skin, where he'd touched her, felt alive.

Finally he spoke. 'My place is no good.'

Why was he suddenly playing hard to get? The anticipation of his touch in the dark made her bold, and she slid her hand onto his knee. Dan's expression was hard to read in the fading light.

'What are we waiting for,' he said at last, and turned on the ignition. The wheels spun on the gravel roadside. In a few minutes they pulled up outside a raised bungalow, a typical Queenslander, with flower beds and an ornamental woven-wire fence. The gabled iron roof was framed by a pale sunset. She didn't know what she'd expected, but it wasn't this. She tried to imagine absent-minded, disorganised Dan pruning the roses, and failed.

They walked up the twilight path and the porch light switched on as if by magic. Timber steps led to a verandah swathed in flowering jasmine. The air hung heavy with its sweet fragrance. 'This is lovely,' said Clare, taking his hand. Dan pulled her into the shadows and kissed her until every nerve in her body screamed for more. She drank in his warmth, his strength, the delicious force of his desire, and her head swam like she'd had too much wine.

As his fingers found the buttons of her shirt, Clare caught a movement out of the corner of her eye. A huge toad leaped from the darkness and snapped up a beetle near her shoe. She let out an involuntary scream.

'I've got it,' said Dan. To her horror, he scooped up the creature and vanished inside, leaving her alone on the verandah. Clare tentatively pushed through the screen door just in time to see Dan disappear into the kitchen at the end of the hall.

'Get that bugger out of here,' yelled a voice, a female voice.

Who was here? Clare tiptoed down the corridor and peeked into the kitchen. A pretty young woman was standing with her back against the fridge. A slight muffin top spilled over the waistline of her low-slung jeans. Wavy blonde hair tumbled to her waist and generous breasts spilled from a tight boob-tube. Who was she?

Dan stood with the toad held out like a sacrifice. The creature lay acquiescent in his hands. 'You're not putting that thing in the freezer,' the woman said defiantly. 'Mum nearly had a heart attack when she found that other one.'

Time for some answers. 'Hello,' said Clare, entering the kitchen and introducing herself. She offered her hand, but the girl just eyed her suspiciously. 'Dan,' said Clare, indicating the young woman with a slight nod. 'I haven't had the pleasure...?'

'This is Bonnie. Bonnie ... Clare.' Bonnie. The name sounded more like a collie than a person. 'This is actually Bonnie's home,' said Dan. 'I just rent a room.'

So that was it. His peculiar behaviour all made sense now. 'Ahh ...' said Clare. 'You didn't tell me.' She made no effort to hide the edge of rebuke in her voice. Dan shrugged and looked a little helpless. 'I'm sorry —' he began, but was cut short by a scream. A middle-aged woman barged into the kitchen, eyes blazing.

'Get that infernal creature out of here,' she shouted. 'I went for the ice-cream last night and found two of them things instead. Stiff as boards, they were. What do you want with frozen toads anyway? Are you doing some sort of mad experiments?'

Clare stifled a laugh. 'I've run out of *Hop Stop*,' said Dan. 'Cooling toads in the fridge overnight, followed by freezing, is the next best way to kill them.'

'Fridge?' said the woman, a look of mounting revulsion on her face.

'You can't put them straight into the freezer,' said Dan, in his most reasonable voice. 'Exposing fully conscious toads to extreme temperatures causes painful ice crystals to form in their skin. It's not humane.'

The woman's horror turned to mirth. 'Humane?' she said with a cackling laugh. 'My George doesn't worry about being humane. He practises his golf swing on the little bleeders.'

The toad squirmed. 'You're putting it in the fridge?' said Clare.

'Not any more, he's not,' said Bonnie.

'The toads don't know they shouldn't be here,' said Dan, calming his amphibian charge by flipping it over and rubbing its belly. The toad appeared to fall asleep. 'Ultimately, all the damage they do is our fault for introducing them. We have to get rid of them, true, but we have to show them as much compassion as we would any other animal.'

The older woman looked pointedly at Bonnie. 'I always said he was a little loopy.'

Dan retreated, complete with cane toad, and Clare followed him out the back door. 'That was interesting,' she said, failing to restrain a giggle. 'Not quite how I expected the evening to turn out, but interesting just the same.'

'I should have said,' mumbled Dan. 'About Bonnie, I mean.'

'Yes, you should have.'

He took the toad to the car, found a cloth bag in the back and placed the unfortunate creature inside. 'I'll drop it off at the surgery after I take you home.' Clare nodded. They sat for a bit, while stars wheeled above them in a show of celestial brilliance. The desire she'd felt when he kissed her in the shadows was undiminished, in spite of the strange scene in the kitchen. Clare reached for him, but he shrank away.

'I can't touch you,' he said in a strangled voice. 'My hands, they're starting to sting. I must have triggered her poison glands.'

'You mean the toad? How do you know it's a she?'

'Size,' he said. 'The females are bigger.' Dan uselessly wiped his hands on his trousers, then settled them back on the wheel. 'I'd better get you home.'

Clare nodded, then leaned over and carefully kissed his cheek.

'Dan,' she said, while buckling her seat belt. 'You really ... really need to get your own place.'

IT WASN'T much past ten when Clare got in, but Grandad had already gone to bed. Clare crept into Jack's room, just like she'd done each night since she'd been at Currawong. Almost a month now. It was hard to believe that she'd once seen Jack as an imposition.

She softly scolded Samson, who was stretched out beside the child, sharing his pillow. Jack was squashed up against the wall, one arm flung over the dog's neck. 'Come on you. Back where you belong.' A sheepish Samson commando-crawled backwards, down to the foot of the bed. Clare rearranged the little boy's sleepy limbs, and repositioned his head more comfortably. Jack's fine white-gold hair lay like a silky halo on his pillow. How long it was getting now. He'd need a haircut soon. There was that little place in town with the funny name, but where did she stand on that? Would Taylor mind? Did Clare have the right, as his carer, to take Jack to *Click Go The Shears*? A sharp stab of resentment caught her by surprise. Why should she have to agonise over something so simple, so ordinary? For almost two months now she'd been Jack's mother in every sense of the word, hadn't she? She'd even left her job, sacrificed her life in Brisbane to bring Jack to this place of healing.

A small voice whispered that this wasn't quite true, that she was rewriting history. *You came to Currawong because you were curious*, it said, *and because Adam cheated on you*. She tried to ignore the voice, but it grew more and more insistent. *You have no real place in Jack's life*, it whispered. *It's futile to think along those lines. You're his temporary carer, nothing more.*

That was the law and nobody understood it better than she did. Taylor could come back at any time. If she'd made a fair fist of improving her life, Jack would be hers. And that, of course, was just how it should be. Clare would take the job with Paul Dunbar and her sojourn at Currawong would end. Whatever was going on with Dan would probably end too. She stood there in the dark, still feeling

Dan's touch on her skin, his lips on hers. Maybe Jack's social worker had been right all along. Getting attached to Jack was a recipe for heartache. And maybe getting attached to Dan was just as risky. Her picket-fence fantasy of staying in Merriang, of settling into some kind of life with Dan and Jack, was just that – a fantasy. An idyllic silly dream. Wasn't it?

She sat down on the edge of Jack's bed as a wild, hopeful notion took hold. To hell with her job. To hell with Taylor. If she could keep Jack she would. If she could stay here with him and Grandad … and Dan, she would. She'd stay and build a new life, a different future. Jack stirred in his sleep. Clare swept the little boy's hair off his face, and her imagination took flight. It wasn't an impossible dream, after all. It could really happen. She was suddenly sure that she and Dan would make it. It was early days, and she didn't have much evidence, but her heart was shouting that he was the one. Not the carefully protected heart of her past, but one that had broken free of its safeguards: a heart that longed to recklessly love this boy, this man, this place. A heart that hoped Taylor would not return to claim her son.

CHAPTER 22

The ringing phone jolted Clare from sleep so abruptly, that her dream remained vivid, the horror still real. She'd been miles beneath the earth, swimming in a warm underground ocean. Jack was there too, on the beach, laughing and throwing sticks into the shallows for Samson. A tranquil scene. But while they played, the waves changed direction, breaking at an unnatural angle to the shore. It was then she saw it – a dark stain in the distance, expanding at incredible speed. She'd called to them, but Jack had merely waved and cast a stick into the waves. Samson bounded after it, swimming strongly out to sea. 'Jacky, no!' But like a flash the child was in the water too, dog paddling towards the stain. The black water assumed a concave shape – a monstrous, roaring vortex, swallowing all before it. Samson and Jack vanished down its gaping throat. A primal scream broke from her lips. The whirlpool had sucked the ocean dry, and left her standing in a desolate wasteland. Nothing left but pale skeletons dotting the slimy seabed.

The phone call summoned her home. Clare shook her head, still groggy from sleep, and looked at the time on her alarm clock. Six o'clock in the morning. Who'd be ringing this early? She stumbled out to the hall.

'Jesus Christ, Clare ... You're a hard woman to get hold of.'

'Roderick?' It was preposterous to hear her boss's voice coming from the clunky old Currawong phone. A worm turned in her stomach.

'Don't sound so surprised, Clare. You're on the Darling Downs, not on the rim of the known world.'

Clare didn't know what to say. She was fond of Roderick. More than fond. His encouragement and passion had inspired her ambition for the bar. But she didn't want to hear from him now. Not now. Not here.

'Great news,' he said. 'Taylor's back.'

It was like he'd punched her. 'That's good,' she managed. 'How *is* Taylor? How'd she go in court?'

'She's well and truly headed in the right direction,' he said. 'Good behaviour bond and a treatment order. We've found her safe housing, she's dumped the violent boyfriend and, best of all, she's back on the methadone program.'

'You've been busy,' was all Clare said.

'It's all gone far better than we could have hoped. I reckon our Miss Taylor Brown is a fine contender for getting that kid back.'

Clare's hand trembled. She couldn't hold the phone steady. Bile rose in her throat, while some far distant part of her begrudgingly acknowledged the girl's achievements and commitment to her son.

Clare subjected Roderick to a searching inquisition, desperate for every detail. Roderick mainly met her barrage of questions with silence. Finally he said, 'Settle down, Clare. I've already breached Taylor's confidentiality by telling you what I have. Let's not compound the offence, eh?'

'Of course,' said Clare. 'Sorry.'

'Will keep you posted. I don't mean to raise your hopes too soon. Taylor's got a way to go yet.' She could almost hear him beaming. 'Meanwhile, how about sending me through some photos of John for his mum? And the department's organised for Taylor to go down there for a visit, so just make sure I can contact you, okay. Is this landline the best number to get you on? And what the hell happened to your mobile? It's like you dropped off the face of the earth.'

If only thought Clare. 'My mobile's kaput.' Not a bad thing either. She liked not having a phone, liked not being at everybody's beck and call. 'It fell out of a tree and broke and there are no phone shops in Merriang, but you'll always get me on this number.'

'I will, will I?' said Roderick. 'That's funny ... because I've rung you half a dozen times in the past week. Some old bloke always answers. Your grandfather, I'm guessing? I left messages, but you never get back to me. Why else do you think I'm ringing you so goddamn early in the morning?'

Clare felt a warm flush of love for Grandad. He should have told her about the calls – of course he should have — but she knew why he hadn't. He'd wanted to keep her and Jack close. They were co-conspirators now.

'Grandad's forgetful.'

'That's not good enough, Clare. I need to be able to reach you. And what sort of an excuse is my phone fell out of a tree? It's about as believable as the dog ate my homework.'

Perfectly believable, thought Clare. After all, a dog had eaten her phone.

'You *will* get me on this number,' she said. 'I'll have a word to my grandfather.'

'You do that, Clare,' said Roderick.

There was an uncomfortable pause. 'How's the new guy doing?' she asked. 'Davis. Filling my shoes all right?'

'About that Clare ... It's almost November and we're losing you to Dunbar next year anyway.'

'Yes .'

'I could offer Davis a full-time position now. He's not you, Clare, but he's good. I'd be happy to have him on the team. What do you say?' Clare didn't say anything. 'It will solve next year's staffing problems, and give you time to ease Taylor back into a parenting role.'

His words wrenched at her. It hurt, no doubt about it. Hurt that Roderick had replaced her so easily. But of course he was right. One way or another she was leaving Fortitude Valley Legal Aid. She should be grateful that her position would be so swiftly and capably filled. What was it that Grandad had said the other day? *Nobody's indispensable*. Nobody but Grandad, she'd wanted to say. Clare could no longer imagine life without his warmth and wisdom.

'When's Taylor coming?' she asked.

'That's why I've been trying to ring,' said Roderick. 'She's coming tomorrow, Clare —Thursday. Thank god I finally got hold of you. There'll be hell to pay if Kim Maguire organises this access and it falls through. Stay by the phone, won't you? She'll be calling this morning.'

'Of course,' mumbled Clare and they said goodbye. Clare sat down on a kitchen chair and tried to put herself back together. Part of her was proud of Taylor – in awe of her. How difficult it must have been, struggling alone with her addiction, battling on for the sake of her son. *Her* son. Jack was Taylor's son, Clare told herself. Taylor's son.

CHAPTER 23

Thursday morning. Clare stared at her scrambled eggs with no appetite. She pushed them around her plate, then gazed out the window. The sun shone, but to the north an odd shelf of grey clouds had obscured the Bunya range.

Jack was biting his vegemite toast into the shape of a gun. 'Bang,' he said, and shot her. 'You're dead.'

'Have you told the lad yet?' asked her grandfather. Jack looked up.

She shook her head miserably.

'Want me to do it, love?' Grandad asked.

'No,' said Clare, her voice sharper than intended. 'Of course not.' She hated the look of disapproval on Grandad's face. Currawong and guilt so often seemed to go hand in hand, even if the guilt was self-inflicted. Jack pushed his plate away and hopped down from the table, still clutching his toast gun.

'Bang,' he said, and chased Samson out the door. If only Dan was here. Clare didn't quite know why, but it would have been easier to tell Jack with him around. But he'd left at daybreak to vaccinate dairy cows at Oakey, and wouldn't be back until after lunch. Taylor would be here by then. One o'clock, that's what Kim had said. Taylor had got hold of a car somehow and had permission to take Jack out for the afternoon. Clare could barely let herself think about it. What if Taylor was using after all? She might be high, or drunk. She might shoot up with Jack in the car. She might crash ... She might leave with him and never come back.

'I'm driving out to check the brood mares. Want me to take the lad as well? Once you tell him about his mother, that is. Give you some time to yourself?'

'No,' said Clare swiftly. 'I'm spending this morning with Jack.'

Grandad wrapped his arms around her in a fierce embrace. 'Things will work out, love. I'm only as far as the two-way if you need me.' He whistled and Samson cannoned back into the kitchen, followed by the dalmatians. 'Come on, you lot,' said Grandad, and they all vanished out the door.

Clare had half-expected Jack to answer Grandad's whistle, along with the dogs. She glanced at the time. Nine o'clock. Taylor would have begun her long drive to Merriang. She couldn't put off telling Jack about his mother's visit any longer. Kim Maguire's warning echoed in her ear: *'A child like John probably won't understand when you tell him, but it's still wise to prepare for some acting out, just in case.'*

Jack would understand all right. Clare was woefully unprepared to deal with the situation and, for once, she'd listened carefully to what Kim had to say. *'Access visits can trigger a child's repressed feelings of anger, sadness and despair, all associated with separation, and loss of their parents. This may manifest in tantrums or anxiety. John might be hyperactive and agitated, or conversely quiet and depressed.'*

Great. In other words, anything could happen. That was a big help.

Clare finished her tea. Breakfast dishes could wait. It was time to get it over and done with. The day was bright, with a scattering of high cloud and the scent of jasmine on the breeze. An early chorus of crickets thrummed in the garden, and a courting currawong piped a tune. Such a perfect day, such a pervasive sense of peace. Surely nothing could go wrong on such a day. Maybe she was blowing Taylor's visit out of proportion.

'Jack,' called Clare. 'Ja-cky.' He wasn't building roads in the load of builder's sand that Grandad had dumped beside the stable for him. He wasn't in the feed room looking for mice. He wasn't in the cart shed making cubbies, or playing in the hay, or hunting for eggs in the hen house? Where was he? The big gates across the drive were securely closed. Maybe he was inside after all. But as Clare turned back towards the house, something made her stomach lurch. The little garden gate leading to the paddocks hung open. A spidery fear crept up her spine. 'Jack!' Clare ran out the gate, screaming his name.

Sparky ... that's where he'd be. She ran down to the day yard. Jack's pony dozed in the shade of a myall tree, his satin coat twitching at flies, but the little boy wasn't with him. If only Samson was here. She searched the stables, the stockyards, the turnout paddocks. Nothing. She combed the nearby fields at a run, startling the grazing clydesdales, causing them to frisk away with their big, slow-motion trots and lumbering hooves. Not a sign. With lungs bursting, with breath rasping in shallow, painful spurts, Clare sprinted to the dam. No — not that. Not her dream.

'Jack!' She yelled for him so hard and so long and so often, that her voice grew hoarse and faded to a husky whisper.

Wrenching herself from the search, Clare pelted back to the homestead. She slammed in through the door, allowing herself one wild, hopeful sweep of the house before calling her grandfather on the two-way. Then she called Dan. Then she called the police, the rural fire service, the state emergency people. Lastly she called Kim Maguire and left a brief message. 'It's Clare Mitchell. I've lost Jack.'

CLARE SAT SLUMPED in the kitchen chair, staring out the window into the middle distance.

'What was Jack wearing?' asked Grandad. He took pen and notepad from a sideboard drawer, along with a large sheet of heavy, folded paper, its edges curled and yellowed with age.

'A long-sleeved blue T-shirt with penguins,' said Clare. 'Blue cotton trousers with yellow stripes and black elastic-sided boots.'

Grandad noted it down and then spread the old survey map of Currawong out on the kitchen table. 'You head west on the quad bike, out the laneway and up this hill.' He pointed to the map. 'I'll take these eastern paddocks along the creek.'

Clare licked her lips, but they wouldn't stay wet. Currawong Creek began high in the Bunya watershed. In places it flowed dark and deep between steep banks and its course was choked with snags. So much danger for a little boy lost. The creek, the dam, the snakes. The wild dogs and dingoes … the vast, indifferent Australian bush.

'I'll keep Samson with me,' he said. She was about to protest, when it dawned on her: Grandad wanted Samson because he was searching the creek paddocks. In her mind's eye, the dog stood barking at a small figure floating face-down, wedged between rocks, pale hair fanned out on the water.

'Don't forget to take the two-way,' said Grandad. A vehicle pulled up outside the house, then another. Neighbours rallying to help. It felt so good to see them there. 'You get going,' he said, nodding towards the cars in the driveway. 'I'll fill them in.'

A group of five riders on horseback arrived, along with a boy on a motorcycle. Clare ran down to the cart shed for the bike, while Grandad held Samson's collar. The dog leaped and barked and whined - straining to race after her as she roared out the gate and up the hill towards the Bunya range. Clare scanned the ground for tracks, scanned the trees for movement, scanned the horizon - praying to see the boy's slight silhouette against the sky.

She checked the time. Quarter past ten. Taylor would be here in a few short hours. Where would Clare find the words to tell the young mother that her precious four-year-old son was lost and alone in the bush? Where would she find the strength?

'Mick to Clare … Mick to Clare.' The two-way crackled to life, making her jump. Clare was clumsy in her haste, sweaty hands fumbling with the receiver. 'Grandad, any news? Have you found him?

'No, love, no luck yet, and I've bloody well gone and lost Samson as well. Was up in the front paddock near the road, when the dog just took off through that scrubby bit and I couldn't keep up.'

'Near the road?'

'That's right.'

'Do you think he picked up on Jack's scent?'

'Might have done, love. I just don't know,' he said, unable to disguise the despair in his voice.

'I'm coming home, Grandad.'

THE DALBY STATE Emergency guys had arrived by the time she got back. Clare gave them a description of Jack and his clothes. She was going inside to fetch a photo when Samson came galloping down the drive, barking his head off.

'That's Jack's dog,' said Clare. 'I think he wants us to follow him.'

'What,' said one bloke. 'Like Lassie?'

'Yes,' shouted Clare, over her shoulder. She was already pelting down the drive. 'Just like Lassie.' Samson led them out to the road. The emergency vehicle pulled up beside Clare, whose heart was bursting in her chest, trying to keep pace with the racing dog. She climbed in, gasping for breath, terrified she might lose sight of him. Samson detoured through an open, steel-framed gate leading into a paddock on the other side of the road. Not a farm gate, more like one you'd find in a commercial enterprise. Beyond the gate lay some sort of earthworks, an expanse of bulldozed ground in the middle of open pasture. The dog suddenly vanished from sight. One minute he was tearing across the rough, broken ground, and next ... he was gone.

The wheels sank into the soft earth, losing traction. Clare leaped from the car and ran to where she'd last seen Samson. And there, standing below her in a shallow pit, arms locked around the dog's shaggy neck ... there was Jack. Clare felt a lightness in her limbs: weightless, unanchored. She slid down the steep bank and swept the little boy into her arms. Jack looked at her reproachfully, face smudged with dirt. 'You lost me.'

Clare nodded, smiling through her tears. 'But I've found you now.'

Jack scrunched shut his eyes and buried his face in her shirt.

'I won't lose you again, Jacky,' she said. 'I promise.'

CHAPTER 24

Clare rushed into the bathroom with a towel and clean clothes for Jack. Dan was back, sitting on the edge of the ancient, clawed bath, washing Jack's face and helping him to build a bubble bath tower. The little boy was giggling and squealing as if nothing out of the ordinary had happened at all.

Dan stood and gave Clare a swift kiss. 'I'll clear off. Give you some time to talk with Jack.' Clare nodded absently, still in a daze, barely registering Dan's lips against hers, the burn of them. She hoisted Jack from the tub and wrapped him in a towel. Please let the clock on the wall be fast. It couldn't be one o'clock already. She had not told Jack about his mother's visit yet.

It hadn't helped that she'd been on the phone to Kim Maguire for half the morning. Clare had rung her the minute she'd found Jack. She'd meant it to be a brief call, informing Kim of the good news. She'd hoped recriminations could wait. No such luck.

'What happened today is completely unacceptable,' Kim had said. There was an air of exaggerated outrage about her words, but Clare could hardly disagree. 'I'm writing a full incident report as we speak.'

You'll enjoy that, thought Clare. People like Kim were much more at home filing forms than dealing with people.

'And I have a great many questions,' said Kim.

Clare had spent a humiliating half hour admitting her neglect, only to discover that Kim's concern was more for herself, than for Jack. 'You've betrayed my faith in a major way, Clare. You've exposed the department, and potentially me, to a law suit.'

Should Clare argue? Should she point out that Jack was back home and had suffered no harm? Should she advise the social worker that, having properly placed the child with Clare, she was not responsible for breaching any duty of care? Not like when Kim had tried to place Jack at Brighthaven. That was a textbook case of failure to protect.

But Clare knew how to play this game. 'I can't tell you how sorry I am, Kim,' she'd said. 'You bent over backwards to accommodate me, rushed through the kinship assessment. You've been so wonderful, and then I go and cause you all this grief.'

Kim sounded mollified. 'Can you tell me what steps you'll take to ensure John doesn't wander away again?' As Clare talked about child-proof gate locks and not allowing Jack outside unsupervised she pictured Kim ticking off the boxes. Kim asked if there was a garage door that allowed access to the street. She'd clearly forgotten that they were talking about a country property, where you couldn't even see the street from the house. She'd also forgotten that Clare had a dirty, tired, frightened little boy to deal with, one who was currently rocking on her lap. 'Well goodbye, Clare.' At last. 'Thank God you found the child before his mother arrived.'

That was one thing, at least, that they both agreed upon.

THE DOGS WERE BARKING NOW, signalling a visitor. She glanced out the window in time to see Taylor emerge from a battered blue Holden station-wagon. Surely that thing wasn't roadworthy? Dan greeted Taylor and waylaid her with conversation. Good, that would buy her some time. Clare finished dressing Jack and sat down on the bathroom floor beside him. 'Listen to me, Jacky. We have a visitor … Mummy's here.'

The little boy stopped trying to climb back into the bath and just stared, his eyes large. Why on earth hadn't she told him earlier, given him some time to get used to the idea? Clare ran through the possible reactions she'd been warned to expect. For some reason, the one reaction she wasn't prepared for was one of unbridled joy. Jack ran from the room. Clare scribbled Grandad's landline and mobile numbers on a piece of paper and followed the boy outside.

Jack was already wrapped in his mother's arms. The four dogs romped around them, but Taylor didn't seem to be the least bit perturbed. Clare took a closer look at the young woman. She looked much healthier than the first time they'd met. Her long chestnut hair was clean and brushed. Her face, once so pale, was flushed pink with pleasure. Her limbs were a little rounder, her face a little fuller ... her eyes, still hard, but much brighter. And right now those eyes glowed with unmistakable love and pride as she gazed at her little son.

Taylor looked up as Clare approached. '*So* sorry my kid ran off on you. He can be a little bugger like that.'

Clare was stunned. It was an absurd apology. She was the one who'd lost Jack. It had all been her fault. Nevertheless, the girl sounded perfectly genuine, heartfelt even. But there was something much more confusing. How did Taylor know about Jack's disappearance in the first place? Both Clare and Kim had hoped to keep that quiet.

'Where'd you find him?' Taylor directed that question to Dan.

He ruffled Jack's hair. 'Clare will fill you in.' With a nod, he left. She tried to make sense of it. Dan? Dan must have told Taylor that she'd lost Jack. He'd handed Taylor a powerful weapon to use against her, something even that witch Kim Maguire hadn't been prepared to do.

'Come inside,' said Clare. 'I'll make you a coffee and explain what happened.' If she could just convince the girl to spend her visit here at Currawong.

'Nah,' said Taylor. 'It doesn't matter.' She put Jack down and lit a cigarette. 'We're going to the circus.'

'What circus?'

'Toowoomba, was it? I love Jacky's hair. It's long now, isn't it? He looks like a little girl.'

'Toowoomba?' Clare's mouth went dry. Toowoomba was more than two hours away. 'You can't ...' started Clare, brain scrambling to find a logical excuse for keeping Jack home.

'He's my son,' said Taylor, eyes narrowing. There was a new edge to her voice. 'I can take him if I want.'

'Of course,' said Clare, forcing herself to smile. 'It's been such a long drive, that's all. I thought you might like a coffee first ... or maybe a cold drink?'

It wasn't working. Taylor looked wary now. 'No thanks,' she said, avoiding eye contact.

Clare pulled the piece of paper from her pocket and handed it over. 'You can get me on these numbers,' she said. 'My old one won't work. I lost my mobile.'

'Same here,' said Taylor. 'I always lose them things.'

'You don't have a phone?' asked Clare, feeling sick. 'But what if I need to talk to you?'

Taylor shrugged and shoved the piece of paper into her pocket. She dropped the smouldering butt of her cigarette to the ground and trod on it.

Such a filthy habit. Clare bit her tongue, trying to keep track of where the butt lay on the drive, so she could retrieve it later.

'I'd better go,' Taylor said.

Clare's hands tightened into fists. It was intolerable to think this girl could just strap Jack into that deathtrap of a car and drive off. Clare looked to Jack. Maybe he wouldn't want to go? Maybe he would fight and scream to stay.

'Bye bye, Clare.' Jack waved and climbed into the car with heart-breaking alacrity.

Taylor's eyes lit up. 'He's talking? Does he talk much?'

'More and more each day,' said Clare.

'Cool,' said Taylor. She secured Jack in his seat, then turned back to Clare. Her hard eyes softened. 'Very cool.'

'Samsam,' called Jack. The dog leaped into the car and took up his customary position beside Jack, on the cracked linoleum back seat.

Taylor stroked his head. 'Can we take the dog ?' she asked. 'That'd be fun. Jacky loves dogs.'

'No,' snapped Clare. She dragged her hands through hair, limp with sweat and desperation. Take it easy, she told herself. If you're not careful you'll make things worse. 'Samson better stay here,' said Clare. She meant to sound bright and upbeat, but her voice was wavering. 'They wouldn't let a dog into the circus.' For a moment Taylor looked like she wanted to argue the point. Then she turfed Samson out of the car. Jack whined and began to bang his head. Taylor shoved a lollipop in his mouth then climbed into the driver's seat.

'When will you be back?'

'See ya.' Taylor turned the key and the engine sputtered to life.

'I need to tell you about his routine.' Clare could hear the desperation in her own voice. 'Jack needs to be home by six.'

Taylor lit another cigarette, wound up her window and took off down the hill, wheels spinning on the gravel. Samson launched off after them and Clare grabbed his collar just in time. The dog howled. Clare choked back a sob. She'd broken the solemn promise she'd made to the little boy less than two hours ago. She'd promised not to lose him again, and yet now, for the second time that day, Jack was gone.

CLARE SAT at the kitchen table with Samson's head cradled in her lap. How many hours to fill? The minutes crawled by. Clare checked the clock so frequently that sometimes no time seemed to have passed at all. The worst thing was that Taylor hadn't given any indication of when she'd be back – or even *if* she'd be back. Clare fought back tears. A huge chunk of her seemed to have vanished into a vast black hole, along with the child. This must be how it felt to have your legs amputated, or your house burn down. The shaft of sunlight streaming through the open window dimmed and then disappeared altogether. Clare shivered and hugged herself. Jack didn't even have his jumper.

Grandad came in, hung his hat on the peg by the door, then pulled up a chair opposite. 'Jack's mother came for him, then? When's he due back?'

'Tonight sometime,' mumbled Clare.

Grandad reached across the table for her hand. 'It'll work out, love. The lad will be home in no time.'

'You don't know that, Grandad. Taylor might never come back. This is killing me, and all you can do is say stupid things about something you know nothing about.' She stood and paced the room. For a moment she didn't realise that she'd translated her mean-spirited thought into words.

Grandad withdrew his hand and slumped a little in his chair. He rubbed his brow as if warding off a headache. 'You might give me a bit more credit,' he said. 'I've done my fair share of waiting for people.'

Clare swallowed hard. He was right. Grandad had been waiting for his daughter - Clare's mother - for a very long time. Waiting for Ryan ... waiting for her.

'I'm sorry.' She sat back down. 'I didn't mean it.'

'I know you didn't, love.' He extended his hand again, and this time she took it. 'We're all on tenterhooks. I'll make you a cup of tea. That always helps.'

Clare gazed into her grandfather's worried eyes and felt ashamed. This was hard on him too. She had no monopoly on loving Jack. Today had been one heart-wrenching drama after another, and yet she'd barely given a thought to how Grandad was feeling.

Clare threw her arms around him, kissing his rough cheek. He smelt comfortingly of horses and sweat. 'How about I make you one instead.' She was rewarded with a smile. She loved the way his hollow cheeks filled out when he smiled. He was suddenly a young man again, with a twinkle in his eye.

Now Samson licked her hand. His expression was one of almost human concern. Maybe she should stop worrying about Jack and start appreciating what she still had. Grandad, Samson ... Dan. But did she really have Dan? He'd betrayed her, blurted out to Jack's birth mother, of all people, how Clare had lost her son. How she'd let him wander away. There was one good thing, though. Jack was no longer in care on a voluntary basis. She was grateful that Kim had moved so quickly on that front. The state of Queensland was now Jack's legal guardian, and Taylor would be technically kidnapping her son if she failed to return him to Currawong.

Clare made the tea, scalding her hand with steam in the process. A glance out the window showed Dan's jeep, still parked down the hill outside the surgery. 'I'm going for a walk,' she said, handing Grandad his tea. His smile had vanished, replaced with a look of great weariness. 'Won't be long.' Clare kissed him again, called Samson, and headed out the door.

DESPITE THE SUNSHINE, a cold breeze had blown in from nowhere. Swirling twigs and fallen leaves formed sad little willy-willies, which died as soon as they began. Clare rubbed her goose-bumped arms. Dan wasn't at the clinic. A *closed* sign hung on the surgery door and a chain stretched across the car park entrance.

Samson padded restlessly about, whining and sniffing the breeze. She crouched beside him, burying her face in his dark ruff, thinking about when he first came to her. She'd only taken him on from a sense of duty to her dead father. When Samson had first arrived back in Brisbane, he'd seemed like such a silly pup: destructive, demanding, annoying. On more than one occasion Clare had wished him gone. And now? Now she adored him, and between the two of them, Samson seemed by far the cleverest and wisest.

The dog pricked his ears. Clare heard it too, the thrum of an approaching car. She checked her watch. Only two o'clock, but perhaps Taylor had changed her mind and was bringing Jack home early. Her heart made a joyful leap and she ran for the Sunshine gates. But as the vehicle came into view, Clare's hope died. It was her grandfather's tray-back truck, with Dan at the wheel. Clare reached him as he got out to open the gate.

'I want to talk to you.' She was shouting, but she didn't care.

'You okay?' asked Dan.

'No,' said Clare. 'I'm not. I want to know why you told Taylor about me losing Jack?'

'Righto,' he said, climbing into the cab. 'We'll talk at the house. Want a lift?' Clare shook her head. Dan leaned across and opened the passenger door. 'Are you sure?'

'Certain.' Dan frowned, slammed the door shut and took off up the track, with Samson racing along beside. Clare trudged uphill, a growing ball of fury inside her. It was as if he didn't care at all that Jack was gone, didn't care that he might never come home. It was as if he didn't care about her. When she reached the house, Dan was unloading the truck like nothing was wrong. Jack was gone and he'd gone shopping. Unbelievable.

'Look out below.' He turfed a roll of chicken netting to the ground. There were more rolls of wire and some panels of steel fencing.

Grandad came out of the house with his mug of tea and gave them a wave. 'Hope you put that stuff on my account, Dan.'

'No way, Mick. This lot's on me.'

Clare couldn't believe it. Now they were both behaving like nothing was wrong. She wanted to scream. Dan manoeuvred the steel panels to the edge of the truck. She hadn't seen him in a singlet before, and the strength of his arms and upper body was on display. If she hadn't been so furious, she would have been impressed. 'I asked why you told Taylor about me losing Jack.'

Dan straightened his back and wiped his brow. 'I assumed she already knew ... that you'd told her.'

'And give her ammunition to use against me?' said Clare, itching for an argument. 'Why the hell would I do that?'

'First,' he said in a measured voice, 'I didn't know it was a fight between you two. And second, I thought you'd told her because she's his mother, and has a right to know what happens to her kid.'

'He's got a point, love,' Grandad said.

Clare shook her head in disbelief. Dan was one thing, but her grandfather? Whose side was he on?

Dan went back to work as if the matter was closed.

For the first time Clare focused on what was being unloaded from the truck. A tall chain-link gate, about two-metres high. The sort you might find in a factory fence or a dog run. Beneath the gate lay dozens of tall pine posts. Grandad emerged from the cart shed with a post-hole digger and long-handled shovel. Dan jumped off the truck and kicked a roll of tall wire mesh towards the sagging, garden fence.

For a few moments she couldn't make sense of what she was seeing, and then it hit her. While she'd been moping around, imagining worst-case scenarios, blaming everybody else and feeling sorry for herself, they'd been planning to build a fence. A fence to keep Jack safe. Such a simple thing. Such a simple, loving practical thing to do. It left her completely overwhelmed.

Dan caught her eye and smiled. Clare smiled back and threw herself into the work at hand. No more simmering in an emotional stew. It felt so much better to be doing something constructive. Nobody talked much. Dan took a few calls from clients, but after determining they weren't emergencies, he postponed their appointments or asked them to go elsewhere. By the time Grandad declared afternoon smoko, the new fence was half-finished.

An unfamiliar car turned in the gate, and for a moment Clare's heart leapt with hope. 'That's just my mate, love,' said Grandad, looking almost guilty that it wasn't Jack. 'He's come to lend a hand.'

The visitor looked familiar. It was Sid, the wiry old whip man with the bushy white beard – the saddler from the Cobb & Co Museum at Toowoomba. He recognised her straight away. 'I should have known your boy had something to do with Mick. He had too keen an eye for them whips.'

Sid pulled some cold beers from an esky and handed them around. Clare took one, letting the bitter bubbles slide down her throat, letting the tension drain away. A high wind had swept the curtain of cloud from the Bunyas, framing their timeless peaks with a backdrop of infinite blue. An eagle soaring high overhead somehow put things into perspective. Eagles had hunted these same hills for thousands of years. One person's problems didn't amount to very much in the grand scheme of things.

Clare sat down in the sun, her back against the cart shed. Her arms ached and her shirt was damp with sweat, but the beer tasted good and things suddenly didn't seem so dire after all. Not sitting out here in the sunshine, watching gangly foals play hide and seek around their patient mothers. Sid was telling some story about driving an eight-horse hitch back in the fifties, while Grandad shook his head. 'You're dreaming,' he said. 'That was never more than a six-horse outfit.' Then Grandad's phone rang and, for once, he heard it. Everybody froze. Clare held her breath while he fumbled a little in answering it. 'I'll just get her for you ... Taylor,' he mouthed.

'Hello?' said Clare. Don't ask if everything's all right. Don't act worried.

'My car's buggered,' said Taylor. 'Me and Jack won't be back till tomorrow.'

Clare's stomach dropped like a lift with a broken cable. 'Are you both okay?'

'Yeah.' Taylor sounded uncertain. Clare could hear a child screaming in the background. 'Jack's being a little turd, that's all.'

'Where are you?' asked Clare. 'I'm coming to get you.'

'Nah, don't worry.' The screaming stopped. 'We'll be right.'

'I'd better come,' urged Clare. 'You don't have permission for overnight access. Jack's on a guardianship order. The department might issue a warrant.'

'No, that's all sorted,' said Taylor. Now Clare could hear a rhythmic thumping sound. 'Kim said I'm allowed to keep him.'

That couldn't be true. Either she'd misheard Taylor or the girl was lying. 'Where are you?' This time she couldn't hide the panic in her voice.

'I don't know the name,' said Taylor. 'It's real nice, but.' There was a loud crash and a cry. 'Got to go.' And that was that. Clare longed to crawl down the phone. She ignored the curious expressions of the others, and rang Kim. Damn it, an answering machine.

She was about to leave a message when Kim picked up. 'Clare? I was about to call. Taylor's car broke down and won't be fixed until the morning. I found some funding for her to stay at a motel in Toowoomba.'

'What motel?'

'You know better than that, Clare.'

'Just tell me, and I'll go get John. What if she doesn't bring him back?'

'Apparently Taylor calls him Jack, Clare. From now on, you should use the name favoured by his mother.' Clare had neither time nor energy to point out the absurdity of this last statement. 'You don't have to worry about her bringing the boy back,' said Kim, reading Clare's mind. 'Taylor's doing much better, but she still finds it difficult to parent her son. He's proved to be quite a handful, and she hasn't coped very well.'

'Is he all right?'

'I think Taylor's the one who's not all right. She's been glowing in her praise of you though, Clare. Says you've done wonders with the child. Says she doesn't know how you do it. His behaviour at the beginning of the access was apparently impeccable ... but Taylor said it wore off, and she blames herself. Frankly, I think she'll be secretly glad to give him back.'

Clare could have cheered. 'That's wonderful.' Bless Jack and his disruptive heart.

'How is it wonderful that Taylor can't manage her son?' asked Kim. 'She's made some positive changes in her life and was understandably hopeful of regaining custody. I'm afraid this access has been a disappointing reality check for her.'

And a welcome reprieve for me, thought Clare. 'Jack does have some extremely challenging behaviours.'

'Don't I know it,' said Kim. 'You're a braver woman than me. I've no doubt that Taylor will return the boy tomorrow. Call if there are any problems.'

Clare handed Grandad the phone, then pressed her palms against her eyes, gathering her thoughts. 'Well,' said Grandad. 'Don't keep us in suspense.'

'Taylor's car broke down.' Clare took a steadying breath. 'She and Jack are staying in Toowoomba overnight and they'll be back tomorrow. She's had a lot of trouble handling him, and said some really nice things about me. Apparently she can't wait to bring him home!'

Grandad's face spread into a slow smile. 'I told you it would work out, didn't I?' She gave him a quick kiss. 'Dan, why don't you take Clare out somewhere? Help take her mind off things. She's such a worrier. Takes after her grandmother, I guess.'

'But we haven't finished here,' said Dan.

'Sid's the fastest damned fencing contractor in Queensland,' said Grandad. 'Between him and me, we'll be done in no time.'

Clare glanced at Dan. His eyes held an invitation, and all the feelings that had been swamped by the day's dramas flooded back. In her body was a low ache, a longing to be with him, somewhere shady and cool. A longing for his touch on her skin.

'Go on,' said Grandad. 'Off you go.'

'What will we do?' Dan asked her. 'Anything you want.'

'Let's go riding,' said Clare, the desire seeming to come from nowhere.

'Riding it is,' said Dan. 'Great idea. You ride Sparky and I'll take Fleur.'

'Sparky?' she said. 'I want to ride Fleur.'

'Well, I can't ride a pony,' said Dan. 'My feet would touch the ground. Are any of your clydies saddle-broken, Mick?'

'There's the stallion, Goliath. Although he hasn't been ridden in a while.'

'How'd he be riding out with a mare?'

'Level-headed enough, as long as the mare wasn't in season.' Mick chuckled. 'Then you'd have a job on your hands.'

'Goliath?' Sid slapped his thigh in amusement. 'Your feet won't touch the ground on that fella. He must stand eighteen hands.'

'Are you game, Dan?' Mick asked.

'My oath.' He grinned at Clare. 'We're going to have a ball.'

CHAPTER 25

Clare scaled the stockyard rails and scrambled onto Fleur's broad back. This was the first time she'd been in the saddle since childhood, and she was a little unsure. Fleur seemed impossibly high. 'Give it some time, Clare Bear,' her grandfather told her, rubbing the mare's cheek. 'You were always a terrific little rider. Gutsy as well. It'll come back to you.' She leaned down to stroke Fleur's broad neck. Dan strapped on a saddlebag, then hopped around on one leg trying to mount Goliath, who refused to stand by the fence. He was a mountain of a horse, rich bay in colour, with a wide blaze, magnificent feather and four tall white socks. It looked like Dan was trying to mount an elephant.

Grandad disappeared into the cart shed and emerged with an old wooden mounting frame. Dan scaled its steps and was finally aboard. He sat his horse with the easy grace of a man at home in the saddle. Straight back. Strong thighs. Steady fingers, firm on the reins, but soft on the mouth — the embodiment of *good hands*. Goliath pranced sideways, muscles rippling beneath his satin skin, ears pricked and head held high.

Dan's expression was one of calm control and Clare saw him in a whole new light. Man and horse moved with the grandeur and grace of a medieval knight and his charger. Grandad opened the gates, a look of pride on his face, and they moved off down the drive. Clare was tentative at first. It was a long way to the ground, and she wasn't exactly sure what her mare wanted to do or how to read her signals. But while she was busy thinking things through, her body was responding all by itself. Call it muscle memory, call it intuition: she didn't know, but once she got used to it, riding on the Percheron mare's broad back seemed as comfortable and familiar as sitting in an armchair.

They reached the Sunshine gates, which were closed, of course. They were always closed these days. Clare gave Dan a rueful smile. 'Someone's going to have to get off.'

'Maybe not.' Dan manoeuvred his giant horse parallel to the gates. It was obvious the pair spoke the same language. In a few moments he'd swung the catch and, barely shifting in his seat, hauled the gate open.

Goliath arched his neck and Dan waved them through. 'Very gallant,' Clare whispered to Fleur, with a smile. Dan expertly closed the gate. They headed out onto the road and turned right. The horses walked abreast to start with, but the stallion's long legs and impatience soon saw him forge ahead. Clare urged Fleur into a timid trot to catch up. Late afternoon sunlight fell in dappled patterns across the road. Goliath shied at the shadows, but Dan easily kept his seat. Thank goodness Fleur had more sense. 'I love riding this horse,' said Dan, turning in the saddle and parking his right palm on the stallion's round rump. 'I absolutely love it. It's like floating on a couch in the clouds.' Clare nodded agreement. Fleur's gait was also slow, smooth and easy, yet there was something thrilling about sitting astride this magnificent mare. Clare was riding tall, and couldn't remember the last time she'd had so much fun.

The road rose before them in a gentle incline. 'Let's trot,' said Dan.

Clare shortened her reins a little, and pressed her heels to Fleur's side. Goliath began calmly enough, but soon he was pulling and tossing his great head.

'Can we canter?' asked Dan.

Clare took a deep breath. 'Go ahead.' The stallion took off, and Fleur followed suit. Clare gave an involuntary scream. Exhilarating and scary, to thunder down the road on these huge horses, manes and tails streaming, plate-sized hooves pounding, striking sparks from the road like fire from flint stones. A pure, physical adrenaline rush, the likes of which she couldn't remember. Really good sex perhaps, or an important, improbable victory in court. Fleur put on a sudden burst of speed, almost leaving her behind. She gasped and laughed and tried to find her rhythm … there it was. Grandad said it would come back, and he was right. The knowledge was latent not lost, how to meld with her horse and read its mood.

Dan wheeled Goliath about. The mighty stallion half-reared in a shaft of sunshine and the sight took Clare's breath away. Even Fleur looked impressed. She nickered and pranced, sidling up to Goliath against Clare's instructions. The horses touched noses. Fleur squealed and pawed the ground while Clare laughed and tugged at the reins. 'Where are we going?' she asked, breathless.

'It's a surprise,' and Dan swept away. Clare and her mare followed like they were drawn on a string. Dan turned into the gate leading to the mysterious earthworks where Jack had got into trouble that morning. The horses plodded across the soft ground. Clare dared not look into the pit. She half-expected to see Jack there, his clothes dirty and his face streaked with tears. Real tears. He'd learned to cry at Currawong.

'What is this place?'

'Pyramid's building a new waste water pond,' said Dan. 'Quimby Downs already has thirteen coal seam gas wells.' Quimby Downs. Where had she heard that name before? 'Mick was gutted when Pete left.' That was it. Grandad's friend. The one who'd raised six kids and lost his wife. The one who said he'd been driven out by the gas wells.

'So nobody lives here any more?'

Dan shook his head. 'Pete still runs a few head of brangus breeders. Mick and I keep an eye on them for him, but he doesn't take the cattle side of things too seriously now. The wells give him a guaranteed annual income.'

Fleur ducked her head to snack on a patch of fresh grass. Clare gave her mare a loose rein. 'That would be one good thing at least, if the wells come to Currawong,' she said. 'Grandad won't have to work so hard. He can sit around and listen to the cricket, or go on a holiday while the money just rolls in.'

Dan moved his stallion close to Fleur. 'Do you know why Pete moved out?'

'Not exactly.'

'Come on,' said Dan, heading up the hill. 'I want to show you something.'

DAN DISMOUNTED his horse in one sure, swift movement, then helped Clare down. His hands encircled her waist as she slipped from Fleur's back. It was a shock to feel them, rougher than expected, in firm control of her descent. Clare's heartbeat quickened. She landed a little awkwardly, and stumbled into the mare's warm neck. For a fleeting moment she was sure she felt Dan's hard body pressed against her, his breath on her neck. But when she turned around, he was leading Goliath into a large stockyard, its rails overgrown with willow jasmine. The stallion tore eagerly at the long grass, while Dan unbuckled his girth and hauled the mighty saddle from his back.

'What are you doing?' asked Clare.

Dan unstrapped the saddlebag and took out a bottle of champagne and a huge punnet of strawberries. He held them up to her, eyebrows raised. Clare laughed and tugged Fleur across to the yard. Soon the horses were both unsaddled and grazing contentedly.

'This is such a lovely place,' said Clare. The timber homestead's pretty portico led to a wide verandah. A profusion of purple flowering bougainvillea almost obscured the decorative white balustrade. Above the front door, a stunning fanlight of etched, coloured glass depicted a sunrise. 'How could Pete bear to leave?'

'How, indeed?' said Dan. 'Pete built this house out of pit-sawn timber. He felled the cedar and blackwood himself, up in the Bunya Mountains. See there?' Dan pointed to the roof. 'You can still see original hand-cut shingles beneath the corrugated iron.' Clare murmured her admiration. 'Wait until you look inside. It's a real showpiece.'

Clare didn't doubt it. 'The house is truly beautiful,' she said. 'I want to live here myself.' Fantasies of her and Dan came to mind, sitting out on the porch at twilight, sipping wine and watching Jack play.

'You might think differently after you see this.' Dan led her along the side of the house. A vegetable plot, rampant with weeds, stood across the path to her left. They stopped beside an outside tap, with a simple garden hose attached.

Clare looked around. What was she was supposed to see? 'It wouldn't take much to clear out those weeds and start growing vegetables again,' she said.

Dan frowned, retrieved the end of the hose from under a yellow daisy bush and turned on the tap. The faint waft of chemicals replaced the fragrance of bougainvillea on the breeze. Dan took a cigarette lighter from his pocket. He gripped the garden hose and held it at arm's length. Then, holding the lighter beneath the arc of water escaping from the nozzle, he flicked it on. Clare couldn't believe what she was seeing. A tongue of fire flashed from the end of the hose. It erupted like dragon's breath right before her eyes. The impossible flame, liquid and sinuous, licked along the water arc, transforming it into a burning bow. 'No way!' The unnatural spectre flared steadily in the late-afternoon sunshine. It was more than a minute later when Clare told Dan to turn it off.

'How is that even possible?' asked Clare.

'The bore's contaminated with natural gas, mainly methane. Two years ago Pyramid fracked half the wells on Quimby Downs.'

'Fracked?' asked Clare.

'Hydraulic fracturing. It's used to speed up the flow of coal seam gas from underground. They pump a mixture of water, sand and chemicals at high pressure into the gas-bearing formation below the water table, fracturing the strata. It causes little earthquakes that open up pathways for gas to flow out of the rock and into a well ... or a bore.'

'But I went to Pyramid's office in Dalby,' said Clare, still overwhelmed by what she'd seen. 'They insisted that less than four percent of their wells had been fracked.'

'Who knows?' said Dan. 'But Pete's wells were.'

'They said it was safe.' Clare cringed. How foolish and naïve she must sound.

'For Christ's sake, Clare. They're drilling straight through the aquifers of the Great Artesian Basin. They're injecting millions of litres of water and hundreds of tons of chemicals each time. They say these sites are sealed, but the pressure's staggering. There've been cases where fracking has split concrete bore casings and even sheared right through them. Who knows where the bloody gas and chemicals go?' He kicked the tap, frustration evident in his rigid shoulders and clenched jaw.

Clare put her hand on his arm. 'I'm sorry.'

Dan shook his head, as if to chase away the anger. 'Let's go inside,' he said. 'Have that picnic.'

LATE AFTERNOON WAS DRIFTING into evening. They sat in Quimby's lovely old dining room, eating strawberries and drinking warm champagne. Clare took in the pressed metal ceilings, the carved fireplace surround, the intricate shutters gracing wide casement windows. There was no air of decay; it was more like the homestead was holding its breath — waiting for its family to come home. Clare ran admiring fingers across the table's polished surface, making a wavy line in the dust. 'Handmade,' said Dan. 'Like just about everything else at Quimby. The top's carved from a single slab of hoop pine. You'd never get a tree that size these days.' Clare topped up her glass. 'Let's go sit on the comfy chairs.'

They moved to the lounge room, sitting side by side on the couch. 'Tell me what happened here,' she said.

Dan poured her the last of the wine. 'Not long after the wells arrived, Pete noticed an odd taste to the water. When he filled the sink to wash dishes it fizzed like Alka-Seltzer and smelled funny. He didn't want to drink it of course, so he complained to Pyramid. The company came and confirmed the contamination, and then, you know what they did? Installed methane alarms in and outside of his house. A red light warned him not to go inside if the levels rose too high.'

Clare forgot to breathe. 'You mean there's gas in the house?'

'It's safe enough,' said Dan. 'I checked the meters when we came in.'

'They're still here?'

'Of course,' he said. 'If the alarms weren't here, we wouldn't be here either.'

'Pete could sue.'

'No, he can't. Pyramid gave him a bucket of money and had him sign a confidentiality clause. They trucked clean water to Quimby Downs and monitored the alarms. According to the terms of their agreement, that amounts to making good the damage. Fact is, there's no way to fix this. When it rains, gas bubbles up through the puddles. And yet when Pete left, they said it was his choice.'

'So this beautiful old homestead just goes to waste,' said Clare. 'It's a crime.'

He pulled her across to his lap. She relaxed against his body, feeling his energy pulse through her. The hairs stood up on the nape of her neck, as Dan kissed her there. His teeth grazed her skin, and she trembled. This felt downright dangerous.

As she sank back into his chest, a loud, imperious neigh sounded from outside. Dan pushed her aside, with a quick apology, and headed for the door.

'I don't believe it,' she heard him say.

Clare followed and looked past him. 'Oh my lord. Are they doing what I think they're doing?'

'Yep,' said Dan. 'They sure are.'

'Shouldn't we stop them?'

'If you want to get in the middle of that,' said Dan with a grin, 'you're a braver person than I am.'

CHAPTER 26

It was a truly magnificent sight - Goliath rising in slow motion. There was no doubting his immense strength as he reared on pillar-like hind legs and landed with surprising precision on Fleur's broad back. The impact of the stallion's bulk on the smaller mare was considerable. Fleur staggered forwards a few steps, before managing to steady herself. She braced against the powerful grip of the stallion's forelegs upon her flanks, and his swift forward thrusting.

Dan glanced at Clare. She stood open-mouthed, transfixed by the spectacle. In a minute the mating was over. The stallion rested for a moment on top of his mare, then dismounted. Fleur assisted him by stepping forwards and sideways. The pair companionably nibbled each other's wither, in a gesture of equine, post-coital affection.

'That was so quick,' said Clare, with a faint, teasing smile 'Poor Fleur.' She touched his arm and smiled, face a little flushed, moist lips parted. That was it. Dan pulled Clare close, sensing in her the same anticipation. He tipped back her head and closed his mouth over hers. Clare's soft lips moved against his. She tasted of strawberries and smelled of saddle soap. Dan was instantly hard. His breath grew tight and urgent.

Desire made him reckless. Dan pulled her from the porch and

down into the garden, ignoring her half-hearted protests. He lowered Clare to the grass, praying he wasn't rushing things, praying she wouldn't say no. Dan stared into her smiling green eyes. His head swam with longing, light-headed, desperate to see her naked and willing beneath him.

Where was his brain? He wrenched himself away. Slow down, for goodness sake. 'Clare …' His voice sounded hoarse. She shushed him with a forefinger to his lips, pulse fast at her soft, white throat. Then she undid the top button of his shirt. Yes. He flung off his clothes and stripped Clare, impatiently, like he was opening a present. Everything about her was more than he had expected: her breasts more luscious, her skin smoother, her waist narrower than in his fantasies. Her beauty stopped him in his tracks.

Clare knelt up and slipped her slim arms around his neck. Tiny golden hairs stood erect on her skin, gleaming in the light. 'If I were you,' she said, 'I'd kiss me.' He pulled her to him, lips pressing against her mouth as she yielded to his shape. God, she was lovely. He had the strangest sensation of their bodies dissolving, melting into each other. When he entered her, they both cried out, and she arched her back to drive him deeper. The smell of their combined heat mixed with the scent of bruised leaves and crushed earth. It blended with the heady perfume of bougainvillea and jasmine. Here was paradise on earth.

Afterwards, they lay for the longest time, entwined in each other's arms. He traced the shape of her breast with his finger, astonished by its perfect form. 'I love you,' he said.

Clare raised herself on an elbow. 'What did you say?'

'I love you.'

'You can't,' she said. 'Not yet. We barely know each other.'

'Do you usually have sex with people you barely know?'

She punched him lightly on the arm. 'You know what I mean.'

'I don't actually,' he said. 'I feel I know you very well. We've seen each other every day for weeks now.' He kissed her, and his desire stirred again. 'Anyway, haven't you heard of love at first sight?'

'You didn't fall in love with me at first sight. You barely even noticed me. You left me stuck up a tree.'

'I'm a vet,' he said. 'I've taken an oath. My patient's welfare is paramount.'

Clare smiled. 'An oath?' She sat up and pulled on her shirt. 'I thought the Hippocratic Oath was for doctors.'

'It is,' he said. 'But we vets have our own.' He placed her hand on his heart. 'Being admitted to the profession of veterinary medicine, I solemnly swear to use my scientific knowledge and skills for the benefit of society through the protection of animal health, the relief of animal suffering...'

She moved her hand from his chest and placed it over his mouth. 'Enough.'

He burst out laughing.

'Okay, I believe you have an oath,' said Clare. 'But I don't believe you love me.' She gathered up her clothes and retreated to the house.

Dan lay back in the grass and stretched, every inch of his body deliciously spent. He rested his head in his hands and closed his eyes. Life had never been sweeter. Clare would learn to trust him. It was merely a matter of time.

CHAPTER 27

'Sit down, Dan.'

It was unprecedented, having lunch with Mick in town like this. It made him nervous. How could the old man know about Dan's tryst with his granddaughter yesterday? Had Clare told him? What other explanation for this meeting could there be?

He sat at a table by the window of the only café in Merriang, while Mick ordered at the counter. Big bay windows overlooked the creek. Barely a trickle. After last year's horrendous floods, they'd had an unusually dry winter. Now, more than a month into the wet season and still no real rain. If not for the bores, drilling down into the infinite waters of the Great Artesian Basin, this year's summer crops would be in serious trouble.

A jeep sped down Merriang's main street, narrowly missing Milly, the café's tiny terrier. She had a dangerous habit of sunning herself on the road. The jeep hadn't slowed a whisker. Traffic in sleepy little Merriang wasn't usually so fast, or so ruthless.

Leila, who owned the shop, rushed outside and scooped the dog up in her arms. 'Bastards,' she said, giving Milly a hug. 'A few seconds later, Doc, and my Milly here might have needed you.'

'Keep her off the road,' said Dan. 'The traffic's only going to get worse around here.' As if to prove his point, a convoy of Pyramid water tankers roared past, heading for the gas fields at Laredo. Dan imagined the vast, hidden aquifers, far beneath his feet. He could almost feel their ebb and flow.

'Dan,' said Mick. 'Dan.' This time more sharply. 'Where's your head, son?'

Maybe it was the unkind glare of noonday sun on his face, etching each wrinkle and line into sharp relief. Maybe it was the odd pallor under his weather-beaten skin. Whatever the reason, Mick looked much older than usual - looked every bit of his seventy-three years.

Leila brought over coffee for Dan and a pot of tea. 'Pies are on their way.'

'We'll have them outside please, Leila,' said Mick, getting to his feet. 'I could use a smoke.'

Dan couldn't believe his ears. Whatever had prompted Mick to take up smoking again after thirty years? When quizzed, all he said was, 'It's one of life's pleasures. Surely, at my age, a man's entitled to his pleasures.'

'Not if that man wants to live long,' said Dan. They settled themselves at a sunny outside table. Mick produced a tobacco pouch and began rolling a cigarette. Dan couldn't stand the suspense any longer. He was ready to defend his relationship with Clare. 'Quit stalling, Mick. What do you have to say to me here that you couldn't say back at the house?'

The pies arrived, surrounded by mounds of golden chips, but neither Dan nor Mick touched them. Mick struck a match. He lit the cigarette and leaned back in his chair, enjoying the first long draught. Then he smoked the whole cigarette slowly and without a word. Each puff was taken with such deliberate care that it added a curious import to the occasion. Dan wasn't going to hurry him again. The old man could take his time.

'Remember that trip I took to Brisbane last month?' said Mick at last. 'Well, it wasn't to go meet with the bank, like I said. It was for some tests.' Mick stubbed out his cigarette. 'There's something on my brain. Some kind of tumour.' Mick read the question on Dan's face.

'No mate, there's nothing they can do. I could spend the next few months in hospital, sick as a dog, with radiation treatments that won't work anyway. Or I can stay here, in the place that I've loved all my life, and enjoy each day I have left with my granddaughter and her boy. Those two coming … well, it's a blessing I never expected before I died. Sometimes I feel my Mary looking down, fairly weeping with joy about them being here.'

Dan was numb from the news. He poured Mick a cup of tea with an unsteady hand.

'Now son, what would you choose? Tell me. Currawong or the hospital?' Mick took a big bite of his pie.

'And there's no chance they're wrong?' asked Dan, his breath hardening in his chest.

'No, mate,' said Mick. 'I've had my second opinion. More pessimistic than the first. But on the plus side, I'm not in much pain yet. Some headaches … they'll get worse apparently. I feel dizzy sometimes. Confused, lose my legs. The steroid tablets help with that, though they make me cranky. Best news is, this tumour could take me one day in my sleep, when I don't even know it.' Mick finished his pie. 'Can't barely taste a bloody thing any more,' he grumbled, then used the serviette to wipe his mouth. 'So, Dan, now you know the score, you can answer my question. Currawong or the hospital?'

What could he say? He was a vet. One of the advantages of being a companion animal, he'd always thought, was the opportunity of a peaceful death before remorseless suffering set in. It was more than most people got. More than Mick would get. His throat was tight with emotion, and for a moment he couldn't catch any air. Affection for the old man rose up in a warm wave that threatened to wash him away. If Mick had asked him for a decent dose of horse tranquiliser at that very moment, he would have given it to him. 'How long?'

'Six months, if I'm lucky.'

Dan had never smoked, but he suddenly wanted one of Mick's roll-your-owns. 'Mick,' said Dan. 'You have to tell Clare.'

There was no reading Mick's face, not a flicker of emotion. He rolled another cigarette, lit it and took a bottomless drag, like he was smoking a joint. He expelled it from his lungs in neat smoke rings and cracked a smile. 'I'd love to show Jack that trick,' he said with a chuckle. 'But it's not kosher these days, is it, mate?'

Dan shook his head. 'No, Mick, it's not.' He skulled his coffee. 'We were talking about Clare.'

'You're fond of my granddaughter, aren't you Dan? How fond?'

'I love her,' he said simply.

Mick looked well satisfied. 'Give us some time, Dan. The truth will be out in the open soon. Give us this special time together, before the grief sets in. I dare say it'll be brief enough.'

What could Dan say? Who was he to take something so important away from Mick? And anyway, he was right. Why break Clare's heart ahead of time? He bit his lip. 'Okay, Mick. You have your time.' He reached over and grasped the old man's hand. 'Anything you need, it's yours,' he said, his voice breaking. 'Anything at all.'

A welcome, familiar twinkle came into Mick's eye. 'You going to eat that pie, lad?'

Dan pushed his plate across, and idly took a chip. The food lodged in his throat, choking him. He forced it down.

'What about Fleur, eh?' said Mick. He hoed into the flaky pastry. 'Here I am wasting my time, sending her over to Macca's horse, when all along she's got a thing for Goliath. Or maybe there's something more than methane in the water over at Quimby, eh Dan?'

Dan gave him a sharp look. Was that a dig at him? He decided to change the subject. 'Looks like you'll be getting yourself a clydie-percheron colt next year. Could be nice cross.'

'You'll have to look after that little 'un for me,' said Mick. 'I won't be around to see it.'

Oh. What a fool he was. 'I'm sorry —' Dan started to say.

Mick held up his hand. 'The reality hasn't sunk in for you yet. God knows, it takes a while. I don't want you walking on eggshells around me. Promise?'

Dan felt the unfamiliar stab of tears behind his eyes. 'Promise.'

'There's something else I'd like from you,' said Mick. 'Other than your pie.' There was that twinkle again. 'I want you to come and live at Currawong. There's plenty of room, and Clare will need somebody when I go. You are serious about my granddaughter, aren't you son?'

'I'm going to marry her,' said Dan.

Mick raised his eyebrows. 'Does Clare know?'

'Not yet,' Dan said with a grin. 'It's early days. Wouldn't want to scare her off.'

Mick nodded approvingly. 'Take it slow, Dan. Take it slow.' He stubbed out his cigarette. 'Will you do it then? Will you move into the house?'

'Just try and stop me …'

Mick let out a long relieved sigh. 'Come on then, lad. Let's get back to Currawong. See if Clare has got little Jack back. I can tell you, Dan, that girl's going to need you more than ever if Taylor takes the boy away.'

Dan nodded. It would hurt Clare to lose Jack now. It would really hurt, but he'd be there for her. Mick could depend on him to stay right by her side.

CHAPTER 28

Clare sat out on the verandah, watching the sun rise towards its zenith, grasping for a handle on her seething emotions. Vignettes of her and Dan together in the garden at Quimby Downs crowded her mind.

Samson stood on watch beside her. Jack still wasn't back. Clare ignored the kernel of fear buried deep in her belly, buried behind the images of her and Dan and the sweet smell of the grass beneath them. Nothing would go wrong today. Jack would be home soon, she just knew it. The phone in the hall rang. Clare tripped over Samson in her rush to answer it. Hallelujah, it was Taylor.

'We're just about to leave Dalby,' said Taylor.

Dalby was an hour away. It still seemed like forever to wait, but in the mood Clare was in, it was easy to stay positive. They were on their way home, that was the main thing.

'How's Jack?' asked Clare.

'He's okay.' Taylor sounded doubtful. Was that a child yelling in the background? 'He's been naughty though ... in a shop. Can you speak to the lady?'

'Hello?' An unfamiliar voice came on the phone. 'I'm Jane Palmer. I own the gift shop in Main Street, Dalby. There's a little boy here who's done some damage. Broken quite a lot of china. My husband has had to restrain him to let his mother make this call or else there'd be nothing left intact in the store.' The woman stopped talking, giving Clare time for the information to sink in. 'His mother says you know her?'

'Yes,' said Clare swiftly. 'Yes, I know her.'

'She says you might be prepared to pay for the damage and the stolen item. Otherwise, I'm calling the police. I'm afraid she allowed the boy to leave with a ceramic figurine hidden beneath his shirt.'

Taylor was on a good behaviour bond. A theft charge would be a breach of that order. It would be so easy to put her back in court. So easy to put Taylor out of contention for custody. But that wasn't the way that she wanted to win Jack. 'Yes, of course. I'll pay. Let me fetch my credit card.' Ten minutes and five hundred dollars later, Clare hung up the phone. It didn't matter about the money. All that mattered was that Jack came home and, from the sound of things, that was what Taylor wanted too. Clare turfed the dogs from the kitchen and took some cold meat from the fridge. A few biscuits on a plate wouldn't be enough. Taylor would need something more substantial before she began the long drive back to Brisbane. Clare pulled out lettuce, some tomatoes, and began buttering slices of bread.

Dan. A momentary lapse in concentration and the insistent idea of him almost chased Jack from her thoughts. Sex with Dan had been mind-blowingly amazing. Clare considered herself a woman of the world. She'd had her fair share of lovers. Adam had been the best of them – up until yesterday. Adam was experienced and considerate in bed. He took an immense degree of pride in his work, for that was how he approached it. More than once, when their relationship hit a rough patch, Adam's talent in the bedroom had brought her back to him. Hands down the best make-up sex she'd ever had. The best sex she'd ever had, for that matter.

But now? Now Clare knew she'd just been going through the motions. Adam was a skilled technician, nothing more. By contrast, sex with Dan was a wild, multi-dimensional ride, her lust and emotions tangled together so tightly that they could not be undone. Never before had she so truly inhabited each inch of her body. A constant, all-consuming desire for him ran through her veins, blotting everything else out. At times it even blotted out her yearning for Jack. And to top it off, in the soft afterglow, Dan had said that he loved her. He'd confessed it so earnestly, so early, so convincingly. He'd taken her completely by surprise. No matter how involved Adam was in the moment, no matter how many times an *I love* you was ripped from his ecstatic body, there had always been a time of him pulling away afterwards. How she'd craved for Adam to say those three words and really mean them. How she'd hoped it might be more than sex and convenience.

But Dan? Dan turned her inside out with emotional and physical passion, then calmly announced that he loved her, as if it was the most normal thing in the world. She hadn't believed it at the time. It had been too soon, too unexpected, but she tingled now at the memory. This is what she'd been missing. A straightforward, genuine man who wore his heart on his sleeve. A man who rejoiced in simple animal pleasure, then fell in love just as naturally. Clare laughed out loud with the sheer delight of it all.

The phone rang again. What sort of trouble had Taylor got herself into now? But it wasn't Taylor. It was Adam. Adam, who thought himself such a stud in bed. Adam, who didn't actually have a clue about the rapturous, satisfying experience that was top sex. She banished another image of the sunlight on Dan's bare back, and tried to concentrate on the call.

'How are things?' She guessed already that things weren't good. There was a side of Adam she hadn't seen before - a fragile, needy side. His text messages invariably described how low he felt and begged her to come back to Brisbane. *We could try again*, he'd say. *This time will different*. Clare had ignored them. They weren't in the spirit of 'staying friends'. Time to end this pretense; it was only giving him false hope. Still, part of her would miss talking to him. It offered a window on the world back in Brisbane, a chance to catch up on the latest legal news. Currawong was heaven on earth, no doubt about it.

She loved the space and the silence, but she remained curious about her old life.

'How's your new job?' she asked.

'Boring as watching two flies crawl up the wall.' He snorted. 'God, I miss it, Clare … the challenge of the courtroom. The thrill of it. Pyramid have got me monitoring compliance, advising on law changes that might impact their business, drafting contracts, that sort of thing. It's deadly dull."

Clare froze. Pyramid Energy? Adam was working for the enemy? 'What are you doing right now?'

'Redrafting confidentiality clauses on their contracts with land-holders. Strengthening penalties. By the time I'm finished, those poor saps will be tied down so tight they won't be able to tell their mother what they had for breakfast without being sued.'

She felt her jaw tense. *It's not Adam's fault,* she told herself. It's his job. In the same circumstances she'd do the same thing. If she hadn't been to Quimby Downs, that was. If she hadn't seen the water there turn to liquid fire. If she didn't know that a man named Pete Porter, her grandfather's dear old friend, was living out his twilight years in effective exile. Forced from the graceful homestead he'd built with his own hands, forced to leave his land, his livelihood, his community, his connections … and threatened with loss of his compensation payout if he complained.

The dogs began to bark. Was Jack home? 'I have to go,' said Clare.

'So soon? When the hell are you coming back to Brisbane? I miss my job, Clare, but I miss you more.'

Absence, apparently, really did make the heart grow fonder. Or was it merely Adam's ego still smarting from their breakup? But she didn't ask him to stop calling. She didn't ask him to stop his lovelorn texts. It was just too intriguing, him working for Pyramid. So instead she said, 'Good to hear from you, Adam. Don't be a stranger.'

Jack burst in the door and hurled himself into her arms. She fell to her knees and embraced him, speechless with delight. Samson arrived and covered them both with doggy kisses. Jack squealed and hugged him tight. 'Samsam,' he declared, and turned to Taylor. 'Mummy,

Samsam.' The young woman stood uncertainly in the doorway. She looked like she'd been crying.

'He's happy to see you,' said Taylor. It was part observation, part accusation. Clare wrested herself away from Jack, leaving him wrestling on the floor with Samson. 'That's a nice dog,' said Taylor. 'I like dogs. So does Jack.' She took out a packet of cigarettes. 'Can I smoke?'

It was ironic. Taylor had run off to have a cigarette when they'd first met and Clare had wound up with Jack. How grateful she was for that now. Maybe Taylor would do it again. Go out for a cigarette and not come back. Part of Clare wanted that, a big part, but then she looked at the girl's drawn face. She looked utterly exhausted. 'Go on,' said Clare. She looked for a saucer in the kitchen dresser to use as an ashtray, and found something unexpected: a proper ashtray. It was tucked in behind Grandad's little teapot, the one he used when making a cuppa just for himself. She put it on the table. Taylor gave her a nervous smile and lit up. Clare pulled out a chair, indicating for Taylor to sit. 'Coffee?' After a few moments hesitation, the girl nodded and took a seat. 'Are you hungry?' Clare put on the kettle and took the plate of sandwiches from the fridge.

'I think he missed your dog.' Taylor pulled a small, pottery German shepherd dog from her bag. 'Now I know why he took this.' She pushed the figurine towards Clare. 'It's yours now.'

Clare poured two coffees and sat down. 'Thank you.' She ran a finger down the little dog's smooth back.

'I saw that hot guy again down the drive. Dan. Why's he got a rifle?' asked Taylor.

'He's a vet,' said Clare. 'My grandfather has an old cow that's sick…'

'So, what, he's going to shoot it?' asked Taylor.

'He's going to put it out of its misery.'

'That poor cow.' Taylor looked like she was going cry.

'There's something I want to ask you,' said Clare softly. 'Jack's father … is he dead?'

Taylor nodded, her expression hard to read. 'An overdose. Jacky found him ... He was only two, he wouldn't remember.'

The little boy heard his name and ran over, cheeks rosy with excitement. 'Bikkies?' Clare took a tin down from the cupboard and gave the boy two malt-o-milks, one for Samson and one for himself. 'Ta,' said Jack, and began playing keepings off with Samson, who seemed determined to get both biscuits. She offered the tin to Taylor, who took two as well and dipped one in her coffee.

'Now there's something I want to ask you,' said Taylor. 'How do you do it - get him to behave so well I mean? What's the trick?'

The question caught her off guard. 'It's not that simple,' said Clare. How to describe in a few sentences the fraught process that had underpinned Jack's progress? So much had been trial and error. All the puzzling and problem-solving. All the time and thought and gentle boundary setting. Samson and Currawong and Dan's amazing equine therapy - with maybe a bit of magic thrown in. All these things had played their part.

'Jack was real good when I picked him up,' said Taylor. 'Talking and everything. But he went crazy at the circus, yelling and kicking people. By this morning he'd stopped speaking. I couldn't get him to do anything. Then he trashed that shop ...'

'I think it's mainly this place,' said Clare. 'All the room ... and he loves Samson, and the other animals.'

Taylor nodded. 'I always wanted to get him a dog.' She butted out her cigarette and took a sandwich. 'I told you he liked dogs, didn't I?'

'You did,' agreed Clare.

'Could you teach me how to do it?' asked Taylor.

'Do what?'

'Get Jack to do what I say?'

'I said it's not that simple.'

'You just don't want me to know,' said Taylor. 'You don't want me to have Jack.'

There was plenty of truth in that last bit, but Clare felt obliged to protest.

Jack came over and climbed on her knee. 'Don't fight,' he said and pinched Clare's lips together.

'You tell her, Jacky,' said Taylor, looking pleased with her son.

Jack ducked under the table and appeared on Taylor's knee. The girl tried to cuddle him, but he hit her in the face and ran off. Taylor's face fell and Clare's heart went out to her. 'I didn't know much about kids at first either,' she said, 'but I did read a lot about parenting.' Clare went into the lounge room and came back with a book. She gave it to Taylor. '*Transforming the Difficult Child.* You can have it if you like.'

Taylor's face lit up with pleasure. 'So this taught you how to get Jack to behave?'

'It was a big help,' said Clare.

'I'm not usually that great with books,' said Taylor. 'But I'll read this one. I don't care how long it takes me.'

Clare couldn't help but like this girl.

'I'd better get going,' said Taylor. 'Can I take some sandwiches?'

Clare stood up and packed two rounds of sandwiches in a paper bag. She threw in some biscuits, a banana and a boxed juice. Taylor needed someone to look after her almost as much as Jack did.

'Um, can I borrow some petrol money? Twenty dollars would do.' Clare found her bag and handed over a fifty. 'Thanks,' said Taylor. 'Bye, Jacky. Mummy has to go.'

Jack ran over and wrapped himself about her leg, just like he used to do with Clare. 'I'll see you soon, Jacky. Be good now. Maybe Mummy could ring you up and tell you a bed-time story one night?' She opened up the little boy's clenched fist and put her lips to the palm of his hand. 'Put this kiss under your pillow for when you need it.' She closed his fingers. Jack stared at his hand for a second and then punched her.

Taylor looked pleadingly at Clare, who helped her disengage the little boy. Jack ran to the corner, where he began to rhythmically bang his head against the wall, accompanied by an angry singsong wail. 'Just go,' said Clare. Taylor disappeared out the door, face white as a sheet. A few seconds later the old Holden coughed to life and roared off. Taylor must have lost her muffler somewhere. Clare went to sit on the floor beside Jack. He hadn't behaved like this in weeks, but she knew better than to interrupt him until he calmed down. Every time his head hit the wall, she flinched.

Samson trotted over, whining his displeasure. Firstly he squeezed in between her and Jack, and then between him and the plasterboard, so that the little boy's head thumped into his soft back instead of against the hard wall. 'Good boy,' said Clare, stroking Samson's fur. A few head bangs later, Jack collapsed against Samson and started to cry. Proper crying, with proper tears. Clare heaved a big, relieved sigh. She knew how to help Jack back from this. She'd done it before. Her thoughts turned to Taylor driving home to Brisbane, smoking and eating sandwiches. Clare imagined her reading the book. She suddenly wished she hadn't felt so sorry for Taylor, wished she hadn't given her that book. What was it her father had always told her? Yes, that was it. No good deed goes unpunished.

CHAPTER 29

Swathes of sweet-scented wattle perfumed Bronwyn's bush garden. Bright blossoms abounded: magenta callistemon, scarlet grevilleas and a colourful collage of day lilies. High up in the air, Clare could hear the refrain of a butcherbird piping a tune; on the ground, the buzz of bees on nectar-laden flowers. Merriang in late October was truly glorious.

Clare sat out on the verandah with Bronwyn, watching Jack and Timmy play in the wading pool. Samson kept leaping in and out, showering the boys with water and provoking squeals of delight. 'I hope you don't mind me bringing Samson along.' They both smiled as Jack tipped a bucketful of water over the dog's head. 'Those two are inseparable,' said Clare. Samson shook himself in a rainbow of spray, showering Jack with water all over again. Jack screamed with laughter, and chased Samson from the pool.

'I can see that,' said Bronwyn. 'Timmy loves Samson too. He'll miss him when you go back to Brisbane.' She indicated the fresh pot of brewed coffee on the table. Clare poured herself a cup.

'I'm not going back.'

Bronwyn gave her a searching look. 'But that job you were telling me about. That dream job ... You can't just turn your back on it.'

'Why not?'

Bronwyn stared.

'Go, on.' Clare didn't mean to sound defensive, but that was how it was coming out. 'Tell me why I can't turn my back on that job?'

Bronwyn's mouth gaped, but for a few moments nothing came out. She twisted a stray lock of dark hair in her fingers. 'I wanted to go to university, you know. I wanted to study fine arts. Had fantasies about being some sort of designer.'

'What happened?' asked Clare.

'The course was too expensive. Dad sent me to the agricultural college in Dalby instead. I met Jordy, got married and landed right back on the land where I started. I'm not complaining, mind you. I love it here, but part of me always wonders what would have happened if I'd moved to Brisbane after school and studied art.'

Clare sipped her coffee. Was Bronwyn right? Would she regret her decision to stay? Sometimes it did seem like a mad choice, to throw away all that Paul Dunbar offered. Then she thought of Jack and Dan and her grandfather, and she was sure that leaving Currawong would be the truly mad choice.

'Everybody's different,' said Clare. 'And I didn't say it was an easy decision, but we can all play the *what if* game. Maybe you'd have been miserable studying in Brisbane. Maybe you'd have been deliriously happy. How will you ever know? One thing's for sure, you wouldn't have Timmy.'

'I know,' said Bronwyn, 'And of course I wouldn't be without him, or Jordy. But to tell you the truth, I was pretty jealous when I heard of your brilliant career. I was so impressed by your ambition.'

'I think it's easier for us than for our mothers,' said Clare. 'Mine studied accounting and always wanted a career. I think she resented having me and Ryan because we got in the way. Mum left us when I was eleven.'

Bronwyn whistled. 'That's tough.'

'It was different for her generation. She thought she was a failure for *just* being a mother,' said Clare. 'I'm not like her. I don't have anything to prove.'

'I never thought about it like that,' said Bronwyn. 'It came as a shock, that's all, to think that someone like you would rather have my sort of life.'

Timmy and Jack ran over and helped themselves to homemade muffins.

'Merriang can't be that bad after all, eh?' said Bronwyn.

'No,' said Clare, taking a muffin before the kids finished them. 'Merriang is paradise.'

Bronwyn was beaming now. 'I should appreciate what I've got,' she said. 'Don't take any notice of me. It sounds like I'm trying to talk you into leaving, when that's the last thing I want.'

'Isn't it funny,' said Clare, 'how we always think the grass is greener on the other side? She topped up her coffee cup. 'Dan's moving into the homestead tomorrow.' Bronwyn shot her a smile as if to say, *Well, that explains everything.*

CHAPTER 30

Sunday morning, and she and Dan would be living under the same roof by nightfall. Clare had been gearing up to ask whether he could come and stay, but before she did, her grandfather had made the offer. *I've given the back room to Dan,* he'd said. *It makes sense for him to be here.* She could have kissed him. The thought of having Dan so close all of the time sent a quiver through her. Clare poured herself a cup of tea. 'Want another cuppa, Grandad?'

'No thanks, love. Got a bit of a headache. I'm going to have a lie down.'

He'd had too many headaches lately. Clare took her tea onto the verandah as Dan's jeep came up the drive. He'd already made a trip to bring his things over from Bonnie's. He certainly travelled light. One suitcase, two green garbage bags full of who-knew-what, and a dog kennel. But then he'd gone out again for some reason. Red bounced along the path ahead of Dan as he climbed the steps to the verandah. He carried a big bucket and a bag of groceries.

Clare followed him into the kitchen. 'What have you got there?'

'Where's Jack?' he asked.

'Digging in the sandpit with Samson.'

Clare looked into the bucket on the floor. It contained a pile of large nuts, like the ones she'd found in the Currawong box at the top of her wardrobe.

'Boiled bunya nuts,' said Dan. 'I'm cooking bunya nut pie for dinner, but I need Jacky.'

'Why?' asked Clare.

'You'll see,' said Dan. He went back to the jeep and returned with a big hammer and a small mallet. 'You haven't lived until you've made bunya nut pie, Currawong style.' He pulled an ancient cookbook from the shelf. It was one of Grandma's, with favourite pages still encased in plastic sleeves. He flipped to the page he wanted, then unpacked the grocery bag: onions, leeks, broccoli, sweet potato, carrots, and cream. 'Mick showed me the recipe,' he said, 'It's all in the preparation.' He chose a knife from the block and expertly sliced a carrot. Impressive. The man could cook as well. Dan took some eggs from the fridge. 'Duck out to the veggie patch and get me a capsicum and some tomatoes will you…? And mushrooms. See if Mick's got any under the house. About two cupfuls.'

Clare fetched the old wicker harvest basket her grandmother once used. She touched his shoulder as she passed him and felt a familiar tug of desire. Dan looked so at home in Currawong's kitchen, and she loved how well he fitted in, but part of her longed for it to be just him and her. Between Jacky, Grandad and the surgery, it was difficult to steal time alone.

Clare returned with the fresh garden vegetables and got to work on the chopping board, casting the odd sneak peek at Dan. She loved the way his tongue poked out slightly when he concentrated. She loved his steady hand as he brought down the knife on a sweet potato. For a while they sliced and diced in companionable silence. Occasionally Dan pointed to a line in the recipe, and Clare wordlessly set about the indicated task. She put the leeks, broccoli and sweet potatoes on to steam.

'I'll go get Jacky.' said Dan. 'We'll need him for this next bit.' Clare washed the sharp knives and put them away, wondering how a four-year-old could help. And what were the hammers and nuts for? A few minutes later Jack and Samson burst through the door, with Dan chasing after. They were all laughing, even Samson. The dog, tongue lolling, wore a distinctly self-satisfied grin.

Jack's attention was drawn to the big bucket by the door. Dan took down a heavy cast-iron pan from the shelf. He cleared the sink, then tipped out a cascade of nuts into it. Next, he played some sort of magic trick, extracting a nut from behind the little boy's ear. Jack's face glowed with delight. 'Nothing up my sleeve,' Dan said, and another nut materialised from Jack's pocket. Now Clare was laughing too. Dan gave her a swift kiss and, with great ceremony, placed a single nut onto the worn, timber tabletop. 'Now watch me,' said Dan. He hefted the big hammer and smashed it down on the unsuspecting nut with an enormous bang. Jack squealed and Clare screamed. The shell lay splattered around its smashed heart. Dan picked out the bits of kernel and threw them into the pan.

Grandad emerged from the hall. 'What the bloody hell's going on?' he said. 'I'd just nodded off.'

Dan chose another nut with a flourish, put it on the table and gave it the same treatment. '*Only way to make bunya nut pie.* Isn't that what you said, Mick?'

Grandad chuckled. 'Did you boil them well, son?'

'Boiled them to billy-o,' said Dan.

'Go on,' said Grandad. 'Do another one.' Dan obliged. Bits of shell skimmed along the floor, providing Samson with a lovely game. The dog slid along the floorboards after the woody pieces, pouncing and wolfing them down. 'That's one way to get your fibre,' said Grandad.

Clare captured Samson by his collar and hauled him outside. When she returned, Jack was standing on a chair at the kitchen table, a look of glee on his face, and brandishing the small mallet in his hand. Dan deposited a nut in front of the little boy. 'Drum roll, please.' It didn't seem right to teach the little boy to bash things with hammers. Clare started to speak, but Dan held up his hand for silence. 'Objection dismissed,' he said with mock solemnity. 'Think of it as an exercise in hand-eye coordination.' Clare smiled, felt her stomach flip over again at the sight of Dan, and held her tongue. Jack was poking the nut with his mallet; it skittered around the table. Dan observed for a while, then put his own nut on the table. Jack stopped to watch him smash his target to smithereens, then, with a determined glare, planted both hands firmly along the handle of his mallet.

'Keep your eye on the nut,' advised Grandad.

With a sweep of his arms, the little boy scored a bullseye, caving in the hard shell and exposing the creamy white kernel beneath.

'Bravo, Jack,' cried Grandad. 'Bravo. That's the same technique your uncle Ryan would use — the double-fisted slammer.'

A memory crept into Clare's consciousness. A memory of Grandad and Ryan, jumping and shouting and slamming away in the kitchen. She tried to catch hold of the recollection; it threatened to slip away like a half-remembered dream. There, she had it again. She was a child, with her hands over her ears and a big grin on her face. Grandma was there too, laughing until she cried, but always a little shy to pick up the hammer.

'I want a shot,' said Clare.

'Good on you, love,' said Grandad.

Dan placed a nut in position. She lined it up and delivered a killer blow, splitting the shell in one shot, and leaving the kernel exposed and intact. It took more force than she'd expected.

Grandad clapped. 'That's the way. Not too hard. Not like this mad bugger.' He pointed to Dan. 'There's nothing much left after he finishes. And not too soft, or you'll never get through it.'

She gave him a thumbs up. This was a lot of fun. 'More nuts,' she said. Soon she and Jack were yelling and thumping and laughing. Grandad and Dan were an enthusiastic audience, rescuing the kernels and throwing them into the pan.

Grandad took the hammer and held up a nut. 'I name this nut *Pyramid Energy*.' Bang, it was gone.

'Let me,' said Clare. Soon she was smashing her way through all the people and institutions in life of which she did not approve.

Dan raised his eyebrows. 'You have a long hit list.'

'And I haven't finished yet,' she said, through tears of laughter. 'I name this nut *Adam*.' Bang. I name this nut *Veronica*.' Bang.

Was that the phone? Its ring was barely audible over the noise. She ran into the hall. 'Hello?' Nobody spoke, but there was somebody on the end of the line. She could hear them breathe. 'Hello? Who's there?'

'Clare? Is that you?' It was hard to hear over all the banging but she'd recognise that prim, self-righteous voice anywhere. It didn't make any sense, but Veronica was on the phone. *I just smashed you to bits,* Clare wanted to say, but restrained herself.

'Yes,' said Clare.

A long silence ensued. 'I found this number in Adam's phone,' said Veronica at last. 'I didn't know whose it was.'

Clare tried to make sense of Veronica's words. Why would she ring an unknown number she'd found in Adam's phone? And why did she have Adam's phone in the first place? Then it struck her. Of course. Veronica was still seeing him. Here was Adam, professing his undying love for Clare in every phone call, when he was still screwing around with Veronica.

'I'm wondering,' said Veronica, 'considering your very public breakup with Adam, why there have been a number of calls between his phone and this number ... your number.' There was a challenge in her voice. 'It's not been one-sided. Recently you've matched him, call for call.'

Of course Clare had. She'd been trying to get some dirt on Pyramid Energy, so far without success. 'I'm not seeing Adam, if that's what you're wondering,' said Clare. 'Not after what he did.' She couldn't resist a little dig. 'I wouldn't be so stupid.'

'No, I suppose you wouldn't,' said Veronica, her voice bitter, 'but I, evidently, would.'

Clare almost felt sorry for her.

'Is he ... is he pursuing you?'

'Yes,' said Clare. 'He is. At first he just asked if we could stay in touch.'

'Because he's so depressed and needs a friend,' said Veronica.

'Why yes. Then he said he loved me and what a mistake you'd been. He'd only been with you-'

'Because I threw myself at him and, hey, he's only human.'

'That's right,' said Clare. 'I guess he said the same thing about me?'

'Precisely. I can't believe I fell for it. I really can't believe it.'

A huge shout came from the kitchen, followed by a tremendous bang.

'What on earth's going on there?' asked Veronica.

How odd that particular explanation would sound. 'It's a bit hard to describe,' said Clare, 'but don't worry, everything's fine.' Veronica hung on the end of the phone without speaking. 'What about you?' said Clare. 'Are you okay?'

'I will be,' said Veronica. 'Once I get back at the bastard ... like you did.' This conversation was getting more and more intriguing . 'There were times I wasn't fair to you, Clare. I'm sorry.' Clare gasped. Veronica was famous for never apologising. 'Truth is, I was jealous. You're such a natural in court. You're brilliant.'

'This is insane,' said Clare. 'You always went out of your way to make me feel like an idiot.'

'I said I'm sorry,' said Veronica. She sounded genuine; even the tone of her voice had changed. 'I want you to forgive me for being such a bitch. I imagine you're the kind of person who can do that, Clare, the kind that's gracious in victory. And it's been a comprehensive victory, hasn't it. Adam, Paul Dunbar ... even Roderick. You're always the favourite.'

'Veronica —'

'Call me Ronnie. It's what my friends call me.'

'Okay ... Ronnie. This was never a competition.'

'No ... I suppose not,' said Ronnie, with an unhappy sigh. Clare took a deep breath. What other astounding things might her newfound friend say next?

'I was so in love with Adam that I couldn't see straight. Thoroughly, stupidly, blindly in love. I won't be able to sleep until I settle the score with that pig,' she said. 'And don't go all holier-than-thou on me, Clare. You swung some serious payback yourself. You destroyed his career. I do so wish *I'd* had that privilege.'

Clare was about to say that she hadn't planned it that way, that she'd behaved on an impulse, when she bit her tongue. Perhaps she could turn this bizarre situation to her advantage?

'Ronnie.' The nickname sounded wrong on her lips: too casual, too friendly. 'Adam's working for a coal seam gas company that wants to put wells on my grandfather's land. Under ordinary circumstances there's nothing Grandad can do to stop it.' Words spilled from her mouth as if they had a mind of their own. 'I've been pumping Adam for anything that might put a spanner in the works. Some sort of corporate non-compliance maybe, something that might trigger the unconscionable conduct provisions – whatever might slow the process down, or better yet, stop it altogether.'

'So that's why you've been calling him,' said Ronnie. 'Any luck?'

'Not yet,' said Clare. 'Listen.' Her tone was urgent and low. 'You want to get revenge? Then help me and my grandfather. Dig up some dirt on Pyramid Energy and leak it to me.'

'You mean spy on him?' asked Ronnie.

'That's exactly what I mean.'

'You're on.' The answer came clear and unambiguous, just as the ruckus in the kitchen reached a crescendo. 'What *is* that?' asked Ronnie.

'Hold on,' said Clare. 'Promise me you won't hang up.' She rushed down the hall and slammed the door. It would be impossible to draft a battle plan on the house phone. Too many curious ears. What she needed was some privacy. Tomorrow she'd drive to Dalby and get a new mobile. 'It'll be tough,' she told Ronnie. 'You'll be playing a charade. You said you love Adam.'

'I thought I did, yes. How foolish can a person be?'

'Don't do this if it hurts you,' said Clare. 'I shouldn't have asked.'

'It will hurt more if I don't do it,' said Ronnie. 'Now, tell me more about these gas wells ...'

CHAPTER 31

Dan put down the phone. 'Why is it,' said Dan, his voice raised in frustration, 'that the minute a vet touches an animal, he's held personally responsible for every bad thing that happens to it from that moment on? That was Ray Sharp. Yesterday I treated a cow of his that'd been sick for two weeks. Two bloody weeks. I almost told him to ring his neighbour instead, the one that had been doling out free but completely useless advice ever since the cow went down. I get there and can see straight off that she's going to die. They've pulled her dead calf using a bloody tractor and then left her all this time with a torn uterus.'

Clare put the kettle on. She hated hearing these stories. The life and death of a production animal could indeed be a brutal one. But she knew how much it helped Dan to have a sounding board. He felt for each and every one of his patients, no matter how hopeless their case, no matter how close to the end of their life they might be. It was one of the reasons that she loved him. The bell over the door rang. Another client on an already busy Thursday surgery.

'The cow was in shock,' he continued. 'Covered with flies … her body racked with infection.' Clare put her hand on his arm. 'I told him straight out that she'd die. *Let me put her out of her misery*. But no. To hear Ray tell it, that poor cow that he'd left untreated for weeks — that cow suddenly meant the world to him. So I did what I could: painkillers, intravenous fluids, anti-inflammatories, antibiotics.' Clare pressed a coffee into his hand. 'That was him on the phone. The cow died last night. He says I must have killed her, so he's not paying the bill. Next time I'm at the produce store, it'll be *I hear one of Ray's best cows had calving trouble. He got you out and it died.*'

Clare wrapped her arms around Dan's neck and kissed him. Even here, with him in scrubs and clients waiting, she still felt the sizzle when their skin touched. 'Nobody with any sense listens to Ray.'

'Maybe so, but unfortunately there's a heap of folks without any sense around here.'

She smiled. 'Lucky you happen to have a waiting room packed with sensible people then.' He gave her a wry grin and called in the next patient.

Clare was settling down to the thankless task of sending out bill reminders, when the phone rang. Ronnie again. It was two weeks now since that first conversation about Adam. Since then they'd been in constant touch, partly to discuss industrial espionage strategy, and partly because Ronnie needed a friend, and friends were apparently a bit thin on the ground back in Brisbane.

It was still hard for Clare to get her head around it. That the stylish and sophisticated Veronica Fisher had been jealous of her. This new Ronnie was embracing their fledgling friendship. She'd even forgiven Clare for snatching the Paul Dunbar readership out from under her. 'You're better than me, right now anyway, but I won't give up,' she'd said. 'I'm going to stick it out at the Valley for another year ... see what happens after that.' Clare was impressed. She was even more impressed with Ronnie's enthusiasm for her new role as a spy.

Clare took her call in the hospital ward, under the curious gaze of an epileptic poodle and a sick swan. 'I've hit pay dirt,' said Ronnie. 'Something that will knock your socks off.'

'Fantastic,' said Clare. 'What have you got?'

'A risk management report Adam used to draft gag clauses in settlement agreements. It's backed up by over a hundred cases of contamination and other damage caused by fracked wells.' Clare sucked in a quick breath. 'Listen to this. *Pyramid Energy must be protected from liability for aquifer contamination caused by recent surface spills and operations underground.* And this. *The fluids involved contain heavy metals, toxic minerals, chemical additives and known carcinogens.* I'm telling you, this stuff is gold.'

'How'd you get it?'

'I stayed at his place last night. Adam left his laptop on when he went for a run. It was all there: the report, PDFs of each case file, everything.'

Clare couldn't help it. She pictured his South Bank apartment. Adam going for his seven o'clock run by the river. The laptop set up by the window with the view to the gardens. But instead of her being there, waiting for the customary gourmet dinner for two which would arrive at precisely eight o'clock – instead of her, there was Ronnie. Ronnie in her place, scrolling through Adam's documents, glancing at the door, slipping in a memory stick to save the damning evidence of Pyramid's treachery.

'Are you okay?' asked Clare.

'I don't know yet. Part of me is over the moon, and the rest of me wants to cry.'

'What are you going to do now? Can you bear to stay with Adam a bit longer? If you dump him now, he'll guess.'

'I suppose you're right. It might be fun to stick around and watch the fallout.'

Dan came in, followed by an elegant Afghan hound. 'Will you weigh Fatima please?'

She held up her hand for him to be quiet. 'Can you email the info through to me?' Clare asked Ronnie.

'Done,' she said. 'It's on its way.'

'I owe you one, Ronnie,' said Clare. 'More than one, actually.' She sank back in her chair, giddy with excitement and disbelief.

Dan regarded her curiously. 'You okay?' he asked. 'Should I be jealous of this Ronnie character?'

She jumped up and slapped a kiss on him. 'No,' said Clare. 'You should be thanking *her* instead. And don't use the internet for a bit. I'm expecting a big download.'

THAT EVENING, Clare lay in bed, trawling through the information Ronnie had sent her. It really was too good to be true. Dan made an effort to tempt her out, even once tried to get into bed with her, but she chased him off. She only had eyes for the report – the report that laid out Pyramid's long-term concerns about public health, pollution and potential compensation claims. Examples were given, backed up by detailed case studies. A school located in a heavily drilled area with asthma rates ten times the state average. A well site blowout that spewed methane for sixteen hours. A drunken dozer driver who accidentally released thousands of litres of chemical-laced wastewater into nearby creeks. Wells contaminated by methane and benzene. The list was endless and she knew just who to give it to.

Clare skimmed through the conclusion. *Area managers will project pollution catastrophe scenarios for their regions to ensure Pyramid has sufficient insurance to cover the costs of these types of events ... comprehensive, iron-clad confidentiality clauses will be used in settlement agreements to gag potential claimants.* She lay back in bed, listening to the night time serenade of frogs on the dam. Her dream came back to her, the one where a black stain had fouled the prehistoric waters of the Great Artesian Basin before the vortex drained it dry. That nightmare would never come true. Not if she could help it.

Grandad poked his head around the door. 'Not often you hit you hit the sack before me, Clare Bear. Is everything all right?'

Clare jumped out of bed and hugged him tight. 'Everything's better than all right,' she said. 'Everything's perfect.'

THE NEXT MORNING Clare began calling. Gordon McCrae had been surprisingly accessible. Less than an hour of ringing around and she had the man himself on the phone.

'I have a leaked Pyramid Energy report,' she told him, 'documenting a cover-up of contamination in the Darling Downs gas fields.'

'Email me the material,' said Gordon. 'I'll be in touch if there's anything in it.'

Clare did as he asked, then sat down to wait. Gordon was a busy man. He might not look at the documents straightaway. It might take weeks for him to get back to her. Maybe she should go directly to the media. She tried to distract herself by tackling one of Grandad's half-finished crosswords. *Another word for blessing?* Seven letters ... with D as third and last letter? The phone rang just as she penciled *godsend* into the squares.

'Clare Mitchell?' It was Gordon. 'That report you sent me ... it makes very disturbing reading. I'll be raising it in parliament next week.'

'Will it stop the expansion of the gas fields?'

'There's every chance,' he said. 'When people see this, it'll be a brand new ball game.'

Gordon rang off. Clare sat for a while, trying to grasp the implications of what he'd told her. Every chance, he'd said. There was also every chance that Pyramid would trace the leaked documents back to Adam. She felt a twinge of regret, but then hardened her heart. It couldn't be helped. Adam had made his bed ... let him lie in it.

Clare went to find her grandfather. He was in the lounge room, going through stud records. 'Grandad? I think you'd better sit down.' She waited until he was settled in his favourite old armchair. Claire took a place on the frayed couch and launched into her news.

The story was hard to tell. She was leaving bits out, some of them on purpose, and talking too fast. Her grandfather listened in silence, occasionally tugging at his ear. 'So,' she concluded, 'Gordon McCrae says there's a good chance that this could stop the gas wells.' Clare wet her lips and waited, wound tight, awaiting his response.

A slow smile crinkled across his face. 'I can't believe you did this,' he said, his voice quivering. 'For me, for Currawong.'

Clare felt a catch in her throat. The emotion in her grandfather's voice overwhelmed her. If she could do this, if she could save Currawong, it would be some kind of atonement. She sat on the arm of his chair and buried her face in his shoulder.

When she looked up there was a joyful light in his eyes. 'I'll not ask you how you came by this report,' he said. 'There are some things a grandfather shouldn't know about his granddaughter, eh?'

She gave him a grateful smile. God, how she loved this old man.

CHAPTER 32

Sunday morning, first day of November. Spring sauntered towards summer, but it was still cold this early at Currawong, lying as it did in the shadow of the Bunya range. Early sunbeams streamed in the window, bathing the room in a cool, golden glow. Clare stretched, then snuggled back beneath the blankets

Dan's silly secret knock came at the door, and he slipped in. He wore satin boxers sporting a serpent design, and carried a plate of mangos, sliced checkerboard fashion, and a damp facecloth. He sat on her bed and they feasted on the luscious fruit in silence, exchanging glances. Juice ran down her chin. Occasionally he stroked her face and décolletage with firm sweeps of the washer, lingering on the swell of her breasts. He kissed her mouth, tasting of sweetness and sun and sin. She shivered. Jacky could burst in the door any minute. That was the only reason Clare didn't pull Dan into her bed then and there.

In some ways, having him under the same roof was more frustrating than having him at Bonnie's. He was always so tantalisingly close. Sunning himself half-naked on the lawn after a swim in the dam. Working with Jack and Sparky in the ménage, a look of calm concentration on his rugged face. Playing fetch with Red. Swinging in after work in his sexy scrubs – it didn't matter; Clare had the permanent hots for him, and he for her. But the old Currawong homestead wasn't a big house. It didn't have thick walls. It didn't offer much privacy. Their rendezvous were limited to when Grandad took Jack out on morning paddock rounds or late at night, when they hoped the others were asleep.

Even then, they couldn't be certain of uninterrupted time together. Grandad might be away for ten minutes or two hours; he was notoriously unpredictable. 'The old bugger's doing it on purpose,' complained Dan once, while putting on his trousers, hopping around on one leg and swearing. Then there were the *walk-ins* at the surgery. Depending on how urgent the case or how pushy the client, these often ended up at the house when the surgery was closed.

So far their close encounters had happened mainly in the cart shed, among the hay bales, beneath the massive, gleaming harnesses hanging on the wall. They closed the high timber doors for privacy and to keep the curious dogs at bay. Dan's bare body, the sight and scent and feel of it, was inextricably linked in Clare's mind to summer gardens and the warm smell of hay and saddle leather. They had swift, silent, urgent sex in the dark. It was about as far as it could be from the slow, sensuous lovemaking that Clare craved. But even so, these hurried trysts with Dan were more exciting than anything she'd known before. Without fail they left her restless and hungry for more.

Dan's fingers slipped the strap of her singlet from her shoulder, just as Jack rocketed in the door, followed by his shadow, Samson. The pair leaped onto the bed and Jack started his favourite tickling game. Clare took refuge beneath the covers and Dan rescued her by hoisting Jack aloft, so his wriggling fingers couldn't reach. 'I think she deserves a Sunday sleep-in,' said Dan. 'How about I take you for a ride on Sparky?'

'My pony,' yelled Jack. 'My pony.'

Clare emerged from beneath the blankets and whispered a thank you.

'No worries,' said Dan. He gave her a quick kiss and shepherded the little boy and his dog from the room.

That old adage about it taking a village to raise a child made perfect sense to Clare now. You needed other people to share the load: Grandad, Dan, Bronwyn and Timmy — even Samson. They preserved her sanity, and Jack needed extended family and friends around as much as she did. Each person showed the child a different way of being in the world. How did she ever think she could have managed him all by herself in Brisbane, just her and the Happy Elves? It seemed so stupid to her now. She yawned, snuggled back down onto her pillow and closed her eyes. Life was good.

LATER, over breakfast, Clare watched Grandad. He seemed years younger. The furrows had fallen from his face and been replaced with smile lines. Gordon McCrae and that leaked report was all he could talk about.

'I'm mighty grateful to you, love. Mighty grateful,' he said for the umpteenth time. Simple words for so heartfelt a sentiment. 'You've given me a whole new lease of life.' He piled an extra helping of bacon on his hot, buttered toast.

'Happy to help,' she said, feeling a warm glow of pride. She gave her grandfather's bony shoulders a big bear hug, then stood him at arm's length to examine his face. 'Have you been smoking?' The faint, acrid smell of cigarettes clung to his clothes.

'Won't lie to you, love. Sid gave me a packet of Drum. Just been having the odd one every now and then, I swear.'

'The *odd one* is one too many,' said Clare. 'After all the effort you said you put into giving up. Maybe that's why you're getting those headaches.'

'Funny thing is,' said Grandad, 'the fags seem to help.'

'Don't give me excuses,' she said, unable to stay stern. 'You're old enough to know better.'

'That I am, love,' he said, with a chuckle. 'Where's Jacky?'

'Having a lesson on Sparky.'

Grandad scowled. 'Well, tell Dan to get the lad back here,' he said. 'I'm handling Bessie's new foal today. It'll be a real treat for the boy.'

'Sorry,' she said firmly. 'Jack's got a play date with Timmy. I'm really looking forward to spending the morning with him.' She shook her head. 'Between you and Dan, I barely get a look-in with that boy.' Her grandfather looked so put out, she gave him a kiss.

'That's enough of that lovey-dovey stuff.'

'Nonsense,' said Clare. 'You lap it up.'

He put his gnarled old hand over hers, where it rested on his shoulder. 'That I do, love' – a smile breaking through his frown – 'That I do.'

Out the window, a sparkling early summer day beckoned; fairy floss clouds floating in a sea-blue sky. Clare finished packing her bag and went out the screen door, just as the hall phone rang. Should she leave it? No, Grandad only heard the phone half the time these days. An important mare was coming to stud today. It might be the owners asking for directions. When on earth was Grandad going to get hearing aids? She ran back in. Grandad sat oblivious, lost in the latest *Heavy Horse World* magazine, newly arrived from the UK.

But when Clare answered the phone, she wished she hadn't. 'Kim?' A dart of fear pricked her happy mood. 'How are you?'

'We need to talk.'

Clare had never known good news to follow such a phrase. She braced herself.

'I've been approached by a solicitor representing Taylor Brown. She's suing for custody of Jack.'

It didn't make any sense. 'But he's on a twelve-month guardianship order.'

'She's challenging it.'

'On what basis?'

'On the basis that her circumstances have changed and that the child will no longer be at risk in her care.'

Clare didn't trust herself to speak. If a single word came out of her mouth, she was bound to break the golden rule when dealing with Kim: don't show how much you care.

'There's another thing, Clare, another basis upon which she's challenging the order …'

doubting Jack's guts, and his courage made her brave. Sharing her news with Dan would help too. What was it Grandad always said? *A trouble shared is a trouble halved.*

Dan lifted Jack down and the little boy ran to her, eyes shining. 'Did you see me?' he said. 'I galloped.'

'Cantered,' said Dan, leading Sparky over. He looked at Clare as if she might scold him for it. 'The canter was a bit of an accident.'

Clare lifted Jack's helmet from his head and smoothed a stray lock of hair. 'Yes, I saw you. You were fantastic, and so was Sparky ... and so were you, Dan.' Jack hugged her leg for a moment, and then tried to climb back into the saddle.

'No, that's all for now,' said Dan, hoisting the boy off the pony. 'Come and help me unsaddle him.'

Force of habit made Clare brace for the tantrum that used to so often follow the word *no*. The yelling and hitting. The small taut body hurling itself to the ground. But instead Jack calmly positioned himself at Sparky's near shoulder and took charge of the reins like Dan had shown him. 'Walk on,' said Jack, and led his pony off towards the stable. Dan walked by his side and Clare trailed after them. She longed to tell Dan about Taylor's custody grab. Ached to vent about her outright lies. But it was impossible with Jack there.

'I need to take Jacky to the house now,' she said. 'Then I'll come back. There's something I want to tell you.'

'No way,' said Dan. 'Feeding and grooming Sparky is as important a part of Jack's therapy as riding. More important, actually. It cements the bond between them.'

'Just this once,' she said. 'I *really* need to talk to you.'

Dan's phone rang and Clare groaned. 'So you have both feet but no head,' he said. 'Which way are the hoofs flexed? Do they point down or up ... down? Good, it's not a breech birth then.' He took Sparky's reins from Jack, handed them to Clare with an apologetic shrug, and continued his conversation. 'I'm on my way. In the meantime make the mare stand and walk. This will help the foal slide back into the womb a little and make it easier to reposition.' Clare combed Sparky's mane with her fingers. 'She's up? Good work. Wash and lubricate your arm anyway, in case I'm not there in time. If she goes down and starts straining again before I arrive, you'll have to help her with directions from me over the phone. Okay? Hopefully it won't come to that.'

'I know, I know,' said Clare. 'You've got to go.'

'The life of a country vet,' called Dan over his shoulder as he sprinted down the hill.

'Well, Jacky.' The little boy hugged her. 'It's just you and me, kid.'

IT WASN'T until after dinner that Clare finally found herself alone with Dan. All day she'd struggled alone to cope with the idea that Taylor might soon reclaim Jack. Clare had toyed with telling Bronwyn in the morning. She'd almost confided in Grandad on countless occasions during the afternoon, but each time she'd bitten her tongue. How would she bear Bronwyn's sympathy or her grandfather's very own grief at the thought of losing the little boy? It was Dan she needed, Dan who'd understand. So instead she'd waited, each second seeming to take an hour.

Sid arrived in the afternoon to check out the new foals, and then disappeared to the pub with Grandad. Clare fed Jack his dinner, listening for Dan's footstep on the porch. He arrived in time to read Christopher Robin to Jack, while she washed up. At last the little boy was asleep, and there they were, out on the verandah, with beers in their hands. It had been a dreary day, a gloomy one, but for a single, magnificent moment, the sun flared bright on the horizon. It rimmed the dark clouds in dramatic crimson. In almost the same moment it mellowed and lost its hold on the sky. Stray rosy rays slanted across the ancient Bunya range, like they must have done for aeons past. Clare usually loved this mysterious interlude between night and day, this transition point between worlds. But tonight it unnerved her, with its promise of imminent change. What she really wanted was for nothing to change - nothing at all.

Dan put down his drink. His expression was intense and searching. ' I can tell something's wrong. Spill.' That was all it took to release of shadow. He pulled out a chair and sat down, seeming suddenly frail. Clare braced against the wrench in her guts. 'No,' she said. 'I can't stay.'

Jack leaped onto Grandad's knee and glared at her. 'I won't go,' he yelled. 'I won't bloody go.'

Grandad hugged him briefly, got to his feet and put the little boy down. 'Don't talk like that,' he scolded. 'Clare will bring you back for a visit soon. Won't you love?'

She couldn't bear to look at them. 'Yes.' Clare inspected her shoes. 'Of course.'

'Come on then,' said Grandad, giving Jack a smile. 'Time to go.'

Dan stepped forward, hoisting the little boy aloft, carrying him to the car and strapping him in. 'See you, champ.' Tears glistened in Jack's eyes like silvery snail trails, pasting his lashes together. Samson took his place on the seat beside him. The little boy had already begun his rhythmic head thumping, eyes shut tight, lost in some other world.

'Goodbye love.' Clare embraced her grandfather, and he stroked her hair. 'I'm coming to that court hearing about Jacky,' he said. 'No arguments. Just tell me when it is.'

'You don't have to.'

'I'll hear none of your back talk,' he said firmly. 'I'm coming, and that's that.'

Thank you, Grandad.'

When she turned to go, Dan was by her side. On an impulse she extended her hand. He seized it with such force it hurt. His eyes bored into her, as if he could make her stay by sheer force of will. They held each other's gaze for the longest time. Was there nothing more to say? Would it really end this way?

Dan opened his mouth and closed it several times, like he was struggling to find the right words. She hung on the moment, waiting, watching his Adam's apple bob up and down. He rubbed his hand through his hair. 'Goodbye Clare.'

'Bye Dan.' Clare swallowed hard and drove away without a backward glance.

CHAPTER 34

She'd hoped to slip into *Fortitude Valley Legal Aid* that first morning unnoticed. No such luck. 'You're back,' squealed Debbie, running out from behind reception to give Clare a hug. 'And you've even got yourself a tan,' she said. 'It looks so natural.'

'That's because it *is* natural,' said Clare. She pulled up the short sleeve of her shirt, exposing the white skin.

Debbie looked horrified. 'I'll take you to *Bronzilicious* at lunchtime,' she said. 'They'll even you up, no worries. And there's a Supa-Dark tanning-bed special on – buy ten sessions, get ten free. You'd look great with a proper tan.'

Clare smiled and thanked her for the advice. It was somehow reassuring to discover that Debbie hadn't changed. Isaac emerged from the corridor with a fat manila folder under his arm and a familiar frown creasing his broad forehead. He did a double take at the sight of her, and broke into a grin. 'So you're back.' A fresh-faced young man that she didn't recognise came out of her old office. Isaac introduced him as Davis. Clare inspected her replacement. He looked about fifteen. She must be getting old.

'I'm back part-time until the end of the year,' she said, shaking Davis's hand. Ronnie walked through the glass doors, fabulous in a dark, geo-print dress that looked both chic and corporate at the same time. At first, the expression on her flawlessly made-up face was as snooty as ever, but when she saw Clare it changed to a pleased smile. 'Let's do lunch,' whispered Ronnie.

Clare nodded. 'You're on, but right now I want to speak with Roderick.' And with that she escaped down the hall.

RODERICK LOOKED TIRED. There was nothing unusual about that, but there was something else behind his eyes. Uncertainty maybe? Misgivings?

'How's Jack?' he asked

'He's having some trouble adjusting to being back,' she said. 'For that matter, so am I.'

He nodded, as if she'd given him the right answer.

'He's made such big strides these past few months,' Clare said.

'Where is he today?'

'In a new day care place. It offers a therapeutic program for kids with emotional problems ...' She trailed off. Roderick was studying her face. 'Jack doesn't like it,' she said, 'but it's an improvement on Jolly Jumbucks, and it's only three days a week.' Why was he looking at her like that?

'Well, we can certainly use the help leading up to Christmas,' he said. 'Young Davis is good, but he's green.'

He paused, as if expecting her to say something. But what?

'You know who's been a real turn up for the books?' he said. Clare shook her head. 'Ronnie. You wouldn't know her, not since that business with Adam Grant. She's been twice as hardworking and ten times as clever. I'm afraid I underestimated her.'

Exactly what *business with Adam* was he talking about? How much did Roderick know?

He was smiling at her now. 'Why the change of heart, Clare?' His voice was kind, concerned. 'Last time we spoke you were determined to stay up country till next year. You said you were so happy you mightn't ever come back, remember?' He picked up a perfectly sharpened pencil and tested its point with his finger. 'What changed?'

'That's none of your business.' Clare felt anger flushing her face. Then she stood up, horrified that she'd spoken like that to her old friend. 'I'm sorry,' she said, 'but I'd rather not talk about it.'

'That much is obvious.' Roderick's manner became businesslike. He patted a fat pile of folders on the desk. 'Overflow files we could use a hand with. Nothing too complicated.'

Clare picked them up.

'I've partitioned off the large storeroom and put a desk in there. It doesn't seem right to turf Davis from his office.'

'That's perfectly all right,' she said, but her voice was not quite steady as a wave of longing for Currawong overcame her. Part of her wanted to apologise to Roderick, collect Jack and Samson and find her way back to Clydesdale Way and through the Sunshine gates. But instead she turned on her heel and left. There was no going back – not now.

Clare threw herself into work, rating the files before her in order of priority. She made brief notes on each one, appraising the probable strength of the cases and flagging folders where, at first glance, a guilty plea seemed appropriate. This preliminary sorting stage was something she normally enjoyed, a kind of legal lucky dip. You never know what interesting cases you might come across. But today she found the process tedious. Her mind kept turning to the looming custody hearing. What would Taylor's lawyer do and say? How would Jack's psychological assessment go? What sort of witness would Taylor make?

By the time Ronnie knocked on her door at lunchtime, Clare had only worked through half the files she should have. Ronnie flicked through the documents in her out-tray with a curious eye. 'My, we are in a bad mood, aren't we?'

'What do you mean?' asked Clare.

'According to you, in each of these cases our client is guilty as charged and should cop a plea. Remind me never to appear before you if you decide to switch sides. Her Honour, Clare Mitchell - the hanging judge.'

Clare threw her a sarcastic smile. 'Do you want to have lunch or not.'

'Absolutely. I wouldn't dream of getting on your bad side,' she said in mock fear, tapping the pile of files on the desk. 'Not after seeing these.'

THEY SAT down on the chrome and glass chairs at the tapas bar. Adam would have loved it here, Clare thought. Just as she suspected, the menu was wildly overpriced.

'Shall I order for you?' asked Ronnie, with a faint look of pity. Clare nodded. 'The drinks too?'

'But I don't drink at lunchtime,' said Clare.

'You must,' said Ronnie, 'or you'll offend Chef Diego .'

And that apparently was that. Ronnie clicked her fingers at the waiter. 'Miguel, we'll have the champinones al ajillo, the clams, patatas aioli, chorizo sausage and the dancing flamenco.'

'Very well, Madam.'

'And some Basque cider to begin with.' Ronnie snapped the menu shut.

'We only have an hour,' protested Clare.

'That's plenty of time. And lunch is on me, by the way.'

As the clams arrived, their conversation turned to men. 'So Adam never suspected that you leaked the Pyramid report?' asked Clare. 'I was worried for you.'

'Adam didn't have a clue. He did suspect *you* however, but couldn't quite figure out how you managed it.'

'Well he'll figure it out pretty quickly if he sees us together.'

'Don't worry, Adam's gone,' said Ronnie. 'Pyramid traced the leak to his computer. He offered to resign without entitlements in return for them not pursuing a breach of contract claim. Right now, Adam's working at his uncle's practice at Bankstown in Sydney.'

Clare raised her brows and whistled. She tried to imagine Adam as a humble solicitor in a down-market suburban shopping strip, and failed. 'What sort of practice?'

'Wills, tax, conveyancing,' said Ronnie. 'Oh, and family law.' Neither of them could stifle their laughter. 'What about you?' asked Ronnie. 'You and your vet patched things up yet?'

'Dan?' Clare shook her head. 'No.'

'So it's all because of his attitude to Jack?'

'I suppose it is,' said Clare, finishing her cider, and starting on a crisp dry white that had miraculously appeared before her.

I don't understand,' said Ronnie. 'You never struck me as the maternal type.'

'With respect, counsellor,' said Clare. 'I don't think I struck you as much of anything.'

'Well, I think you're crazy,' said Ronnie. 'To give up a scrumptious man because he thinks a boy belongs with his mother?' She shook her head. 'He's probably right about that, Clare. And how on earth will you combine motherhood with being a barrister?'

Clare put the last mushroom on a piece of bread, 'I have no idea,' she said. 'No idea at all.' She ate the bread and finished her wine. The waiter put a little plate of sausage in front of her. 'If I eat this,' she asked, 'do I have to have another drink, yes? Tell me,' said Clare, as Ronnie pointed out an item on the wine list to Miguel. 'Why do you care so much that I get together with my *scrumptious vet*?'

'Isn't it obvious?' said Ronnie. 'If *you* make a tree change to play house with Dr Doolittle, *I* get your job with Paul next year. Although it was actually my job to begin with, so we'd simply be restoring the status quo, wouldn't we?' Ronnie's hair had come loose from its sleek chignon and her fingers were not quite steady on her glass.

'Yes, we would,' said Clare, slowly and thoughtfully. 'It was your job, and I did take it from you, and you've been very, very nice about it.'

Ronnie brushed her hair back from her face and picked up her glass. 'I propose a toast,' she said. 'To our unlikely friendship … and to being back late in the office.'

They clinked glasses. 'He's been calling,' said Clare. 'Dan. Calling, texting, emailing …'

Ronnie raised her exquisite brows. 'And?'

'And I've been ignoring him.'

Ronnie rolled her perfectly made-up eyes. 'You could at least *talk* to the poor man.'

'No' said Clare, recalling Dan's heartbreaking words. *What's best for Jack is to be with his mother.* 'There's nothing to say.'

CHAPTER 35

Clare had been back in Brisbane for two weeks, and it was finally the day of Jack's pre-hearing assessment with the court psychologist. She was a bag of nerves. For the first time her dubious, self-taught parenting abilities would be clinically assessed. Not only that, she'd be seeing Taylor for the first time since the young woman's visit to Currawong.

Clare took a deep breath, then knelt down on the floor to extract Samson from the chewed-up-land under the bed. She grasped his collar and dragged him out. Damn, she'd caught her skirt on something and brought the hem down. She tied the dog to the table leg and quickly pinned it up. Next job was to extract Jack from under the battered couch. Ouch … she'd kneeled on the pin. Biting her lip, Clare reached under and tried to grab him. Jack kicked out and began to wail. 'Please, Jacky, give me a break.' She pulled him out by his shirt, feeling guilty and justified all at once. She was already late. What was she supposed to do?

With practised precision she slung her bag over one arm, tucked the little boy under the other, and groped for Samson's lead. The quick-release knot Grandad had taught her allowed her to free the dog one-handed. Very useful that. Clare hitched Jack up higher and reached awkwardly for the doorknob with her left hand. This couldn't go on. She needed a house. A place with a yard and a swing and a lemon tree. She intended to spend the weekend searching for just such a house. Maybe then she wouldn't feel like it was her and Jack against the whole world. Maybe then they'd be happy again. She took one last look around the chaos that was her flat, and backed out of the door.

THE WAITING ROOM was airy and spacious, with floor-length windows that let in the light, and a well-equipped play area. Jack was on edge, choosing a toy, then discarding it moments later. He glanced at Clare often, as if he thought she might sneak away while he wasn't looking. How many times, she wondered, had he been through this sort of thing before?

Clare was on edge too. She'd had a long, sleepless night to rehearse her fears. What would happen when Taylor walked in?

The glass had turned the room into a hothouse full of emotion. A young woman approached the doors and Clare held her breath, but it wasn't Taylor. Maybe she wouldn't show. Jack began to jig from one foot to the other, like he needed to wee. Clare swooped and encouraged him towards the toilet, but he wouldn't move. When Clare turned around, Taylor was standing behind her.

'Jacky,' cried Taylor. The little boy made an excited beeline into his mother's arms.

'Hello, Taylor,' said Clare.

'You can go now,' said Taylor. 'The shrink wants to see me and Jacky, not you.'

'I think you'll find she wants to talk to both of us.' Clare sat back down.

Taylor glared at her, and cuddled Jack harder. He pulled away and Taylor looked stricken. Jack began to line up wooden cars along a pattern in the carpet, but his mother made no attempt to join in. When Jack gave her a car, she tried to pull him back onto her lap. He threw the car at her.

'You've turned him against me,' said Taylor.

Clare remained silent. Unnoticed by Taylor, a middle-aged woman had emerged from a side door and was quietly watching them. 'You must be Taylor Brown,' she said, with a kindly smile. 'I'm Stella Martin, a court-appointed psychologist. And this is your son Jack?' Taylor nodded. She looked well. She'd put on weight again and had some colour in her cheeks. 'If you two would like to come with me,' said Stella.

'Come on Jacky,' Taylor said hopefully. 'We're going to speak to this nice lady.'

Jack looked like he was in two minds. After an interminable pause, he followed Taylor into the room and Stella closed the door.

Clare stared out the window. The sun was pitiless, blazing uninterrupted against the glass. What was happening behind that door? Oh, to be a fly on the wall. It seemed to take hours before they emerged. 'So, you're Clare,' said Stella, offering her hand. 'Do you happen to have an extra pair of pants? Jack's had a little accident.'

'Yes,' said Clare. It felt like a test. 'Yes, of course. I always carry a spare, just in case.' She fossicked around in her bag and produced a small pair of jeans. Taylor was glaring at her.

'Would you help Jack change please, Clare, and then meet me in there?' Stella pointed to the room she'd just come from. Thank god Jack hated being wet these days. Clare waved the pants at him and he followed her promptly to the bathroom.

When they emerged, Taylor was sitting in the waiting room. 'We'll be some time,' Stella said to her. 'Do you want to say goodbye now?'

'I want to have a visit with my son when he comes out,' said Taylor.

'I'm going back to work after this,' said Clare. 'I'm afraid there won't be time.'

'Work?' said Taylor, looking puzzled. 'I thought you'd be taking Jacky back to the farm. He likes it there. He's got a dog.'

Clare wanted to strangle her. *Yes*, she felt like saying. *He does like it there, and so do I. But since you told everybody that Currawong was a violent death trap, crawling with armed men and dangerous dogs, I've had to make other arrangements.*

'I'm living back in Brisbane now,' said Clare. 'Come on, Jack.'

The boy didn't move. He'd been watching the exchange between Clare and his mother with a defiant look on his face.

Taylor must have sensed a mutiny. She called Jack herself. 'Come to Mummy, sweetie. Come and say goodbye.' To Clare's horror, Jack climbed onto his mother's knee. Taylor beamed at Stella, who was watching the scene with great interest. Any minute now she'd start taking notes. Stay calm, don't make this into a contest. Clare waited with a fixed smile on her face, while Taylor and Jack played a tickling game. It was stupid and immature to be jealous, but she couldn't help it.

'We really must get on,' said Stella at last. 'Clare?'

What was she supposed to do? Drag the boy from his mother's arms? She dared not call him again, in case he refused to come. What did she do when Samson ignored her? Of course, she offered his ball. Clare took Jack's box of Pokémon from her bag. 'I thought we might show Stella your toys,' she said. 'But I can't remember this one's name.' She extracted a figure and took a few steps towards Stella's office. Jack looked torn. 'It's Pikachu, isn't it?' asked Clare.

'No,' said Jack, unable to resist correcting her. 'That's Squirtle.' He struggled from Taylor's grasp and ran to Clare. She offered the box to him. He rummaged through it until he found a little yellow figurine. '*This* is Pikachu.'

'You'd better come, Jack, in case I get it wrong again,' said Clare. The child took her hand. Taylor looked close to tears.

'Good,' said Stella brightly. 'Let's get started.'

STELLA WATCHED Jack arrange his Pokémon toys on the desk. 'He spoke,' she said, sounding puzzled. 'I didn't see anything about him speaking in his file.'

'That's because his file's wrong,' said Clare. She took an iPad from her bag. 'Take a look at this.' It was the video of Jack at breakfast. '*Samsam stole my sausage,*' he said, clear as a bell.

Jack peered at the screen. 'That's me,' he said with a broad grin.

Clare smiled too. For a shutter-blink of time she wished Dan was there to share the moment. The mutinous desire sneaked in before she could cast it aside.

The rest of the assessment went just as well. Jack liked Stella and wanted to teach her about his Pokémon. She was a willing student, putting Jack in an amiable mood. Clare answered all the psychologist's questions as reasonably as she could, keeping a firm lid on her emotions. By the time Stella escorted them out, Clare was pretty sure she'd made an excellent impression.

'You manage him very well,' said Stella, with genuine admiration in her voice. 'Jack has made astonishing progress in the few months he's been with you.'

Clare allowed a wave of warm relief to wash over her.

'He could even be at the point where his mother might manage him,' said Stella. 'With a little help, of course. What do you think? You know the child better than anybody.'

Clare's smile died on her lips. Surely not? Surely this woman wasn't suggesting that Jack's improvement was a reason to hand him back to Taylor? 'I don't know,' Clare mumbled, trying not to let her misery show. 'I'm sorry, but I'm late for work.' Stella nodded and waved them goodbye.

Great. She thought she'd managed so well during the assessment. But she might have just shot herself in the foot instead.

CHAPTER 36

Friday afternoon. Clare checked the clock. Home time at last. During the last two weeks she'd performed her duties, represented her clients, gone through the motions – but her heart wasn't in it any more. The crawling days, the restless nights, the ever-present burn of tears and loneliness. Clare had never been more miserable. She missed Dan. His absence stung her every hour of every day. Bed was no comfort any more, and neither was work. Where had her drive gone, her energy, her commitment? Clare listened to her clients' sad stories. She listened to their tales of alcoholic fathers and disabled mothers, and could barely muster an ounce of sympathy. How was she supposed to present a plea of mitigation to the magistrate, when she wasn't convinced of its merits herself?

The drunk drivers and drug users, the teenage car thieves and shoplifters that she used to have sympathy for? Now she saw them as foolishly bent on self-ruin, destroying their loved ones' lives in the process. Their anguished parents and grandparents, their neglected children – all of them collateral damage in a desperate, downward spiral. Thank goodness the job was only three days a week. How would she ever manage full-time in this frame of mind? How could she possibly do her clients justice? She tried not to think about the life of a criminal barrister that awaited her next year. That was full-time. That was more than full-time. It was an all-encompassing career choice, a commitment that would entail a complete lifestyle change. Where would there be room for Jack, even if she could hang onto him?

Clare shook her head to clear it, squeezed her eyes shut against the sting of tears. 'I'm out of here,' she told Debbie as she hurried past the desk. What a relief to get outside. The day was bright and hot, the sky an empty, punishing blue, but the city buildings hid the sun. Heat shimmers rose from bitumen and cement. Late-afternoon shadows lengthened across the road and crept up the facades of skyscrapers, as if trying to climb out of the concrete jungle and escape across the rooftops. The city felt like a prison.

She clicked the remote on her key ring. The roll-a-door to the basement car park glided up and she hurried to her car. Damn Jack, damn Currawong – damn Dan. He'd made her feel like a fish out of water in her own life. *We've only been city creatures for a few hundred years,* he'd said one night, staring up at the stars. *That's just a blink of evolutionary time*. He was right. She didn't belong here in Brisbane any more, but she didn't belong back there either – not while Dan took Taylor's side. Not while he expected her to hand over Jack without a fight.

Clare fumbled with her car keys and they slipped to the ground. This tiny frustration was almost enough to tip her over the edge. She wanted to weep. The phone rang. Dan again. Clare didn't answer it. Instead she dug the heels of her hands into her eyes until it hurt. She had to pull herself together. The hearing was only a week away. She daren't lose courage now. Jack was depending on it.

CHAPTER 37

Mick offered Dan a second scoop of curried lamb, but he waved the pot away. 'You have to eat,' said Mick, piling up the plate anyway. 'Christ almighty. Anyone would think it was you with the cancer.' He took a second pot from the stove and ladled out sticky rice without asking permission.

The two men ate in silence, growling at the dogs in turn each time they poked their noses through the kitchen door. 'You have to speak to the lass,' said Mick at last.

'I've tried ringing,' said Dan miserably. 'She won't answer.' They both picked at their meals again. '*You* could, Mick,' he said hopefully. 'You could talk to her.'

'Don't put me in the middle. I can't tell her what she needs to hear.' Mick took another mouthful, staring belligerently at Dan. 'You're the one who needs to grow a backbone.'

Ever since Clare left, a pall had descended on Currawong. Nothing Dan did gave him pleasure any more. His patients weren't so bad. At least they let him get on with the job. It was their owners that he couldn't abide. He hauled himself from bed each morning, dreading having to make small talk, thrown by the simplest, *How are you, Dan?* He'd never been one to abide pretence. His natural instinct was to answer the question honestly. How was he? He was gutted, that's what he was. He missed Clare so badly, it was a constant physical ache. Nothing seemed worthwhile without her. Each day was empty - a dreary matter of going through the motions.

Inevitably his dreams were of Clare. The unbearable thing was that in these dreams things always worked out. Either she'd never left, or she came back, or he rescued her from bears that had shredded her clothes ... and the dream then turned deliciously X-rated. However weird the scenario, they always ended up living happily ever after.

How appalling then to wake up each morning and, like in a perverse version of Groundhog Day, have to confront his heartache all over again. Consequently he didn't want to sleep. He watched movies late into the night or played online computer games, building himself a gorgeous avatar lover who looked suspiciously like Clare. He drank too much bourbon, hoping it might provide a respite from dreaming. It didn't, but it did provide him with a sore head in the morning. Life had become a living nightmare.

He'd misjudged things badly, he saw that now. Expecting Clare to see things from his point of view, without giving her any basis for doing so. And why the hell should she anyway? Her life wasn't his life. How could she possibly appreciate the danger of taking a child from his mother the way he did?

'Dan,' said Mick. 'I reckon it might be easier for you to talk to me, kind of a practice run.'

'I can't.'

Mick pulled out his tobacco pouch and rolled a cigarette. There was a certain gravity in the air, like something important was about to happen. 'This is difficult for you, Dan, I can see that.' Mick stood stiffly and rummaged through the pantry. 'Here it is.' He pulled out a velvet-lined display box and placed it on the table. It contained a dusty bottle of whisky. 'My old dad won this fifty years ago at the Royal Sydney Show. Currawong horses took out every championship in sight that year, including Grand Champion Stallion. First and last time that honour's gone to a clydie, I reckon.' He smiled to himself, like he was remembering. 'I've been keeping it all these years ... don't

has safe, supported housing. She's passed every drug screen, and she's stuck with the methadone program so faithfully that the doctors have lowered her dose. She's participated in parenting classes and, as far as we can tell, she's cut off all contact with the violent boyfriend. And she's in counselling.'

Oh. Taylor had jumped through every hoop the department had presented her with. Clare couldn't help it. There was that grudging admiration again.

'On the plus side for us, Jack has now been in care for a cumulative total of eighteen months. It means he's a candidate for a stability plan.'

An SP was an official plan for long term out-of-home care for a child. 'If only we had one of those,' said Clare.

Grace whipped a document from her wallet. 'We do,' she said. 'Here's your copy. You really should have seen this before, but there just wasn't time. It was only finalised this morning, courtesy of Kim Maguire. I trust there's nothing in there that you disagree with?'

Clare read the pages. The plan proposed, among other things, that Clare become Jack's long-term carer, and that he be kept on a guardianship order for now, with a planned transition to permanent care. There was provision for Taylor to have generous access. Clare couldn't believe it. Kim had really come through for her. *Transition to permanent care.* The prospect was too good to be true. 'No, said Clare. 'There's absolutely nothing that I disagree with. This is wonderful.'

'Right,' said Grace. 'I was hoping Kim could be here as a witness, but she's giving evidence in another case. Instead I have a comprehensive affidavit from her for the court. Kim speaks glowingly of you, by the way. But don't get your hopes up,' warned Grace. 'We're still in for an uphill battle, and Magistrate Jackson is known to be sympathetic to birth parents.'

Clare groaned. Not Joe Jackson. She usually cheered when she wound up in his court, but that was when she was acting for the other side. Clare recalled the time she'd won back custody of twin girls for their single mother on her latest release from jail. Even she hadn't expected to win that one. The three-year-olds had been in a stable, loving placement for two years. Their foster parents had wept at the decision. It made her ashamed now to think about how she'd treated them.

Ronnie helped herself to the document in Clare's lap. 'Permanent care?' she asked in astonishment. 'Is that really what you want?'

'Yes,' said Clare, keeping her eye on the lift. 'It's what I want more than anything.'

Clare wasn't only on the lookout for Taylor. Her grandfather had promised to come. Of course she'd told him not to bother. She'd told him that it was too far for him to drive, especially with those dizzy spells of his, and she'd meant it, but a big part of her still hoped she might see him walk through that door. And then there he was, large as life, clutching his hat, looking out of place in the windowless hall. His bewildered expression transformed into a sunny smile the moment he spotted her.

Clare leaped to her feet. 'Grandad, you shouldn't have.'

'Yes, I should have,' he said, embracing her.

Clare introduced him to Ronnie, wondering what she'd make of him.

'How do you do, Mr MacLeod.' Ronnie looked him up and down. 'I love your style. Pure R. M. Williams. That look's very in right now.' She glanced over at Clare. 'Perhaps you could give your granddaughter some fashion tips.'

TAYLOR STILL HADN'T ARRIVED and Clare allowed herself to hope. They were first on the list. If she didn't show soon, it would be game over.

Then it happened. The lift door opened, framing two people inside. Clare's heart faltered. Taylor … and Dan. What on earth? She turned, open-mouthed, to her grandfather.

'Don't start, love,' he said. 'Dan drove me up here.' Grandad was speaking in the tone that he used for nervous, young horses. 'He spotted Taylor in the lobby and they got talking.'

Taylor noticed Clare. They eyed each other warily, and then Dan spotted her too. What would he say? What would she say? But she needn't have worried; he didn't approach her.

Clare felt sick. Her heart ached at the sight of him, but she couldn't stop staring. Devastatingly handsome in a charcoal suit and tie. The tailored clothes emphasised his height, his square shoulders, his lean hips. Her body responded to him in spite of herself. She folded her arms across her chest. The only thing worse than Dan not being there to support her, was him being there to support Taylor.

'It's not what you think,' said her grandfather.

'Good,' said Clare as she stood up. 'Because if it's what I think, Dan's a dead man.' She marched off down the corridor to compose herself. Sarah called Taylor over. Clare moved closer - close enough to overhear the barrister's last-minute instructions to her client. She eavesdropped shamelessly, but Sarah wasn't giving anything away.

'You'll be asked to take the stand,' said Sarah. 'You can either swear on the bible, or simply swear that you'll tell the truth. Answer all questions honestly. If you don't understand a question, ask for it to be repeated. If you still don't understand, ask for the Magistrate to make the question clearer. Address him as *Your Honour* or *Sir*. I'll ask you questions first, then the other lawyer will cross-examine you. Okay?' Taylor looked like a scared rabbit, but she nodded and the case was called.

Grandad stood up. 'We can't go in,' said Clare. 'You're not a party, and I'm a witness.' Her grandfather sat back down.

Dan came over. 'Hello, Clare.'

'Dan.'

'Can we talk?' he asked.

'No,' she said, powerfully aware of his physical presence. Damn that man. She had to keep her wits about her for the stand.

'Leave her be, son,' said Grandad. 'It'll keep.'

Dan gave her one last, longing look, and then sat down a few seats away.

Ronnie's eyes widened and a knowing smile played on her lips. 'You weren't kidding,' she said. '*Scrumptious* is an understatement.' She sneaked another peek at Dan. 'I might pack up and go bush for him myself.'

Clare ignored Ronnie and concentrated on calming down. She

could *feel* Dan, though she couldn't look at him. For a moment she thought she could smell him too: a kind of warm, open air, animal scent She forced her mind away from him. Time slowed, along with the beat of her heart. She was intensely present in each moment, like in a meditation. When they called her, she'd be ready.

The sound of the clerk saying her name startled her. Surely it wasn't time yet? It was too soon. With a pat on the back from her grandfather and an unexpected hug from Ronnie, Clare entered the court. Grace met her on the other side of the door.

'There's been a change of plan,' she whispered. 'His Honour wants to speak with you.'

What was Grace talking about? Either Clare was giving evidence, or she wasn't. Taylor stood in the witness box with a defiant tilt to her chin. She glared at Clare. Whatever this was, it didn't look pretty.

His Honour Joe Jackson was a cheerful, middle-aged man, with grey hair and fine principles. He was one of the more progressive magistrates on the bench, and liked to pursue what he regarded as a social justice agenda. In other words, he was a bit of a sucker for the underdog. That normally suited Clare just fine, but not today.

'Ms Mitchell,' he said. 'Always nice to see you in my court, whatever the circumstances.'

'Thank you.' She sized up the situation. To her surprise, Sarah Chapman looked furious. That had to be good.

'Ms Brown has a rather novel proposal. If it should prove acceptable to both parties, it would allow for this matter to be settled with a consent order.'

Whatever was he talking about?

'If you wouldn't mind reiterating your request?' he asked Taylor.

Taylor looked at the Magistrate in confusion. 'Tell us again what you want, Ms Brown,' said Jackson. 'We're all waiting with bated breath.'

Taylor slowly turned her gaze to Clare. Nobody else, just Clare. Her voice, when she finally spoke, was resolute. 'I love my son,' she said. 'Don't get me wrong, he's the best thing that ever happened to me. The truth is, though, I haven't always been the best mother to him. I've always tried. I've tried my heart out for that little boy. I'm still trying.' She stopped.

'Go on,' said Jackson, gently. 'Tell Ms Mitchell what you told me.'

'I hate her,' said Taylor, and Clare forgot to breathe. 'She's a stuck-up bitch. But I know she loves my son ... and I know he loves her too.' Taylor wiped her eyes and looked at Jackson. 'That's probably why I hate her, eh?'

Jackson smiled. 'Quite possibly.'

She returned his smile, and it seemed to give her courage. 'The fact is, Clare's good for Jack. He's talking and everything. I love hearing him talk. He only talks when he's happy.' She turned back to Jackson. 'So I was thinking, 'cause I do love him so much, that I might give him to her.' Clare's breath returned in a heady rush. 'But I'll only do that if Jack can live with her at that farm. He likes it there. He's got dogs and a pony. I want him to have a pony. And I'd have to be able to see him at Christmas and birthdays and holidays and stuff.'

'Well,' said Jackson, beaming. 'As you've now heard for yourself, Ms Mitchell, this is an unusual request indeed. I've never made a consent order before that has been conditional upon the child having a pony.' There was laughter from the court, and Clare felt tears beginning to slide down her face. 'Ms Mitchell, I believe you're poised to take up a position at the bar next year. That would of course be incompatible with Ms Brown's request. Should you wish, we will continue with the hearing. But know that if you are agreeable, I'll have the relevant order prepared forthwith.'

'Yes,' said Clare, smiling through her tears 'Yes, absolutely yes.'

'Then I think we have reached an agreement.'

Sarah could no longer contain her outrage. 'With respect, Your Honour cannot make an order that directs Ms Mitchell to remain at a certain address. Nor can you direct her to give the child a pony.' More laughter. 'I don't think my client understands this.'

'That's very true, counsellor.' Joe Jackson turned to Taylor. 'I can't direct Ms Mitchell to remain at this farm indefinitely. You would have to take it on trust, and of course you would always be free to apply for a variation of the order, should circumstances demand. So, what say you?'

'Sure,' said Taylor. 'I'll trust her.' Sarah threw her papers in the air.

Clare wanted to hug Taylor and never let her go, but the girl looked on guard. Better take things slowly. This was going to be a steep learning curve for the both of them

It was only when they were all directed to rise, and were filing from the courtroom, that she thought of Dan. She was going to be living at Currawong again. How on earth was that going to work?

CHAPTER 39

They were an odd assortment, all gathered in Clare's untidy apartment. Jack and Samson in the lounge room, attempting a game of tug-a-war with an old tea towel. Taylor on her knees, getting in their way, trying to cuddle each of them in turn without much success. Clare smiled. A lap dog and a baby doll would suit Taylor better.

Ronnie and Grandad were perched on bar stools in the kitchen, talking a dime a dozen. Who would have guessed they shared a love of antiques? For the first time ever, the place felt like a real home. Clare cleared the clutter away in the kitchen, until she could reach the huge coffee machine squatting in the corner. A present from Adam that she'd barely used, but it might impress Ronnie.

She plugged it in and tried to remember the instructions. 'Don't worry about that, love,' said her grandfather. 'A cuppa will do me fine.'

'Tea?' asked Ronnie. 'Yes, tea sounds like fun. Do you have one of those pots?'

For a moment Clare didn't know what Ronnie meant. 'You mean this?' She extracted a large and very beautiful old teapot from the back of the cupboard, a present long ago from her mother .

Ronnie clapped her hands. 'Perfect. We'll have a tea party, shall we?'

'If you like,' said Clare, abandoning the monstrous coffee machine and putting on the kettle instead. 'It won't be all that traditional. I think you're supposed to have scones and jam at a tea party, not take-away pizza, but we can pretend.'

Dan was standing at the window, staring out across the city lights. He'd barely spoken a word since the court case. Was he unhappy with the outcome? If he was, he was the only one. What was it, she wondered, that he'd wanted to say to her earlier on?

Grandad made himself useful, finding plates and distributing slices of pizza. Clare took a marrowbone from the fridge, banishing it and Samson to the training crate.

'That's cruel,' said Taylor, patting the dog through the wire, and feeding him bits from her plate.

'Come on, Jacky,' said Grandad. 'Sit up. How about some garlic bread as well.'

'Pizza,' yelled the little boy, climbing up onto a bar stool. How happy he looked. How content, to have all the people who loved him together in this one place.

'Clare,' said Ronnie, in a wheedling tone. She didn't look entirely at ease, balancing a plate of greasy take-away on her knee, but she was making a valiant attempt to cope. 'What a brave decision you made today. I do so admire you.'

'Do you now?' said Clare sweetly. She held the teapot aloft. 'Tea?'

'Please.' Clare had been stringing this out all day. It was kind of fun, torturing Ronnie. 'When do you think you might talk to Paul?'

'Paul?' asked Clare.

'Oh, come off it,' snapped Ronnie. 'You won't be at the bar with Dunbar next year. Why don't you just tell him? You have an obligation Clare, to tell him this very day. And you must ask him if he'll consider me as your replacement. The job's truly mine, in any case. You stole it right out from under my nose.'

Clare grinned. This was the Ronnie she knew and loved. It was time to put her out of her misery. From the corner of her eye, Clare noticed Dan watching her. Shirt sleeves rolled up. Collar open. He looked very handsome in the soft reflected light at the window. It emphasised his rugged features, his unkempt hair, his watchful eyes. He looked a little wild.

'Relax,' Clare told Ronnie. 'I've already spoken to Paul. He's very happy for your old arrangement to stand. In fact, he wants to meet you for dinner tomorrow night to finalise things.'

Ronnie's expression collapsed into a teary mess, mascara running, smearing her face as she dragged her knuckles across her eyes. She clutched at Clare's hand. 'You're my truest, dearest friend,' she said, sounding slightly unhinged. 'This job is my every dream come true. You have no idea. I'd cheerfully sell my grandmother for this chance. I'd even have stayed another year in the Valley, if Paul had insisted.'

'Thank goodness it didn't come to that,' said Clare. The irony was lost on Ronnie, whose hands fluttered in the air like startled birds as she repeated her thanks.

Clare studied Ronnie's exalted face. It told her something rather surprising, something she was very glad to learn. She didn't really want the job, at least not the way Ronnie did. Ronnie had a fierce, uncompromising hunger for it. She wouldn't have given it up for anything. How hard, then, must it have been for her to forgive Clare and offer her friendship? In spite of Adam, in spite of Paul. They may have started out as co-conspirators, but their connection had blossomed into something far deeper. This was a friendship that would stand the test of time.

Moments later Ronnie was on her mobile, ordering buckets of home-delivered champagne. 'And a bottle of whisky?' She looked at Grandad, who was thoroughly enjoying himself. 'Single malt?'

He nodded, and Ronnie smiled. She cast her eyes around the room one more time, and her gaze settled on Jack. 'And a bottle of non-alcoholic sparkling wine, suitable for a small boy.' She beamed at Clare, apparently pleased with herself for being so child friendly.

'How about I take Jack and Samson for a walk?' said Dan, who had mysteriously appeared at Clare's shoulder.

'If you like,' she said coolly.

Taylor gave up trying to braid the back of Jack's hair, and came into the kitchen. 'Are you going with Dan?' she asked Clare. 'On the walk?'

'No,' said Clare.

'Why not?' asked Taylor.

'I have guests,' said Clare shortly. She turned away to collect the empty mugs, and began to stack them in the dishwasher.

Taylor pouted and took another piece of pizza. 'I should have made you two get married.'

'What?' Clare dropped a teacup. It shattered on the floor. Taylor ignored it. 'Dan's nice. Jack would like having him for a dad.'

'Taylor,' said Clare. 'Whatever do you mean?'

'I mean,' said Taylor, with exaggerated emphasis, as if Clare was a bit slow, 'I should have made you two get married, like I made you go and live back at the farm with Jack.'

'You didn't make me go live at the farm,' said Clare. 'I'm choosing to live there.'

Taylor giggled. 'I did too. And I could've made you marry him. I reckon you love my son that much. Dan should've thought of it when he thought of the other idea.'

Clare's hands went clammy. 'What other idea?'

'I've got a job,' said Taylor, inexplicably changing the subject. 'Out west. They're going to train me to drive those monster trucks at a mine.'

Dan bent down to release Samson from his crate. 'Don't you move,' commanded Clare. She grabbed Taylor's arm and marched her over to Dan. The room went quiet. 'Go on, Taylor,' said Clare. 'Finish your story.'

'The Newstart Centre lined me up for the job weeks ago. I wanted to tell Sarah that you could keep Jacky, I really did, but she was so gung-ho about everything. I was scared she'd think I didn't love him ... so the case sort of kept rolling along.'

'Go on,' said Clare again. Everybody had moved closer to listen. 'Well, I was so confused this morning,' said Taylor. 'What was I supposed to do? If I told people about the job, they'd think I was a bad mother. But if I got Jacky back, I couldn't take the job, could I? I want it that bad. I've never had a job before. I think it would make Jacky proud of me.'

'I think so too, love,' said Grandad. Taylor shot him a grateful look. 'Anyway, Dan saw me crying in the lobby.' Taylor faltered again.

'For God's sake, just spit it out,' said Ronnie.

'Don't you get it?' said Taylor. 'Today was all Dan's idea. I told him that I wished Jacky could live at the farm with you. So he said, why don't I tell the judge? He said nobody would think that I didn't love Jacky. So I did. I wouldn't have been brave enough if it wasn't for him. '

Clare wet her lips with her tongue. 'And ...?'

'And I was just thinking, since Dan loves you and all, it would have been nice if I'd made you get married as well, and then Jack could have a daddy ... as well as a pony.'

'Dan,' said Clare. 'Is this true?'

Dan nodded, his gaze bold and unapologetic. It put her unexpectedly on the back foot.

'Taylor told me she wanted Jack to live with you at Currawong, and I suggested she tell the judge. Simple as that.'

'And you didn't think to tell me?' said Clare.

'I tried. You wouldn't listen. By the time the case was over, you already knew. What would have been the point?'

Clare shook her head in disbelief. She ran over the events of the day in her mind. It was true – he had asked to talk to her. 'And what's this about us getting married?'

He held out the palms of his hands. 'Now that's a new one on me.'

Clare tried to digest all she'd heard. Did the end justify the means? It was true that Taylor had held her over a barrel today, but the end result was that she had Jack. And though she was loath to admit it, it looked like she had Dan to thank. Clare turned to confront Taylor, who was sitting on a bar stool looking miserable.

'You think I'm a bad mother, don't you,' said the girl, before Clare had a chance to speak. 'To want the job so much.'

'No,' said Clare. 'I don't think that at all. But I also don't think you should be keeping secrets and … and blackmailing me.'

'Steady on, love,' said her grandfather. He'd gone all protective of Taylor, and it irritated Clare.

'What business is it of yours, if and who I marry?' asked Clare. 'And wherever did you get the idea that Dan loves me?'

'He told me,' said Taylor. 'Not that he had to. Blind Freddy could see it a mile off. I don't think you know how lucky you are. You've got a farm, and horses and dogs. You've got Dan and he's a hunk, by the way, in case you haven't noticed. You've got Mick. He's the sweetest old man in the world … You even have my son. But instead of being happy, you're storming around like you're mad at everybody.' It was the longest speech Clare had ever heard Taylor make. 'I think you should thank your lucky stars.'

Jack crept over. He climbed the bar stool and nestled into his mother's lap. Taylor folded him in her arms and kissed his hair.

'You know what?' said Clare. Taylor shook her head. 'I think you're right.'

It was the going away party she'd missed the first time round, all her legal aid colleagues gathered together after work on her final day. Roderick thumped the table. 'Will everyone please charge your glasses.'

Clare helped herself to a glass of riesling from the cask and poured another one for Ronnie. Her friend took a sip and made a face. 'The only thing worse than this wine is having to listen to one of Roderick's speeches,' she whispered.

Clare giggled. Ronnie was right. He did go on a bit. She nibbled a cracker topped with gherkin and cheese, while Roderick cleared his throat. 'As we gather to farewell our colleague, Clare, I'm reminded of words spoken by Brutus in Shakespeare's Julius Caesar. *There comes a tide in the affairs of men, which taken at the flood leads on to fortune.* Such a tide has swept Clare from us. We hope that for her, the flood will lead to something better than it did for Brutus and Cassius ...'

A sprinkle of laughter. Debbie looked confused. Ronnie looked bored. Clare would miss these people, these friends. She gazed out the window to the wizened coolabah tree. It was her friend too. She wished she could spirit it away with her, back to Currawong. She wished she could set it free. Ronnie dug her in the ribs just as Roderick finished. '... So I ask you to be upstanding and drink to Clare and her future.'

IT WAS GROWING dark when Clare finally waved goodbye and headed for the car. She clicked the key to unlock it and sat awhile in the dark. Then she got out again, retraced her steps and slipped around the side of the building to her coolabah tree. It stood forlorn on a patch of dead grass, narrow leaves trembling in the breeze. Silhouetted against the sunset, its spindly branches looked like crooked hands reaching skywards, begging for release. Clare ran her finger down its rough furrowed bark. She scanned its sparse canopy until she found what she was looking for. There, at the tip of a low hanging bough. Clare reached up and plucked a drab bunch of grey-green gumnuts. She collected a few more from the ground. 'Don't worry,' she told the tree, before she turned to go. 'Grandad will know just what to do with these.'

CHAPTER 40

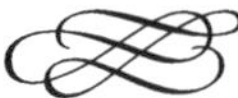

Clare awoke in her own bed, in her own little room back at Currawong. The candlewick spread, the pretty lamp, the lacy curtains - nothing ever changed in this space. It could have been her first night back at the homestead, and all that had happened these past few months might well have been a dream. It was both a comforting and unsettling thought. She was certain of one thing though. Last night with Dan had been no dream.

Clare stretched, cat-like. What time was it anyway? The bunya pine in the yard already cast a shadow on the window. She checked the wind-up alarm clock beside the bed. It was later than she thought.

A knock came at the door. 'Breakfast's up, sleepy head,' said Grandad. Clare hopped out of bed, and into jeans and a T-shirt. She pulled a comb through her tousled hair, slipped on sandals and was ready to go. It took her two minutes. How different from her mornings back in Brisbane, juggling Jack and Samson and traffic: juggling everybody's expectations, including her own. She'd been exhausted before she began. The contrast made her smile.

'What's this?' asked Clare. Beside the bacon and eggs, the buttery toast and the jar of vegemite, was a big bowl of fresh summer fruits.

'Who said you can't teach an old dog new tricks,' said Grandad. 'I learned a thing or two those few days I stayed with you in Brisbane. I learned that I like fruit for breakfast.' He turned to where Jack was chewing on bacon rind. 'I'm going to make you a nice fruit salad, lad.' He searched around in the fridge. 'Now where'd I put that yoghurt?'

Jack pulled a face and escaped out the door, where Samson was patiently waiting for him. The dog gave a joyful bark and the two of them ran off.

Clare smiled and looked round for Dan. Last night they'd spent a magical evening; forgiving, re-joining, falling in love all over again. Grandad had thoughtfully retired early, leaving them to share chips and beer and cherries out on the verandah. They'd talked until way after midnight. About their childhood and families. About their hopes and dreams and the things that made them who they were. They'd reconnected with a deeper understanding.

Mother Nature had turned on a spectacular show, as fork lightning cracked over the Bunyas, dazzling the eyes. A deafening boom of thunder had made Clare jump against him, and Dan had snatched her in his arms. She'd almost cried out at his touch, at how much she wanted him.

Afterwards they'd sneaked down to the surgery and made sweet, slow love. The pair of boobook owls in the recovery room provided the soundtrack — a duet of low, rhythmic mating calls. Clare had stumbled back to bed in the pale light of picanninny dawn, knowing life didn't get any better.

'WHERE'S DAN?' asked Clare.

Pregnancy testing cows at Kingaroy.' Clare smiled, wondering how Dan was managing on hardly any sleep. 'I thought we might spend the day together,' said Grandad. 'Just you, me and Jacky. We could go for a drive into Dalby, maybe have a picnic at Myall Creek. Or what about a carriage ride into Merriang and lunch at the pub. Fleur could use a bit of a run? What do you say?'

'They both sound perfect,' said Clare. 'You choose.'

'A carriage ride it is then,' said Grandad.

'There's something I want to ask you first,' said Clare. She fetched the gumnuts she'd collected from her coolabah tree in Brisbane, and spread them on the table. 'Can I grow these?'

She watched as he put on his glasses and examined the woody pods. Was it her imagination or had he grown more frail? Yes, he had. It was easier to spot after being away for a few weeks. The skin on his hands looked thin enough to tear with a touch, and his eyes seemed sunken. They retained their old sparkle and warmth, though, and he still had a spring in his step.

'What are they?' asked Grandad. 'Black box? Coolabah …?'

'Coolabah,' she said.

'First thing,' he said, 'is to stick them in a paper bag under the verandah until the nuts release their seed.' He picked up a gum nut she'd taken from the ground and rolled it between his fingers. 'This is a good'un. Some trees hold their nuts way past the first year. With these older ones, you're sure the seed is ripe.'

'Wait.' Clare grabbed a pen and paper.

'Plant the seed in pots with a mixture of peat and sand. Stick them in the fridge for six weeks so they think its winter. Then just take them out and keep them moist. You'll have a fine crop of coolabah seedlings before you know it.'

Clare finished writing down the instructions, then leant over and kissed him. 'Thanks Grandad. I knew I could count on you.'

THE PHONE RANG and for once Grandad heard it. Clare cleared away the gumnuts and poured herself a cup of tea, idly listening to the conversation. She put down the teapot. Something was wrong, she could hear it in his voice. 'You buggers will come onto this land over my dead body,' he said, his voice thick with anger. The phone slammed down. It took some time for him to emerge from the hall.

'We'll have to take a rain check on that carriage ride. Those Pyramid bastards are on their way.' His hands closed into fists. 'Going ahead with some exploratory wells, they said. Reckon they've got the paperwork, and I can't do nothing about.'

A flush of guilt scorched her face. She'd been so caught up in her own problems, she'd forgotten about his. 'Oh, Grandad, I thought we'd put an end to all that.'

'So did I, love,' he said. 'Gordon tabled that report of yours in parliament last week and the vote's today. He's crunched the numbers. It'll be close, but it should get through. If it does, he reckons there'll be a moratorium on new wells. But if those buggers get their toe in the door before the vote, they might just get away with it.'

'The vote's today? Surely we can stall them for one day?'

'Buggered if I know how. There's a whole convoy on its way.'

Clare took his arm and smiled. 'I wasn't a student activist for nothing,' she said. 'Ring around. See who can get over here straightaway. Ask them to bring chains and padlocks. We're going to stage a protest.'

'Blimey,' said Grandad, looking more cheerful. 'Why didn't I think of that?'

More than two hundred people turned up, with tractors and cultivators and graders – anything that could block access to the Currawong track. A party atmosphere developed. Women served sandwiches. Someone had brought along balloons for the children. An eclectic collection of farm dogs milled around, some circling each other, stiff-legged, manes up and spoiling for a fight. But one word from an owner was generally enough to stand them down. They soon sorted out a pecking order and formed a rough pack. Samson and Red, Pongo and Perdita – they all joined in.

Clare, along with Bronwyn and a few others, sat chained to the Sunshine gates. She was enjoying herself, reliving the student sit-ins of university days. 'There's nothing like a bit of civil disobedience,' she said. Jack and Timmy thought it was great fun and demanded to be chained up too.

'Not today,' said Bronwyn firmly. 'Maybe next time.'

Clare laughed. 'Chaining children to fences might be going a bit far.' Another truck joined the blockade. 'Let's hope the press get here before Pyramid does. Otherwise they'll never get through.' Vehicles were already parked ten deep.

'It's about time we put up a fight,' said one man, and doffed his hat to the chained women. The hairs on the back of Clare's neck stood up, and a shiver of pride ran through her.

'Have you got that radio?' she asked.

Bronwyn handed over a big, battery-powered Sangean. 'I've set it to the broadcast of parliament.' The modulated voice of an ABC announcer rang clear in the still air. News on the hour of bomb blasts and earthquakes and rebellion in faraway places. Then the droning voice of MPs debating some bill about tariffs.

'Parliament's sitting late tonight,' said Clare. 'It could be ages before we know.'

The sound of a distant motor stopped the general chatter. Not a loud motor. Certainly not trucks in convoy. A car rounded the bend. 'They're from the local paper,' said someone. Good. This was all going according to plan. A young man and woman got out.

'How do you reckon they'll spin it?' Clare asked.

'Are you kidding?' said Bronwyn. 'That reporter—' she pointed to a pretty woman conducting interviews. 'Her parents are here. Her grandparents too. I think we can bank on good press.'

Clare smiled for the photographer.

Now a new, more menacing sound - the rumble of heavy vehicles. Once more the chatter stopped, and heads turned as one. Truck after truck crested the horizon. It was an army. 'Action stations,' shouted an earnest young man who looked vaguely familiar. She had it, Gavin Butler the artist, local president of Shut the Gate, minus the dreadlocks. An uneasy calm settled on the crowd as they waited for the trucks to come.

Ten minutes later the lead vehicle grumbled around the corner. It bore gold emblazoned Pyramid Energy logos and looked brand new. 'That's the first bulldust that bumper's seen,' someone said. Grandad threaded his way through the throng to meet the convoy, flanked by two burly farmers.

Clare was too far away to hear, but if she peered sideways, she

presents, singing the carols, pulling some early bonbons – she was more wide-eyed than Jack. The pair's innocent delight had put extra smiles on all their faces. Last night Taylor had snuggled down on a mattress in the corner of Jack's room, refusing to take her son's bed.

After light's out, Clare had heard them giggling and playing and jumping around, like two kids at a sleepover. When all went quiet she'd peeped in. The camp bed had been moved next to Jack's, and the young mother lay curled up in sleep beside her son. It was a touching scene. Red and Samson stretched out at their feet, the girl's face so angelic in repose, so much like Jack's. Clare had smiled before closing the door, thinking once again that Taylor needed fostering almost as much as Jack did. But she'd be off to her new job in a few days' time; a job which had in fact made Jack very proud, just as his mother had hoped. 'Mummy drives *monster* trucks,' he kept saying, spreading his arms wide.

'She's very clever then, isn't she?' Clare would say.

Jack would nod solemnly and run off to tell someone else.

Another car arrived. All day, an odd procession of vehicles had been arriving, delivering little and not so little presents for Dan. Beer, biscuits, fruit cakes, honey – these were the common fare. But some gifts were more unusual. One client gave him a box of bullets, another a hand-crafted bridle, another a hat and Drizabone, another a rifle to match the ammunition. And Martha had finally managed to offload that pig.

Jack had squealed with delight when he saw it. 'It's Babe. I love him.' The little boy locked arms around the animal's neck. My how that piglet had grown, but Dan hadn't the heart to say no. They'd put it in the day yard next to Sparky, and the two had become instant friends. Her grandfather had shaken his head. 'Why'd you have to go and give Jacky that *Babe* movie, love? I watched it with him last week. How the heck am I going to put that pig on a spit now?' Red received two dog beds and enough treats to last him for a year. Jack got Matchbox cars, a disturbing arsenal of toy guns, and bags of Christmas lollies, which Taylor helped him demolish.

Clare went outside to see what new gift had arrived. But it wasn't a gift. It was Pete Porter, Grandad's old friend from Quimby Downs. A thin, middle-aged woman helped him from the car. 'I'm Faye.' She extended her hand. 'Pete's daughter. Apparently Pete's staying here for a few days? Hope you're expecting him. I didn't like imposing like this on Christmas day, but he insisted on coming.'

'Will you stop fussing, Faye,' said Pete. 'I organised it with Mick last week.'

Faye shot Clare a helpless glance. 'Your medicine's all packed. You will take it on time, won't you? Perhaps if I give it to Clare, she could help you?'

Pete shuffled over to his daughter, and rested his hands on her shoulders. His back might be bent, but it was clear that in his youth he'd been a tall man. 'I'm perfectly capable of looking after myself.' He kissed Faye's cheek. 'It'll do you good to have a break.' He pulled out his wallet and handed her a bank card. 'Take a trip to the Gold Coast on me, do some shopping, live a little.'

She managed a wan smile. 'You sure you'll be all right?'

He kissed her again. 'I'm sure.'

Faye threw her arms around him. 'I love you, Dad.'

'Not as much as I love you,' he said. She pulled back and wiped away a tear. 'Now, now, love. That'll do. You're the best daughter a man could be blessed with,' he said. 'You go and have some fun, for Chrissake.'

'Well, goodbye,' Faye said.

'Goodbye,' said Clare. 'And try not to worry. We'll look after him.'

PETE WATCHED his daughter drive away with an expression of immense satisfaction. Mick put a drink in his friend's hand and said, 'Who's up for a game of backyard cricket?'

'Me, me,' called Jack.

'Righto,' said Grandad. 'The kid has terrific aim,' he told Pete. 'Hits the wicket nearly every time.'

Clare winced. Jack was a good shot all right. Ever since he'd scored that bullseye with the stapler in the centre of Kim's forehead, Clare had learned to duck when he was angry. It was heartening that the boy's talent for braining people had finally found a sporting outlet.

After the game, Sid, Pete and her grandfather sat out on the verandah, beers in hand. Grandad was twisting a new cracker for Jack's whip. Clare came back into the kitchen, where Dan was making himself a meal of leftovers. 'They're *all* smoking,' she whispered. 'I can't believe it. Pete's got lung cancer.'

'I suppose he doesn't think things can get much worse then.' Dan opened his arms and she melted into him. 'He's staying?' Clare nodded. 'That's it then,' he said. 'With Taylor, and Sid and now Pete, it's a full house. I'll be bunking down in the surgery tonight.'

He didn't sound like he minded, and neither did she. Their future stretched invitingly before them. They had all the time in the world.

After dinner Clare had a closer look at her presents. She put on the outfit Ronnie had sent her. All carefully coordinated: skirt, top, jacket, bag, shoes and jewellery. Not that she had any use for high heels in Merriang. Dan was more admiring of the saddle Grandad had given her, his finger tracing its intricate stitching and embossed pigskin seat. She inspected the gold, heart-shaped locket from Dan. It contained a picture of Jack with her grandfather. Clare squeezed the lid shut. It felt cool and solid in her hand and was the best present of all.

She jumped up and wandered around the crowded, festive homestead, taking snapshots with her heart. It had been a truly magical day, a day when Currawong had turned into a real life Shangri-La. What about tomorrow?

CHAPTER 42

Dan shivered and pulled the covers up to his chin. For a moment he couldn't place where he was. One thing was certain though, he'd had a night of it. His head was sore, his back was sore and his tongue was furry. He opened his eyes a crack. The sharp light of summer poured in the window.

He lay on a blow-up mattress in the corner of the surgery, his home for the past week. Not so blow-up any more. His spine lay hard against the floorboards, and why couldn't he feel his legs? He propped up on his elbows. Red lay spread-eagled over the end of the mattress, a dead weight. 'You've got me confused with that pushover, Taylor Brown.' He kicked at Red, who smiled and wagged his tail as if to say, *Don't worry. I know you didn't mean it.* 'Get out of here,' growled Dan. A second kick convinced the dog he was serious.

Dan linked his hands behind his head, and fell back with a sigh on his pillow. New Year's Day, and he'd be back in his own bed tonight. Sid was giving Taylor a lift to Toowoomba this morning, where she'd catch a train to start her new life. He checked his watch. Past nine, they'd have already left. He hauled himself to his feet, drained a glass of water and gazed out the window. The coming year held some nasty surprises, what with Mick's illness and the spectre of gas wells at

Currawong. But it also held the promise of a glorious future with Clare and Jack. He weighed up the odds. They were in his favour.

What was that noise? The door opened a fraction. Clare. She slipped into the room and pulled her oversize T-shirt over her head. Naked except for underpants, her face flushed with desire. He was instantly hard. Wordlessly she locked the door and joined him on the floor.

Afterwards she lay with her head cradled in his arm. 'Marry me,' he said.

She sat up, a shocked expression on her lovely face. 'Is this Taylor's idea?'

He pulled her to him. 'Yes,' he said, 'but it's a good one.' They wrestled together on the floor, laughing and kissing until he was hard all over again. The second time surpassed the first. Clare could joke all she liked, but she'd say yes in the end. It was written in the stars. 'Come on,' she said, jumping to her feet. 'Let's get up to the house, or we'll miss breakfast.'

'SO TAYLOR'S GONE,' said Dan, finishing his cold toast.

'Sid took off with her at seven o'clock this morning,' said Clare. 'I thought she'd never get up in time. She almost missed her lift.'

'She's not a morning person,' said Dan.

Clare laughed. 'I've come to love Taylor, don't get me wrong. But I think she's almost more trouble than Jack.'

Dan poured himself another cuppa. 'Pete still here?'

She nodded. 'Hasn't *he* given Grandad a new lease of life? They're like two naughty schoolboys.'

Grandad came in the back door, followed by Jack and all four dogs. 'Keep this lot here, will you? Me and Pete are heading over to Quimby. He wants to take a look around.'

'Would you like me or Dan to come along?' asked Clare.

'No thanks, mother hen,' he said. 'Us old blokes can take care of ourselves.'

He wrapped her in a hug that took her breath away. Grandad was becoming more sentimental every day. She drew in his scent, warm and familiar, the smell of the earth. How she loved him.

'You two have fun,' she said. What would it be like for Pete, seeing his old home again? The gracious homestead that he'd built with his own two hands, falling into disrepair. The grounds and garden fast returning to the wild. Surely it would tear him in two? She was struck by an overwhelming urge to go with them, in spite of any protests.

It seemed her grandfather could read minds. 'You're not coming.' His voice had taken on a commanding tone, and suddenly she was a child again. He looked her up and down, a satisfied expression on his face. 'You coming back like you did, love, and bringing little Jack ... it's been a blessing. There's much of your mother in you,' he said, 'and of your grandmother. I see the resemblance each time I lay eyes on you.'

The mention of Mum was so unexpected it made Clare miss her. 'If you should speak to your mother ... if you should speak to Patty, tell her how much I love her. How much Grandma and I always loved her. Tell Ryan that too.'

'I will,' she said. 'Now go before you make me cry.'

'In a minute.' He sat down and patted his knee. Jacky was there in a flash. 'Now you be good for Clare,' he said. 'And look after that pony while Pete and me are gone - and Babe the pig too.' The boy nodded gravely and something seemed to pass between them. Samson trotted over and put his head on Jack's knee. 'Keep an eye on my boy for me,' he told the dog, fondling his ears.

Pete tooted the horn of the truck. 'Will you be back for lunch,' asked Clare.

'I don't think so,' said Grandad.

'What will you do for all that time?'

Grandad shushed her, with a finger to his lips. 'Secret men's business.'

Clare laughed, but Samson erupted into a frantic flurry of barking. He stood in the doorway, forefeet spread, barring the way.

'Here now,' said Dan. He slipped a leash on the agitated animal and pulled him aside. Grandad put on his hat, took one last, lingering look around the kitchen and was gone.

What was it, she wondered, that was bothering Samson? Was it the same, indefinable thing that was bothering her?

'THIS IS our first family ride together,' said Clare. She loved saying the word *family*. She loved how it sounded. She loved that that's what they were now. Dan rode Martini, a blue-roan clydesdale filly, sweet-tempered and pretty as a picture. According to Grandad, she was a rare throwback to the Queensland stallion, Hillend Macgregor – a champion during the war. Not that it meant anything to Clare. Maybe she should study the Currawong bloodlines? Yes, she should learn more about breeding these magnificent horses; carry on the family tradition, so to speak.

Martini was only a green-broke two-year-old, but already she stood sixteen hands high: a gentle giant with the heart of a lamb. Little Sparky had a crush on her. Dan barely needed to hold the pony's lead rope, he followed so faithfully at Martini's side. Jack sat his pony with assurance, listening to Dan's occasional instructions, his tiny tongue extending slightly from his lips in concentration.

Clare stroked Fleur's dappled neck, and the mare snorted in pleasure. Jack's aptitude never ceased to amaze her. Had it really only been five months since they'd first met in her office? Hard to reconcile the memory of that traumatised child with this smiling, confident little boy. 'Canter, canter, canter,' he yelled. Dan touched his heels to Martini's sides and she broke into a lumbering, yet graceful, trot. Fleur followed suit and Sparky was forced to canter in order to keep up with the two-time pace of the heavy horses. Jack's grin was a joy to see.

A currawong arrowed across the perfect arch of the cloudless summer sky. Here, in this high corner paddock, they were well and truly in the foothills of the Bunyas. To the left lay groves of brigalow: elegant wattles boasting high, silvery canopies. No breeze stirred their branches. Scattered patches of bright green vines showed in the gullies, remnants of subtropical rainforest that had occupied the brigalow lands millions of years ago. Swathes of pale-gold summer grass bent beneath the horses' drumming hooves, only to spring up behind them. Soon this heavenly hillside might be lost, a bombsite of roads and wells and wastewater dams, all carved into the rich black soil. Her grief, her grandfather's grief, cast a shadow over the golden morning.

They paused at the crest of the ridge. So silent. Spread before them, peaceful paddocks of grazing clydesdales, Currawong's main herd. Goliath wheeled and reared low, acknowledging the horses on the hill. She looked to the north. In the distance, Quimby Downs stood bathed in sunlight. Clare caught her breath. What a magnificent sight.

It was then she heard it. A faint boom, a distant explosion. Thunder? But the sky was a flawless blue. Her imagination? There came the sound of faraway barking. The horses pricked their ears and held their heads on high, staring in the direction of Quimby Downs. Clare glanced at Dan. His eyes narrowed. 'Look.' Flickers of bright flame flowered around the distant homestead and a thin pillar of smoke rose in the still air. Dan leaped from his horse, scooped up Jack and somehow remounted with the child in his arms. 'Come on,' he said, and thundered back to Currawong with Clare in swift pursuit.

CLARE SAT out on the verandah. A subdued Jack played at her feet, lining up his Matchbox cars in neat, obsessive rows. Samson stood chained to the rail, statue still, his gaze fixed to the north.

A second fire truck hurtled down the road, then another. A police car followed soon after. She fingered her phone. Why didn't someone ring? Mick was her grandfather, after all. She had more right to know than anybody. Samson raised his nose and howled to the heavens, the most mournful sound. Why couldn't the bloody dog shut up?

It was another half hour before the phone finally rang and Dan's shaky voice came on the line. 'I'm sorry, honey,' he said. 'Mick and Pete ... they didn't make it.'

JACK WAS HER SAVIOUR, all that dreadful morning. Staying strong for the children, such a cliché, such a fundamental truth. Giving the little boy a bath, making his lunch, going through the motions. It kept her sane until Bronwyn arrived with Timmy, freeing Clare to take the short trip to Quimby Downs.

Dan met her at the gate. They embraced for the longest time, gathering strength for whatever was next. 'What happened?' asked Clare.

'I don't know,' said Dan. 'I just don't know.'

The homestead was gone, razed to the ground, a smouldering ruin of timber and tin. The outbuildings were gone too. Behind the house, a fire still burned with a steady flame, cordoned off with crime scene tape. The earth all around was blackened in a wide circle. Was that where Grandad and Pete met their death? Clare headed towards the spot and was waylaid by two police men. She identified herself, feeling numb and oddly composed, 'If it's any comfort, your grandfather and his friend would have died instantly,' said one of the officers.

'What happened?' asked Clare.

'We think gas leaked from the domestic well and exploded inside the pump house. There's no putting out that fire now.' They all stared at the unearthly flames, burning bright on the scorched ground as if by magic. 'I understand there's a history of methane contamination at Quimby Downs?' asked the officer. 'Did your grandfather smoke?'

Her first instinct was to say no, but that would be wrong. He'd been smoking lately. He'd even given up trying to hide it. 'Yes,' she said. 'He smoked, and so did Pete.'

The officer nodded and made a note. 'Maybe they lit up in the pump shed,' he said to his colleague.

'The homestead,' said Clare. 'What happened to the homestead?'

'My guess is the wind blew burning embers into the roof,' said the officer.

Clare was in a daze. She recalled the vertical plume of smoke, rising straight as an arrow to heaven. There was no wind that morning. *Secret men's business*. 'Oh Grandad', she whispered. 'Whatever have you done?'

CHAPTER 43

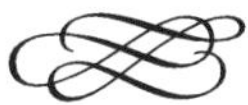

'If only Grandad could see this,' said Clare, waving the newspaper in Dan's face.

'Who's to say he can't?'

Clare gave him a swift kiss. 'Listen.'

The deaths of Darling Downs farmers Mick Macleod and Pete Porter in a gas explosion have shocked all Queensland, and galvanised a state-wide campaign against the coal seam mining industry. Pyramid Energy stands accused of non-compliance with dozens of environmental and safety regulations. It's alleged the company bullied owners of contaminated land into signing compensation agreements with unconscionable non-disclosure clauses. Today the State Government announced a suspension of all ongoing activities and permits relating to coal seam gas mining, and a moratorium on new exploration projects.

Dan smiled. 'Currawong's safe then.'

'It gets better.' Clare smoothed out the creases in the paper with trembling hands.

A bill was introduced into Canberra's lower house last night, calling for the Great Artesian Basin to be included as an environment of national significance. This would give the Federal Government broad powers to intervene for its protection. In the light of the recent Queensland tragedy, this proposal received bipartisan support.' Clare clasped a hand to her chest. Her mother, Ryan, everyone at the funeral service had prayed for this. In death, Grandad had finally brought the family to a common purpose.

'That's fantastic news,' said Dan. 'Unbelievable, fantastic news.' He handed her the funeral urn. 'Now let's get this show on the road.'

Clare waved goodbye to Bronwyn, who was supervising Jack and Timmy in the sandpit, and climbed into the jeep. They drove in silence for a while. 'Grandad loved Jack.'

'Yes,' said Dan.

'I wish you'd told me he was dying.'

Dan shot her an anguished glance that broke her heart.

'I've forgiven you,' she said, laying her hand on his knee. 'You know I have. Do you know what Grandad said to me on New Year's Eve?' Dan shook his head. 'He said that watching Jack blossom had been the greatest gift. He said he wished he could pay that gift forward somehow.' Dan stayed silent. 'Maybe I can do it for him,' said Clare.

'Go on.'

'That course in equine therapy that you did?' she said. 'I'm going to do it too. Let's turn Currawong into a place of healing for other kids like Jack.'

Dan turned to her with a brilliant smile. 'Mick would like that just fine.'

CLARE AND DAN approached the entrance to the rainforest walk. Seen from the outside, this bunya pine forest was a forbidding place: ancient trees standing shoulder to shoulder, limbs entwined as if barring the way. A curtain of vines and prickly plants stood bathed in sunlight at the jungle's edge, protecting the forest, keeping the drying winds and summer heat at bay.

They slipped inside. Domed pine canopies reached to the sky, while elephant-like buttresses held fast to the dappled earth. Each tree was a bridge between worlds. It had been this way since time immemorial, a place where all sorts of magical and dangerous things might happen. Their footsteps made no sound on the soft earth as they walked to the waterfall. A seedling sprouted from the stump of a long-dead forest giant. Death and regeneration went hand in hand in this place.

Clare stood on the ferny bank and scattered the ashes on the water. They dissolved in the dark stream, as it leaped from its course and shattered in a rainbow of spray on the rocks below. Grandad wasn't gone. He lived here now, where she could always find him. She took Dan's hand. With a silent prayer, Clare retraced her path and stepped from the shadows into the light.

ACKNOWLEDGEMENTS

Thanks to the team at Pilyara Press, especially Kathryn Ledson, Sydney Smith and Kate Belle.

I must thank my talented writing buddies of The Little Lonsdale Group for their help and support. Thanks also to the Darklings, a writing group formed while we were all together at Australia's National Writing Centre known as Varuna - The Writer's House. Varuna sent me on a magical writing residency to the Tyrone Guthrie Centre in Ireland where I completed this manuscript.

Thanks to my agent, Clare Forster of Curtis Brown Australia.

And finally, thanks go to my patient family for putting up with a distracted writer in their midst. A special thank you to my son Matthew, for always being willing to brainstorm ideas.

ABOUT THE AUTHOR

Bestselling Aussie author Jennifer Scoullar writes page-turning fiction about the land, people and wildlife that she loves.

Scoullar is a lapsed lawyer who harbours a deep appreciation and respect for the natural world. She lives on a farm in Australia's southern Victorian ranges, and has ridden and bred horses all her life. Her passion for animals and the bush is the catalyst for her bestselling books.

Visit Jennifer's website to enter the monthly prize draw! If you enjoyed this book and have a moment or two, please leave an online rating or review. Reviews are of great help to authors.

www.jenniferscoullar.com

Printed in Great Britain
by Amazon